SHADOWLANDS

MARK E. PRIOR

Copyright © 2014 Mark Edward Prior.
Cover design by Emily Blass.

All rights reserved. No part of this book may be reproduced, stored, or transmitted by any means—whether auditory, graphic, mechanical, or electronic—without written permission of both publisher and author, except in the case of brief excerpts used in critical articles and reviews. Unauthorized reproduction of any part of this work is illegal and is punishable by law.

ISBN: 978-1-4834-1161-3 (sc)
ISBN: 978-1-4834-1163-7 (hc)
ISBN: 978-1-4834-1162-0 (e)

Library of Congress Control Number: 2014907675

Because of the dynamic nature of the Internet, any web addresses or links contained in this book may have changed since publication and may no longer be valid. The views expressed in this work are solely those of the author and do not necessarily reflect the views of the publisher, and the publisher hereby disclaims any responsibility for them.

Any people depicted in stock imagery provided by Thinkstock are models, and such images are being used for illustrative purposes only.
Certain stock imagery © Thinkstock.

Lulu Publishing Services rev. date: 7/3/2014

> If you knew the truth with certainty,
> you would see the fire of hell;
> you would see it with your own eyes.
> —The Koran

Author's proceeds are donated for the assistance of military veterans and Alzheimer's research.

PART 1

CHAPTER 1

MATT

August 2008

Matt shifted his weight to relieve the pressure on his right side, his arm trembling as he supported himself on his crutch. Daylight had barely broken over the Kandahar hills, and the temperature was already building to its shimmering crescendo, the heat seeping through the soles of his dusty boots and rising up his legs like mercury. By the time it reached his remaining testicle, his body would be coated in a fine film of sweat, perspiration bleeding through his fatigues as though he were stricken by a sudden malarial fever. For the rest of the day, especially this time of year, the heat would fight to suck every liquid molecule from any living thing until, at last, dusk brought some relief. At least the heat was predictable, as reliable as the plaintive wails of the muezzin from the minarets, calling the devout to prayers.

Matt stared down at the knuckles wrapped around the crutch's grip, as if his fingers belonged to someone else. His gaze rose to the copse of blond hair on his forearm that shrouded the tattoo he had etched when he was thirteen: "The meek shall inherit the earth." Even now—especially now—it made him snort. All that pain as a kid just to impress his mother, thinking if he came home with this permanent marker of Christian devotion she would be thrilled, perhaps even look at him with newfound affection. He thought about removing it when he joined the military or replacing it with "You reap what you sow." Anyone in the forces who believed the meek inherited the earth needed to look for a new job.

"Here, soldier." Jeremy thrust a flask into Matt's stomach.

Wincing, Matt buckled at the waist, caught by the surprise of Jeremy's motion. The pain around his groin was still excruciating, especially now that he was off the morphine and onto the disappointingly dull Tylenol 3's.

"Shit." Jeremy sucked air through his teeth. "Sorry about that, bud. I keep on forgetting you're not the man you used to be." Jeremy smiled his shit-eating grin and nudged the flask into Matt's ribs, this time more gently. "This oughta help."

"With what?"

"With whatever pain you're dealing with today."

They stood peering west over the runway, in the direction of home, a place they would materialize in a little more than a day. A small sand cyclone at the far end of the asphalt lurched its way toward them, deking from side to side. Back home it was already night, and Amanda and the kids would be getting ready for bed. There would be no more contact with them until he arrived.

His last conversation with his wife had rattled him, something he had rarely felt with Amanda before. She hadn't really said anything, but he had noticed a gradual pulling back in her e-mails and on the phone. It had struck him in that instinctive way couples develop over time, interpreting less what was said than what was left out, parsing the emotional grammar of gaps.

Matt managed a half-smile at his friend's instincts while contemplating Jeremy's offer of a drink. He couldn't help but think back to how in the Graydon household when he was a child it had been a cardinal edict, laid down by Shirley, the alcoholic, unswervingly devout Christian mother (or swervingly, when she was drunk), that one did not drink before noon. He glanced at his watch and shrugged, as if to say, "What the fuck." At least it was nighttime back home.

"Here's to you, man." Matt tilted the flask toward Jeremy. Squinting against the glare of the metal container, Matt raised the flask to his mouth and followed the heat of the Jack Daniels as it coursed down the back of his throat. He swallowed hard, the whiskers on his Adam's apple scratching against the khaki handkerchief tied around his neck, and then shuddered, blowing a long gust through cracked lips.

"Better, Sarge?" Jeremy asked with a wink.

Matt held the flask at arm's length and blinked at it. "I'll be better when I get out of here; that's what *I* think." His voice was suddenly grittier, the alcohol, dry air, and lack of sleep wrestling with each other.

Since the surgery, sleep had been fitful, especially when it wasn't drug-induced. Being confined to sick bed filled the days with too much restless time, time he spent enviously watching his colleagues go back into combat. But his nights ... they were filled with questions, stinging doubts about leaving this place, about going back home. And in spite of what he told Jeremy about being happy to be out of here, he wasn't so sure.

The moment Matt stepped up the plane's ramp, his second, and maybe last, tour of Afghanistan would be over. The military had good enough excuses to send him home early—his injuries, his sister, Gwen's, death—and at least he would be spared the humiliation of sticking around to wait out his pending court martial.

He couldn't go back in time, and even if he could, he still would have shot the Afghan civilian. There had been no time to think about it, no time for rationalization. He had acted on instinct, trying in a split-second to save the boy by shooting the man. And then the kid ended up dead anyway.

He had not expected his tour to end like this. He arrived in Afghanistan like so many other soldiers, intent on his country's mission to turn things around. In all this time, their progress was only measured in the most infinitesimal increments, viewed as though looking through the wrong end of a set of binoculars. You knew something was down there at the end, but you just weren't sure what it was. Setbacks, on the other hand, loomed much larger, magnified by every body that was carried up the ramp of the Herc, the "flying casket." A soldier's final ride home. By the end of a couple of tours, the slow rot of cynicism had infected nearly everyone.

Still, Matt felt more poorly equipped to deal with what awaited him at home than with anything Kandahar in all its surprises could throw at him. He knew he would have to readjust to Amanda and the kids, easing back into a space that had been reshaped over six months into a place that had normalized without him. Like any military family, Amanda and the kids lived with the unspoken fear that he might not return, imagining themselves in a future whose equation had changed; a constant suddenly dropped. It wasn't like that when he had returned from his first tour. They had felt so lucky, so happy to have him home. But he knew he had squandered that time between tours. He had been a shit, and he knew it, distant and odd, never able to recapture the ease he and Amanda had settled into before he left for Afghanistan the first time.

And now he would arrive home only to have to leave almost immediately. With Gwen's death, Matt's mother, Shirley, had suddenly become his charge, and it irked him that he would have to go to the Okanagan Valley to figure out what to do with her. Life in Afghanistan was beginning to seem simple by comparison.

Matt looked at his friend and was suddenly back in the present. Jeremy raised his eyebrow, like he always did when he thought Matt was full of shit. Jeremy had a knack for reading him.

"Fuck off, Rayner. How the hell *should* I feel about going back? My mother is apparently as nutty as a can of Planters, and now she's my responsibility. Oh, and my sister just died, and in every e-mail or phone call I've had from my wife, she's been as distant as Pluto and just about as cold. I think I'd rather stay here and be shot at." He hit the green duffle bag with his crutch, kicking up a swirl of dust.

"I'll shoot you myself if you don't get on that plane and deal with it," Jeremy said.

"Listen, Corporal, don't forget your rank." Matt winked at him.

"Well, at least you won't have to put up with any more jokes from the guys about being nuts to be in the army."

"When I get better, I'm going to wipe that smirk off your face, buddy. You'll see. Or I'll tell all the guys about how much you love opera." Matt could never figure out why Jeremy wouldn't tell him what kind of music he liked until he sneaked a look at his iPod's playlist one day. It was dominated by divas: Callas, Te Kenawa, Bartoli. Jeremy didn't seem to care, though; he would fall asleep at night with a content look on his face, earphones in place while he listened to his ladies.

"Tell you what. When we get home, I'll take you to an opera so you can find out what all the fuss is about," Jeremy said.

"Like a date?"

"Yeah, like a date. You can be my bitch." Jeremy grabbed Matt in a headlock and spat on the tarmac. "No, not like a date! I'll bring Chrissy, and you can bring Amanda."

"Yeah," Matt said, prying loose from Jeremy's grip. He gazed toward the orange windsock that flapped at the side of the airfield. "I'll bring Amanda." A shiver worked its way up his spine in spite of the heat, leaving an empty feeling in its wake. He handed the flask to Jeremy, who pushed it right back at him.

"No, keep it for later. We'll have a drink when we land at Camp Mirage." He put one hand on Matt's shoulder and with his other gave him a couple of quick pats on the chest. "You gonna be all right, buddy?"

Matt looked up at the turquoise Afghan sky. "I can take care of myself," he said. "Besides, I'm sure I'll get back here soon enough, once all this stuff is sorted out." Even as he said it, he felt his chest deflating, along with the contrived optimism.

"It's funny, you know. Isn't your family supposed to give you strength? At least the family you choose." He looked up at Rayner, who stared back at him with intense green eyes, the corner of Rayner's mouth rising in an ironic smile. "No wonder it's so easy for them to shred you like cheese."

"I'm sure you'll figure it all out," Rayner said.

Matt wasn't so sure. But attempting to resolve things from 10,000 kilometres wasn't going to give him any clarity. He wanted to see things right there in front of him. He needed to look Amanda in the eyes, to read her body language. If he could just see her, squeeze his arms around her shoulders and stroke her back while she rested her head on his chest, give her some reassurance …

Even then, he wasn't sure how she would react to his coddling. She had been so shy when he met her as a waitress, barely old enough to be serving alcohol, he first thought. Sure, she had this cheeky act at work, wearing clingy white shorts and a shrunken, green T-shirt cut up above her waist, revealing the cutest little pierced navel. He used to tease her about her clothes being so tight it looked like someone had shrink-wrapped her. Yeah, it was kind of slutty, but it worked for him. Then he would see her out of the bar and all her confidence would evaporate.

He had been so consumed by her, someone he hardly knew.

That was a long time ago.

Matt shook his head as he put his arm around Jeremy's shoulder. "Come on. Let's get out of here." He turned toward the Herc, staring up at the dark cavern at the end of the plane's ramp. His chest tightened, his swampy clothes feeling suddenly cold. He swayed a little.

"You sure you're gonna be okay?" Rayner asked.

Matt turned for a second to look at him, nodding automatically. "Yeah, Rayner," he said as a sick feeling made its way to his gut. "I'll be fine."

Matt sat gazing at the ceiling of the cavernous aircraft, his legs stretched in front of him and the back of his head resting against the vibrating skin of the plane. The interior of the Herc was finally starting to cool with the plane's ascent, expelling the hot, dry air that had seeped up from the Kandahar tarmac.

Every uncomfortable mesh seat was occupied down parallel rows that ran half the length of the plane. The cooling air had not yet managed to expel the body odour—the smell of soldiers—that hung like a thin fog, but the scent was familiar and oddly soothing, in the way a wolf must recognize its pack.

He couldn't wait to get out of his sweaty uniform. Clean, dry underwear would surely be next to godliness; both—the underwear and the godliness—were impossible to maintain in the hell called Kandahar. Everyone at the base measured the sun's intensity in what they called the ASF—the Ass Sweat Factor—which in a southern Afghan summer was always an eleven out of ten, like sitting in a bog all day. He wondered if his old clothes would even fit him when he got home; he had always been in good shape, but what little body fat he once had was now hardened to muscle, a product of two tours of Afghanistan, killing time at the gym between missions and the stomach-turning rations while away from the base. Osama's Revenge, diarrhoea. Or the embarrassing time he just plain shit himself the first time a rocket-propelled grenade whistled by his ear and exploded way too close for comfort, everything in his body screaming *evacuate*. The Afghan weight loss program, brought to you by the Canadian Forces.

As the Herc lumbered skyward, Matt found it hard to turn away from the ground below, in the same way he always found it difficult not to stare at a begging amputee whose limbs had been blown off by a mine. The country had got under his skin, and he was surprised, over and over, at how talons seemed to reach up from the dry earth in an effort to pull him back down, clawing away at his gut. He wasn't sure how much the feeling had to do with simply not wanting to go home, but he found himself grudgingly admitting that he felt a kinship with the rugged solitude of the land, a tacit admiration for the fierceness of the country and its people. He couldn't help but respect their determination; he hoped that at least some of them found the same in him. Even so, even if he had attempted to get close, he found that behind their gaze there was constant suspicion. The people had been subjected to too much, their mistrust built on a history rife with foreigners who had trampled their land and tried to break their spirit.

And a single invader had yet to conquer them.

When he first arrived in Afghanistan, he was in awe of how the elements—the sun, heat, sand and snow—so relentlessly beat down on the land as though intent to destroy it. Afghans had become part of the landscape, a sort of natural selection where they survived on what little there was to sustain them, like stubborn cacti in the desert. He was still surprised how ferociously a rabble of insurgents would fight for their piece of dirt. Even the Afghans found irony in protecting a land so seemingly undesirable—the Pashtuns had a saying: when Allah created the world, he had a pile of rocks left over so he created Afghanistan—but it was as though the land's harshness had been absorbed into their pores. From the dust these people were made, and they would fight for that very dust until it was returned to them, or they back to it. Still, there was a stark and powerful beauty in the contrasts of the land—its lush fields and parched deserts, the monotonous plains and thunderous purple mountains—the contradictions that seemed to live so easily in the country and in its people. Even Afghan men, among the toughest he had ever seen, defied stereotypes by holding hands with each other, or plucking a flower from a roadside to appreciate its beauty or perhaps its tenacity for surviving such desolation. The land beneath him—this place where deep-rooted pride fought with chronic resignation, where the hospitality of its people could be so quickly dismissed by an act of terrorist savagery—was slipping away. And in spite of how desperately he wanted to leave, never had he felt he belonged anywhere so much as he did there.

He avoided looking toward the cargo section of the plane where the flag-draped coffins of two Canadian soldiers lay. Just six months ago Matt had been in this very Herc, accompanying his buddy Adam's body back home, and he couldn't shake the image of his friend's pale corpse preserved on ice for the long journey to Canada.

Rayner had taken a seat farther up the plane, likely guessing Matt needed to be alone for a while. Matt figured he would just take out his iPod, plug in his ear buds and seal out the world, a subtle Do Not Disturb sign. He shifted his weight in the webbed seat, already feeling the waffle pattern pressing into his butt, the pressure pushing into his injury. It was going to be a long trip home.

He leaned down to retrieve his iPod from his kit, accidentally brushing the leg of the young private next to him. He quickly retracted his hand. "Sorry," he said.

"No bother, Sergeant," she replied.

Matt had a sudden sinking feeling. He couldn't conceive of anything more painful than talking to someone for the rest of the trip. He reached back into his bag and fumbled for his earphones.

"Where you headed?" she asked.

His hand stopped in his bag as he shifted slowly to look at her. He forced a smile. "Home, I guess," he replied.

"Well lucky you. You're finished with your tour here?"

"In a matter of speaking, I am," he said, glancing down at her chest, "Private Jacks." Her nametag was perched just above her right breast. She was a pretty thing, likely in her early 20s, no wedding ring, probably just trying to pass some time. He watched her eyes travel from his, sliding down his neck to his shoulders and chest and then quickly up again to their starting point. If she were a tree would have oozed sap. Where were the lesbians when you needed them?

"Where's home for you?" she asked, almost absentmindedly.

"British Columbia." He continued to sift through his bag, avoiding her eyes.

"Vancouver?"

"No," he said, bringing his bag up to his lap, attempting to immerse himself completely in its contents.

"Oh, where then?"

As he answered he turned toward her, giving her a look that he hoped would stop the conversation. "Summerland," he said.

"Summerland? Really?" Mission failed. "There's such a place?"

He sighed and removed his hand from his bag, leaning back in his seat. "Yeah. Kind of idyllic, I know." He paused. "That's where I first learned to shoot heroin."

Private Jacks recoiled as though Matt had just slapped her. He smiled at her, as cherubically as he knew how, and then she suddenly got up and excused herself.

Mission accomplished.

His hand connected with the white wires of his earphones, and he tugged the iPod free from his bag, inserting the buds into his ears. He spun the iPod's wheel with his thumb, searching for the right song to take him beyond the blistered fields below. Coldplay. Snow Patrol. Anything cold. He cranked up the volume with resignation; some hearing loss from the proximity of explosions and rounds of fire was an occupational hazard.

He leaned his head back against the Herc's hard abdomen while he rotated the gold wedding band around his finger, closing his eyes to concentrate on the music. Snow Patrol played 'Signal Fire', competing with the drone of the plane's engines, none of it enough to drown out the sloshing sound he imagined coming from the coffins. He tried to ignore the taste of bile rising in his throat.

His sister had loved Snow Patrol. He couldn't believe Gwen wouldn't be there when he arrived in the Okanagan, even though they had said their good-byes when he was last in Canada. There she was dying of cancer, and she told him to get the hell on with his life and go do his job. Gwen and he had always morbidly joked that his chances of dying first were a lot higher than hers, but now she was dead at the ridiculous age of twenty-seven. He didn't yet know what he would say at the funeral and already felt tears floating just behind his eyes. He was pretty sure his performance at the service wouldn't do anything to bolster his tough-guy image. Gwen Graydon, beloved daughter of Shirley and George, loyal sister to Matt, survived by loving wife, Elizabeth (Lizzie), Proctor. God how he would miss Gwen.

Even under the circumstances he still couldn't wait to see Lizzie. Little "Lizzie the lezzie." He loved taunting her with that, and she always returned the jab with a punch of her own to Matt's arm. It surprised him how nervous Lizzie was when she first met him, anxious about how a military guy would react to a lesbian dating his sister, even though Lizzie knew Gwen had come out to Matt when she was a teenager. And he and Gwen had practically worshipped each other; Gwen had what nearly amounted to a shrine in her home for Matt, a section of their bedroom wall strewn with pictures of him from elementary school through to his latest tour in combat gear.

She was made of strong stock, Lizzie was, which had proven of value over the last year. Gwen was dying of cancer and their mother's, Shirley's, behaviour, he had heard, was becoming more erratic as the dementia grabbed a firmer hold, to the point where she needed nearly constant vigilance. Between Shirley's church group and the girls, everyone had managed to keep a pretty good eye on her, but she was becoming more of a burden for Lizzie, with Gwen herself needing more care. And as much as Shirley liked Lizzie, Shirley often reverted to her pious comfort zone where casting judgment on Gwen and Lizzie's "lifestyle" seemed the right thing to do.

Matt hadn't set so much as a toe on that beautiful farmland since he was 18, nearly 16 years ago when Shirley had told him, again piously, if he was joining the military he should never come back. He never had.

He opened his eyes, and without moving his head, glanced to the right at Private Jacks, who had returned to her seat, her chin now bobbing onto her chest. He looked at the display on his watch. They were now well past the border, scheduled to land in Camp Mirage in about thirty minutes. His heart seemed to be beating faster as they left Afghanistan behind them, a tickle of bile again rising in his throat. He tried to swallow it down, along with the irony that the further they traveled from the place where so many people had tried to kill him, the more anxious he became.

∾

Matt's Journal

April 24, 2006, Kandahar Air Field (KAF)
First Tour of Afghanistan

I am still haunted by the faces of my kids. I see them standing at the door of the house, gazing down at their feet, an unbearable effort to raise their heads or their hands to wave good-bye. I wouldn't let them or Amanda come to the airport with the rest of the families to see us off, to be exposed to all that anxiety and grief in one spot. Bosnia was the only other foreign mission in my sixteen year military career, officially a 'peacekeeping mission'; Callum wasn't even born then, and Baxter had yet to say his first word. In a way it would be easier now if they were still as young as Baxter was then, if only so they wouldn't know I was going. We're guaranteed to see combat here in Afghanistan, and that's no comfort to anyone back home. I know Amanda tried to put on a brave face for me and for the kids, but her shoulders were quivering as she tried not to cry while she stood at the door. Getting on the plane with the company was about as uplifting as a visit to the morgue.

Now that we're here though, we are all desperate to get out there and get on with our mission. I think most of us feel like rodeo bulls, all fired up and ready to charge into the ring. We've been trained for this for years, and it's time to put it all to the test.

I nearly lost my lunch when our plane did its spiral descent into Kandahar Air Field, an aerial manoeuvre that deters anyone from taking a shot at us. I'd managed to get a peak out the window before we started our approach. Whether flying over the rugged, snow-capped Hindu Kush or the desert plains dotted by occasional communities, the countryside offers a daunting harshness and menacing beauty, an alluring quality that seems to seductively beckon you to step inside. Afghanistan must have been nearly impenetrable before access by air but has always been prized for its strategic location. I know it sounds lame, but I find it unbelievably exciting to be here, no doubt the highlight of my career with the Forces up until now, and easily the most exotic place I've been. When we arrived and opened the plane doors, there was even a smell to it, something like jet fuel mixed with dust and cloves; I don't think I'll ever forget it. They say the fruit here is amazing—typical of a guy from an Okanagan farm to pick that up—the figs so sweet you go into diabetic shock just smelling them, and pomegranates that explode their red, bittersweet juice all over your hands when you open them up.

We've spent the first few days since arriving at KAF getting acclimatized, familiarized and briefed. The base, or 'camp', as we call it, is like a small American city with ghettoes of Canadians, British, Dutch, Australians. We have a Pizza Hut, Burger King and a Subway here along with a gym, a basketball court and football field to work it all off.

Speaking of acclimatized it's only April and this place is already a freakin' inferno during the day—I can't imagine what August will be like. They say it's unseasonably warm right now, but there's nothing like coming from an Edmonton April to this. If you're outside you move as fast as you can from one shady spot to another and drink about a litre of water an hour and still barely have to take a piss. We'll be carrying the equivalent of a young teenager worth of gear when we're on a mission, and as well trained as we are, I have a feeling this is going to challenge us beyond what we ever imagined.

I had my 32nd birthday yesterday, and Rayner was the only one who knew about it, but he went and rounded up a bunch of guys, most of whom we didn't know or had just met, and had a party last night. Too much booze, but the higher-ups turned a blind eye. How often do you turn 32 after all, or even live to see it in a war zone? Every waking moment here is one to celebrate that you're alive, everything lived in the here and now, on a razor's edge of anticipation and excitement that no one talks about but everyone feels. The piss-up was a good bonding thing for the boys in the platoon anyways. It knocks their guard down and I get a better idea of the guys whose butts I'm going to be kicking for the next six months.

One of the guys, Hutch, will be in my section, and he's barely old enough to shave. He's a Newfie, so damn funny he had us all rolling around in the tent laughing our asses off, even when we couldn't understand him with his accent getting thicker the more he drank. He'll be great comic relief on the team, and I'm sure we'll need it.

We're in a universe of our own at KAF. You would imagine what would be on everybody's lips is the latest Taliban attack or last night's windstorm that we thought would bury us in a dustbowl, but the biggest deal on the base right now, at least with the Canadians, is the Tim Horton's that's about to open up. Napoleon said an army marches on its stomach and it's still true. I wonder what he would have said about this particular Canadian delicacy. The Americans think we're nuts, but all the guys are sure they'll change their minds once they've experienced Canadian gourmet doughnut holes, Timbits. It reminds me of an old Rick Mercer episode where he was interviewing Americans on whether we should stop cruelly pummelling our moose population with Timbits. Maybe we could try that with the Taliban. Kill them with sweetness.

Yesterday I saw a young Afghan man being marched out of a humvee, his hands bound behind his back. I later found out it was one of our interpreters—'terps', as they're called here—accused of spying for the Taliban. I can't imagine a pleasant future for that guy.

Speaking of interpreters, I'm learning some words in Dari (salaam!) and Pashto. The next few days will be consumed with orientation, but at some point we'll get off the base, onto a mission and into some real action. Everyone is wired and geared for it. I'll try my best not to get killed.

It boggles the mind: here I am a Sergeant, commanding a section in one of the most powerful fighting forces ever seen, on a mission to eradicate the Taliban who turned this country into hell on earth. Pretty heady stuff for a kid from Summerland, British Columbia.

CHAPTER 2

SHIRLEY

August, 2008

Anyone entering the room will think she is asleep; of that Shirley is fiercely determined. Slumping forward slightly in the white stackable chair just in front of the window, her head is bowed, her back toward the room's door, nine paces away. Her floral dressing gown rests limply on her sagging shoulders, which rise and lower almost imperceptibly with her breath, the only outside sign of her body's activity. Earlier she had turned to face the Okanagan Lake, its whitecaps licked by the hot, midafternoon sun. But rather than admire the serenity of a perfect summer day, her eyes are downcast and nearly closed, staring through her eyelashes at the hands resting in her lap. If they think she is asleep, all the better. At least they won't bother her. Numbness has already set the underside of her legs tingling with sleep, except the spot just behind her knees where the sharp edge of the chair's plastic seat bites into her flesh. Even so she refuses to move.

How long has she been sitting here? She feels the cold terrazzo floor seeping up through the pale slippers that stretch around her feet, even though the breeze coming through the crack in the window is warm enough that her hands have begun to lightly perspire. The air feels the way it did during the summers of her youth: heavy and lazy but sweetened with the blossoms of valley fruit. She recalls her unending days spent at Sun-Oka Beach, jumping into the lake's frigid water and then warming herself again in the sun, she and her friends slathering themselves with baby oil, turning when tender like slippery eels in a skillet. Though a mother's pleading could not convince them to leave their precious patch of golden sand, nature would soon enough coax them inside as the sun slid behind the mountains and suppertime approached, she and her friends shivering from the cold water, ravenous with hunger. She would gaze out to the water one last time before leaving—there was a monster in that lake, her grandmother used to say, a dark, sinuous serpent that had been known to overturn boats and drag babies floating on their water wings down to the lake's murky bottom.

There are times she slips back almost too easily in time—she knows this—forgetting so much of what has just happened. But the innocence of those moments attracts her, a time where she had friends and life was frivolous, where she doesn't feel so alone as she does now in this place.

She wishes she could open the window farther, but it is already slid back to its maximum; just wide enough to squeeze a grapefruit through, or maybe if she dared a naked but still-firm breast—at least something in age hadn't failed her—if she wanted to send the staff into panicked fits. The corner of her mouth rises slightly with the thought. How ridiculous that her captors would allow the window to be opened just a crack. Did they really think someone would attempt to jump to her death from the first floor?

Her gaze has locked on the top of her right hand, on a small brown spot that she can't remember seeing before. It sits there almost proudly, she thinks, like a new town on a map—Look at me! Look at me!—staking its claim between two blue veins that could have once formed a Mesopotamian delta, long since dried up. It is just another injustice to endure at her fifty-two years; not only is she cooped up like a deranged hen, but now her body is showing *visible signs of aging,* just like they say in the skincare ads. When she is finally sprung from this place she will have to remember to buy some hand cream that claims something less ambiguous than *helps reduce the appearance of fine lines,* or some other such drivel. Maybe if she had drank less—were they liver spots?—or stayed out of the sun when she was younger. Why is it that what we do in our youth is always performed with the belief that we're invincible, or the denial that we'll ever get old, and then one day you wake up and realize that maybe you should have paid more attention? She would simply have to make her peace with it, the same way she attempted to do with so much in her life these days. Best to recognize the condition, embrace and understand it rather than let it take over your whole life, although it felt like wrestling a hydra: each time you lopped off one head two more seemed to grow in its place. So in an act of magnanimous familiarity she resolves to name the veins on her hand the *Euphrates* and the *Tigris,* and the marauding freckle or liver spot, or whatever it is, will be her ancient Babylon.

"*Mrs. Graydon.*" A chirping voice comes from the far side of her head. She is convinced that, unfortunately, it is quite real. She listens to what she imagines as the clopping of hooves approaching from the door and then feels the hovering spectre of one of the hospital's self-anointed saints, a large, curly topped thing whose name she can't remember but reminds her of an overly friendly, fattened sheep. She knows from experience that nothing will keep the nurse away, although she quickly runs the gamut of alternatives through her mind, from playing possum to biting her so-called caregiver. She'd probably taste like a lamb chop.

As the nurse draws nearer, she feels the tug of her presence much like an asteroid must feel the pull of a larger globe. She decides to ignore its gravity.

"Mrs. Graydon." A hand lights on her shoulder. She imagines herself a horse, her flesh shuddering off an annoying fly. If she sits still long enough she knows the nurse will continue talking to her, unsure whether anything is registering, but Shirley will get the details nonetheless of whatever it is little Miss Nightingale wants.

She decides to stay motionless, unless it is time to eat. Her stomach started rumbling a half-hour ago, even in this meditative state where her metabolism must have slowed to a pace that only a slug would find unalarming. Best to be good and hungry if you want to endure the hospital food; there is nothing else to eat in this prison.

"Your son, Matt, called, Mrs. Graydon," says the voice, now coming from just below her right ear. The nurse has squatted to see if her eyes are open. Shirley blinks.

"There we go now, my dear," the nurse says, patting the defiant freckle on Shirley's right hand further into place. "I can tell you're listening."

Shirley sighs softly through her nose and lifts her head, gazing out the window. She remembers now why she had felt that sense of anticipation, the excitement mixed with the anxiety. Matt is coming.

She realizes she must have been sitting here for some time, watching her thoughts soar lazily, without any seeming threat of them spiralling into a jumble. She can't recall 'drifting off', as she calls it, to some incomprehensible place, not for some time, and the thought buoys her. She tilts her head sideways to look at the nurse and smiles slightly, feeling the skin under her eyes puckering into tiny white pockets as she gazes up.

"How long have I been here?" she asks the nurse.

"You mean sitting in the chair or in the hospital generally?" the nurse asks.

Shirley squints momentarily, her eyes becoming glassy as she reflects the question back at her caregiver. Then suddenly the dreaded bewilderment reenters her brain like a cold draft rushing into a rickety attic. She turns her head away from the nurse and squeezes her eyes shut, tight enough that she can feel her eyeballs swimming hard against the inside of her eyelids. Her chest begins to expand in little bursts as she takes quick breaths, feeling the pressure rise from the bottom of her feet to the top of her head in an instant, like some sadistic muscleman has just struck a sledgehammer against one of those carnival anvils. Not a moment ago she was fine, clear and coherent, but now she tightens her body, her eyes, her mouth, her ears and legs, plugging all exits as if to contain her shredding lucidity, willing it not to escape to wherever it goes in these moments. It had only been a question from an annoying cherub of a nurse, but she feels herself beginning to cower in a dark forest of tangled thoughts: branches and synapses thickening around her.

"It's all right, dear," the nurse says, softly stroking Shirley's hands. "Just breathe deeply, love." She makes little *shushing* noises through her teeth, and Shirley obeys her, like a cobra seduced by its charmer.

Her breathing settles into a slower rhythm, and she notices the droplets of perspiration under her once-warm armpits have now turned cold, sending a shiver up her body as they drop, first on the left side and then the right, paddling their way slowly down the side of her ribcage. She shudders slightly, feeling her heart settle back down into a normal rhythm in her chest and lets her body relax as she realizes she is still all there, still intact.

"I know how long I've been here," Shirley suddenly barks, yanking her hand out from under the clammy glob of saint flesh. "It's more than a week now. A week!" She imagines her voice delivered as a pit bull's bark. "This prison that you call a hospital. At least Matty will come and take me away from it." She continues to look straight ahead, out the window.

Matty. She can't believe she still calls him that, but the name just falls off her tongue. She wants to ask the nurse how long it has been since she has last seen him—perhaps she'll know—but she's not willing to risk the humiliation. She may have asked her that already, only a minute ago. Maybe she just saw Matt yesterday. The only thing she can recall is seeing him once in the last sixteen years, and then it was by accident. She had been visiting Gwen in Penticton when Matt just showed up on her doorstep unannounced, the first time she had seen him since he left home for the military. 'Run off' is how Shirley put it. The sight of him had been a shock, with his hair buzzed short and Amanda on his arm when he strode through Gwen's door. She wished she had been better prepared, although had she known he would show up, she wouldn't have been within 100 square miles.

He had always been a handsome boy, solid and quite serious, although there was an equally mischievous side to him. She often remarked how his brow furrowed, even when he was a boy—too much thinking, she used to say; you're a kid, for goodness sake. All of these years she has not even looked at a picture of him, avoiding anything that would remind her he was there, that he was hers. And then there he was at Gwen's, six feet of blue-eyed, cropped–blond hair, strapping muscles, looking as though he had been chiselled in a renaissance studio. As much as she tried, she couldn't avoid feeling just a little proud of him, that she could have sprung something that attractive from her loins.

Seeing her had clearly been just as much a surprise for him. What might have been a celebration grew as frigid as a Winnipeg winter, and seemed to last as long. She had tried her best to be civil, hard as it was asking him about his life while attempting to avoid any talk of his military service. She even played with his kids, who provided a tidy excuse to divert her attention away from her son. And then they were gone. Years ago it seemed, but she couldn't be sure.

"Well, I'm sure your son will be happy to see you, Mrs. Graydon," the nurse says with a smile. "Why don't you come and join us in the dining room in the meantime? You know you skipped lunch, and I can tell by the way your stomach's talking to me that you could use a little bite to eat." So bloody chirpy, she is. And Matt? Happy to see her? How does *she* know how Matt will feel? She—Nurse What's-Her-Name—has that annoying twang of an interior country girl. Uneducated pop tart, Shirley thinks; her role model is probably Britney Spears. Thank God she at least doesn't expose her donut of a midriff; she's probably got one of those dreadful piercings in her navel. She can just imagine it: the fleshy muffin top hanging over her waistband with some cheap ruby clinging to her bellybutton like a puckered cranberry. But if Nurse Goody has made some lunch for her, her status will rise, if only a little. Although her idea of haute cuisine is probably peanut butter and jam washed down with a vodka cooler. Oh what she would do for a vodka right now.

The nurse leans forward and gives Shirley's arm a small push from behind, nudging her forward in her seat.

Shirley jerks her arm away. "I'm okay, for God's sake," she says, standing. "I'm perfectly fit, you know. You have to stop treating me like some 80-year-old." She feels her voice rising. *Gentle, Shirley, gentle.* She realizes the nurse is just playing the role she was trained for. Most of the patients in her ward are physically hovering just this side of the grave, nearly all of them complete fruitcakes. She won't be treated like that. She is still young and fit, in great shape, although she really would have to remember to eat a little more. And she is 100 percent together about 90 percent of the time, or at least four times out of five, like they say in those government polls.

"When did you say Matt would be getting here again?" she asks the nurse.

"I don't think I did, Mrs. Graydon. But I expect it will be sometime soon. I'll help you pack your things as soon as we know for sure."

"I appreciate your kindness, I really do, but I'm capable of packing up myself," she says as sweetly as she can muster. She has decided to try to be nice. "By the way, I'd appreciate it if you'd stop treating me like a total retard." And just like that, her battle to be little Miss Christian Congeniality is lost. Oh well. And what an awful word, *retard*. She hates using it, but it is the only one she can think of.

She has to get out of here. What the hell will Matt do with her anyway, once he picks her up? She doesn't want to be anyone's responsibility, anyone's burden. She will plot her escape. Right after dinner.

She springs quickly from her chair to show the nurse she is not to be toyed with like the average detainee, and she counts the paces—nine of them—as she walks from the seat to the door. Pausing briefly in front of the door, she takes hold of the handle with the sleeve of her robe, pulls, and then marches into the hallway.

～

September 20, 2007—Shirley's Diary

I wandered off today. Unbelievable! I don't actually remember getting up and doing it, although I do remember baking a blueberry pie in the kitchen while looking out the window at one of those sunny days that descends on the valley like a gift from God. I guess I must have wanted to go for a walk but don't actually remember anything intentional. Apparently some time later, Mrs. Aimsley called Gwen from the 7-Eleven in town; seems I had strolled in there looking to buy a new car! According to her I kept on repeating something about driving to Tofino, of all places. Still had my apron on with pieces of pie dough clinging to it. While I'd like to imagine that they would chalk it up to me just being the kooky eccentric who lives on the farm, I'm afraid I wasn't there (mentally at least) to witness the performance, and the news has probably already spread clear across our fair Okanagan valley.

This is not the first time I've 'come to' after taking a little hike to nowhere, and not even realizing what I'd done until they told me. I didn't really believe them the first time, and this time I really didn't want to. It scares me senseless. But the bouts of forgetfulness seem to be getting a little more frequent. What in God's name is going to happen to me? I know I'm descending into this deep hole of dementia, like falling endlessly down the shaft of a dark well, clawing at the sides as I cling to that last bit of fading light above my head, too scared and ashamed to scream my lungs out the way I really want to. No one would listen anyway, and even if they heard it I'm sure they would just turn their backs, like watching someone drown from shore who you know is too far gone to save.

Lord, please make me whole again—don't let me lose my precious mind! It's the only thing I've got that I ever relied on. At fifty-one years old! How could this be happening?

Poor Gwen. She and Liz (I still have such a hard time believing she actually married a woman) are trying their subtle best to keep an eye on me, and I know how hard it must be. I just can't help but wish Liz was a man. But any time I can have with Gwen now I'll take, as I'm not sure how much lucid time I'll have with her—I never seem to know from one moment to the next. God, how could our family be struck like this? Remember the trials of Job is what I keep telling myself. Uterine cancer, I think she has, but she's only told me about it in such a way that it's what I've had to guess, and she won't talk about it if I ask her. And here I complain. Poor Gwen is only twenty-six. Says she wants to concentrate on me, doesn't want me to put anything more in my head that could be confusing. She's probably hoping I'll end up so totally rattled soon that I won't even remember she's a dyke. So as long as I don't trip over a double-headed dildo or something equally as awful, I'm good. I don't need to be reminded what they do to each other. I try to console myself by hoping that maybe they're actually good for each other, that they might make something of their relationship, which is more than I ever did with George.

They've diagnosed my condition through a process of elimination and declared it early-onset Alzheimer's. Imagine that; 'elimination' as though it was some kind of bowel movement. And they say the deterioration with early-onset most often comes faster than your run-of-the-mill dementia. My mind seems to be becoming holier than Swiss cheese. I love that thought—becoming holier, almost saint-like, as I become more nutty—what would my little church group think of that? I can comfort myself by getting away with all the things I dreamed of doing but never would, and they'll just attribute it smilingly to the batty old broad, like calling Gracie Martin a bitch the way she deserves, or swatting some of those bratty little kids at church.

I've had to give up my nutrition and lifestyle counselling, and even the weekly spot I had on the radio for so many years. It's funny, words fail me so often now, almost as though they're embarrassed to be around me. I try to hoard words and phrases in my mind, like a squirrel gathering nuts for later, and then forgetting where they're buried, or even what they are when I find them. Yet I look back at these entries in my diary and everything seems grand. No occluded thoughts or meandering non-sequiturs, but then I do try to get this down or go back to it when I'm at my best. It almost convinces me I'm completely together, as if my diary will become the stitching that holds everything in place. It's easier than looking in the mirror and wondering what drain it is the best parts of me are swirling down.

CHAPTER 3

MATT

Matt flipped open the cover of his cell phone one more time, trying his best not to look desperate in front of Rayner. No messages. He forced his eyes away from the phone, fighting the urge to call Amanda again. His gaze rhythmically swept the arrivals area of the Edmonton airport. He had tried her—twice? three times?—since they touched down, and each time connected only to her voice mail. Maybe she was busy negotiating traffic, or just out of range, in the parking structure or in an elevator. It was the same voice mail recording she always had; no special message to welcome him or tell him why she and the kids might not be there to meet him. He tried to convince himself there was nothing to worry about.

He looked over at Rayner, who stood with his bags at his side, arms wrapped around his girlfriend, Chrissy's, shoulders as he beamed down on her. Rayner glanced at Matt and did his own nonchalant scan of the arrivals area. Matt couldn't help feeling a little annoyed at Rayner, jealous that this recent girlfriend would come out to meet him where Amanda—the mother of his children—was now missing in action.

He worried that maybe she had been in an accident; a horrible thought, but the denial softened the impact of the almost-certain reality. At least if there had been an accident (*please god, no*), twisted as it was, there was still a chance for optimism; things could look up.

Rayner and Chrissy walked up to him hand in hand. "Let's wait a little while longer," Rayner said as he glanced at his watch. "It's only been twenty minutes."

Matt blew a puff of air through curled lips. "Our plane landed twenty minutes late, Rayner, and it's been half an hour since then. She's not coming." He spoke over his shoulder, in the direction of no one. He felt bad that he was spoiling Rayner's reunion with Chrissy. "Why don't you just go home, buddy? I'll wait a little while longer and then take a cab if I have to."

Rayner looked toward Chrissy. "No, I'll stick around for a bit. We're not in any hurry." Chrissy's face registered her disappointment. "I can always give you a ride to your place. We can drop Chrissy back at work first."

He listened to Rayner remotely, as though through a cloud that had stormed its way into his head. Even his vision seemed fogged as he looked far down the hall, nothing in focus. He hopped a few feet to the left and leaned against the wall, allowing his crutch to slide to the floor. The last kid to be picked up at kindergarten.

What could he possibly have said to make her stay away? Did she give him any clue that she wouldn't be there? What would happen at home, assuming she was there? He found no humour in the irony that he had been dreading the reunion in the first place, given how odd she had seemed in their more recent communications. No, dreading was too strong a word. Anxious, or fearful maybe, tough guy that he was. And where were Baxter and Callum? His mind went to a car crash again. *No, god.*

He checked his watch one more time and then slowly lifted his eyes, trying to focus on Rayner. "Yeah, let's go," he said, his voice detached from his body. But he remained standing as though he were glued to the wall, staring down the hallway.

"It's not a bomb, Graydon," Rayner whispered in Matt's ear, as if the door might detonate if he spoke any louder.

Matt could practically hear the mocking smile on Rayner's face from behind his left shoulder.

He remained in place, his hand poised unflinching on the handle of the metal screen door. In spite of how much he wanted things to be different, he knew no one was home. He'd rung the bell as a warning anyway, or maybe it was just to stall for time.

Looking down at his fingers, white and clenched around the handle, his gaze remained fixed on a small bump under the knuckle of his index finger, a tiny piece of glass embedded under his skin from this very door. He had never managed to pluck it out. It happened the last time he was home between his Afghanistan tours, less than a year ago, when he put his hand through the pane of glass. Amanda swore he punched the door in a rage, but he was pretty certain it wasn't that; he was just in a hurry to get outside, his fist flying through the glass as he reached for the handle. An accident. He hadn't been mad, that much he knew, but he couldn't recall why he wanted to get out of the house so quickly. What he *did* know was that he didn't punch the door intentionally. It was just clumsiness, alcohol mixed with a little carelessness.

"Hey, I don't know why you even bother with a screen door with these kind of holes in the screen," Rayner said, poking his finger through the mesh, his voice driving a hole through Matt's reverie. Rayner was a great guy, one of those people you always wanted by your side in combat, but sometimes—especially now—Matt wished he would just shut up. In Afghanistan, Rayner had driven his superiors crazy, especially the officers, baiting and defying them only to see if he could get away with it. He had been assigned more shit jobs—literally—than anyone Matt had known, mostly because his relationship with the military was inappropriately symbiotic, bordering on the co-dependent: he needed the discipline of the military, and the military loved to discipline him. Matt couldn't count the number of times Rayner had been assigned to burn the shit from the base's latrines for punishment. It was the lowest of the grunt jobs, emptying the muck into barrels and then lighting it on fire and stirring it like a batch of flaming brownies until it burned down into a brown slop. Yet he seemed to do it happily, never for a moment letting on that it might have bothered him. It was the kind of attitude that invariably infuriated the higher-ups but made him everyone else's hero.

Matt was almost always happy to have him around. Except maybe now.

Matt stood back from the door, releasing the handle and crossing his arms over his chest, and stepped back toward the street. He stood motionless at the end of the driveway, peering down the road from the end of the cul-de-sac, and although he saw no one, he felt as though sets of eyes were locked on him from the half-dozen houses that sat on either side of the street.

He and Amanda had dreamed about a house like this when they got married, somewhere they could live off base and raise the kids, a little backyard, a decent school district. At least they had gotten into the market before prices went through the roof. If they had to sell it, maybe the house would be worth something. He was nervously mindful of jumping to poor conclusions but couldn't stop himself from anticipating the worst.

He tossed Rayner the keys. "Here, you open it."

Rayner twisted the key in the lock, standing back to allow Matt to enter first. The house was nearly dark inside, the curtains drawn. It smelled stale, not musty exactly but more the smell of stillness, the air of a house that hasn't been lived in recently. It smelled like dust, if dust had a smell. Not like the fine sandy grit that covered everything in Kandahar. There the dust smelled like shit, like just about everything at KAF. There it was alive, swirling through your hair, your clothes and your shoes, even creeping into your sleeping bag at night, settling under the hair on your arms, legs, chest. Here the dust descended softly and unnoticed, as if trying to cover up any signs their home had once been alive. Here everything was in its lifeless place, like a dimmed theatre set waiting for the next performance with none of the usual chaos or props or performers: no kids yelling as they chased each other through the kitchen, no scattered magazines and newspapers or dishes in the sink, no jacket thrown over the back of a kitchen chair.

Matt moved toward the doorway between the living room and kitchen, standing to survey the contents. Their furniture was an eclectic blend of donations from Amanda's parents mixed with Ikea and The Bay, hardly any of it matching and none of it worth very much. The new 40-inch flat-screen TV they had bought before this last tour was gone, although everything else seemed to be as it was when he left. The keys to the Grand Am sat on the kitchen counter. At least she had left that.

His eyes went to the table by the phone where they had always left little reminders for each other. There was a large orange Post-It note stuck on the phone, six small words written in black marker: "I'm sorry. I'll call you. A."

"You okay, man?" Rayner asked, putting his hand on Matt's shoulder.

He jumped; he hadn't heard Rayner come into the room behind him. He leaned against the cabinet where the TV had been.

Was he okay? Rayner was just trying to be thoughtful, but he wanted to slug him for even asking. He peeled the sticky note off the phone and crumpled it, stuffing it in his pocket.

"Yeah, I guess," he said, although he felt like someone had just stuck his head in a microwave. He looked dreamily around the room, taking in everything and nothing. "I just wish I could talk to her."

Reality was suddenly pushing all feeling down from his head right through his feet, a heaviness that descended on him so hard it caused him to crumple into the hard sofa behind him. He dropped his head into his upturned palms and absentmindedly scratched his stubby scalp, fighting a lack of breath that threatened to rise into a sob. There was a dark-green thread on the piping of the couch that had started to unravel; he wrapped it around his finger and gave it a tug.

"Where the hell is she?" he wailed. He squinted, trying to squeeze every ounce of concentration into his brain as though it could infuse him with sudden clairvoyance or wisdom. But all he could feel besides the hollow in his gut were his eyes, stinging as he fought back emotion.

"Where did she take the boys?" Suddenly he was angry. "She can't just walk away and take Baxter and Callum with her. Where the fuck has she gone?"

He was off the couch, hobbling toward the hallway, toward the bedrooms. He stopped in front of the boys' room, feeling the house rotating around him. The thought that he was at least slightly complicit in her disappearance had suddenly dawned on him, and the idea set him spinning. His anger was no longer directed at her but had started to turn toward himself. He braced himself on his crutch and swung a leg back, ready to kick the wall but stopped, his foot poised behind him. He needed to cool off, stop for a minute, take some deep breaths. As he silently attempted to coax the anger out of his body, his shoulders slumping in one heavy heave, he braced himself against the wall and watched the thoughts tumbling through his head, trying to make sense of things, to understand which of his stupid actions might have driven her away.

He remembered when he got back from his first tour how Amanda had jumped on him at the airport and given him the deepest, longest kiss, right there at the arrivals area. They'd barely said hello and she was all over him. And then she had this stunned look on her face when he pulled away. It pissed him off that she would push herself on him like that, although he probably wouldn't have given her behaviour a second thought before Afghanistan. Later he wondered if he was more annoyed at himself for being such a dick, but instead dismissed it as *her* problem, her lack of understanding, not his. It was only the end of his first tour then, just six months and a war later, but suddenly all that intuition, that near telepathic compatibility that couples develop after being together for a while had evaporated. Other things seemed to have become so much more important, and the images of Afghanistan kept stomping on everything else in his head. He would think of the horrors they had been through and it sickened him. Yet at the same time he so desperately wanted to be back there, in an environment where he was understood, thriving in its immediacy, living in fear and sometimes in horror, but living raw and in the moment with everyone else. Every day in theatre was a day of balancing on the thin edge of a sword, and the things they had thought of as problems at home—the car payments, the mortgage, what to have for dinner—became laughable, not even worth noticing, a pimple on an elephant's butt.

He stood in front of the door to the boys' room and gently pushed it open, as if too rapid a movement would allow whatever essence of the boys was left to slip out the door. The curtains were partially drawn, and he blinked as his eyes adjusted to the muted light. He thought of the long nights before his last deployment, staring at the ceiling while Amanda lay sleeping next to him. He would get up and go to the boys' bedroom, padding softly on the worn path of the rust-coloured carpet, and then stand between their beds looking at them as they slept. Callum was always uncovered. He was the restless one, kicking off his blanket every night and lying on his stomach in his flannel pyjamas. Across from him, Baxter would lie on his back with his cheek resting against his pillow, his covers pulled up around his neck, always with a slight scowl on his face as though he disapproved of whatever was in his dreams, or of sleep itself like it was a waste of time.

When Matt was sure the boys were okay, he would cross the room to the darkened window and close the curtains. The boys liked to fall asleep with them open just in case they could catch a glimpse of the Northern Lights some nights—Callum was convinced they were UFO searchlights—but Matt always felt safer with the curtains drawn closed. He would have stayed there all night, watching them, making sure they were safe, but after a while would force himself out of the room, shutting the door softly and walking into the living room, where he would turn on the TV and scan the news for any reports on the guys back in Afghanistan, the light from the TV dancing across his face in the darkened room. He remembered in one of those half-dazed states seeing an episode of *Extreme Makeover*, where they built a house for a returning Marine in the U.S. No one would ever do that in Canada.

After his last tour, the insomnia was relentless. He knew he was wound-up tight; Afghanistan had stretched and twisted him like one of those rubber bands on a toy airplane propeller. There you had to be alert every waking moment; the only time he fell into a deep sleep in Afghanistan was out of pure exhaustion, when they had been in battle for hours under a melting sun, without food, low on water, under siege. But any other time at the base, or on the ground in their sleeping bags outside their patrol vehicle, sleep was always shallow as his body developed the instinct to keep vigilant, to listen and watch for every sign of danger.

After that first tour he would wander through the house, dazed from lack of sleep and exhausted from the images that would play in his head when he closed his eyes. Finally, on one of his nightly perambulations, he found himself in the basement, unlocking the cabinet where he kept his hunting rifle. He removed it and gently turned it over in his hands, stroking the grain of the wood where it met the metal shaft, raising the sights to his right eye and taking aim at the light bulb, his finger resting lightly on the trigger. Then he tiptoed back up the wooden basement stairs with the rifle—safety on—tucked under his arm, and crept down the hall to his bedroom. He slowly took hold of the pillow beside Amanda, whose back was turned to him, her breathing steady and light, laying the rifle down on the nubby carpet beside the bed. Then he took another look at his weapon and smiled at it, almost affectionately, finally laying it on the ground where he flattened himself beside it, resting the palm of his hand against the butt of the firearm.

The next day he couldn't remember even putting his head on the pillow. He had fallen into a deep, dreamless sleep, the best he'd had in weeks, secure now that he had his weapon beside him and only waking up in the morning when Amanda's cold toes lighted on his bare shoulder as she stepped out of bed.

His body had instantly tensed, and he was up on his feet, screaming, "Get back! Get back!" as he pointed the weapon at her. It wasn't until a half-minute later that he realized he was standing, facing her in his underwear, pointing the rifle at her while she talked softly to him, her eyes welling with tears.

Then the elastic band that had him wound so tightly suddenly snapped, and he crumpled into a ball on the floor, sobbing with the realization of it all, of what he had nearly done, his body heaving in spasms as he cried. Amanda had just stood, staring at him silently. She hadn't even held him. Then she left the bedroom, shutting the door behind her so the boys wouldn't hear their dad's sobs.

"Maybe you should go for treatment," she said in the morning, breaking the long silence over coffee. The wives had all been trained to watch for signs of stress.

"I'm okay," he said, shaking his head. "Really. It's just tension. I'll get over it."

Post-traumatic stress disorder was the last thing any soldier wanted to admit to, and besides, things seemed pretty normal to him. Who wouldn't come back a little fucked up, especially after losing a close buddy? But admitting to PTSD made you look like a wimp, or else the guys thought you were faking it to get out of going back to Afghanistan.

Sure, there might have been some signs: she would bang a cupboard door shut behind his back and he would jump; he couldn't go to the supermarket without being certain someone was around the corner in the other aisle just waiting to ambush him. He knew the signs came across his face, in his body language. But he'd get over it.

"You can't sleep with the rifle next to the bed, Matt. It scares me."

"I know, I know," he had said. But when he'd tried sleeping without it, the long nights awake continued. It had taken him two weeks of sleeping in the living room with the rifle tucked beneath the sofa until he had finally crawled back into bed with her, locking his rifle back in the basement.

Now he sat on Baxter's bed facing the window, smoothing the blanket on either side of him. Matt was a fucking statistic, that's what he was. A walking cliché. He knew forty percent of relationships don't survive when you're shipped off on tour, joking about the "Dear John" e-mails you get from your partner back home. Here you are, fighting your guts out in theatre, stressed out of your mind and living on death's door and your wife decides with impeccable timing to e-mail and let you know that "things just aren't the same anymore." The guys take bets on who it's going to happen to first. Gallows humour.

They all knew about the enormous stress on the partner left at home. So many families lived with their TVs on 24/7, and they scoured the Internet continuously for any news from Afghanistan. It became an obsession, living with the constant stress of an imagined loss, and for some of them the only way to get rid of the anguish was to turf the relationship, or take up with someone else who could be there in living and breathing flesh, someone who could be expected to live as long as you, help bring up the kids together, who would go for walks with you through the park without wondering what was behind every tree.

Maybe he shouldn't have got married at all, except of course for Callum and Baxter. How many times had the thought of them kept him going in Afghanistan, even when he felt like everything else was in danger of collapsing around him?

He looked up from Baxter's bed and caught his reflection framed in the window. He pushed himself off the mattress and threw the curtains shut. He stood for a minute, then turned and walked slowly out of the boys' room, quietly closing the door and continuing down the hall to the open door of his and Amanda's bedroom.

As he paused in the doorway, his eyes went immediately to the old oak dresser, a massive six-drawer antique they had proudly bought for next to nothing at a barn sale in the country, on top of it a framed picture of him and Amanda, Matt in uniform with Amanda swung upside down over his shoulder, his hand on her ass and her hair dangling downward, both of them laughing. At first he felt relieved that it was still there, that she hadn't put it away somewhere. Or she had left it behind because she didn't want it, or maybe had it tucked in the dresser drawer all this time and she had taken it out and put it there when she left, a little dagger aimed at his heart.

Everything looked as sterile as a model bedroom at The Bay, as though it were someone else's photo on the dresser and clothes in the closet. He walked toward the bed, covered in its bright floral-patterned comforter and turned around and sat, slowly raising his feet up over the edge and allowing his head to float down to the pillow, not even removing his boots. He lay staring at the overhead fan, its brass metal chain hanging from its side, the tulip-shaped milky white lampshades pointing toward the corners of the room. His eyes had roamed over every detail of that ceiling on so many sleepless nights in that very position. Only now he closed his eyes, exhausted from his trip and spent from the stress of uncertainty, and fell into a long, restless sleep.

∽

"Hi, Matt," Amanda said. Her voice was soft, dreamlike. At first he wasn't sure if he was really awake or not. He switched his cell phone to his other hand and glanced at his watch: nine-thirty at night.

"Amanda, where are you?" All the clever things he had thought to say to her, all the sarcasm and anger, slipped away in the fog of his half-awake state.

There was no response, except for a faint sigh over the phone.

"What's going on, Amanda?" he asked. "Why weren't you at the airport? Is everything all right? Are the boys okay?" He tried not to let the anxiety show in his voice, grasping instead for a thread of hope in whatever she said next.

"The boys are fine, Matt. They say hello."

"They say hello?" he said incredulously. "Amanda, I need to see you. I need to see the boys. What's going on? I get home and all there is, is a stinking note by the phone from you. What are you telling me?"

He could hear her breathing on the other end. Finally she said, "Me and the boys have moved out for a while, Matt. It's something we needed to do."

"What the fuck? Why?"

"Oh, Matt." She sighed, as if he was a four-year old who should know better. "I was afraid of how things would be when you got home." She drew a long breath. "Things were so bad last time. I didn't think it was fair or safe to put the boys through that again. And I think it's better if you have some time on your own to figure things out. You've got your mother to worry about too, and I think you need to make that part of your family a priority right now."

"But you *are* my family." He felt his voice rising, but he couldn't help it. "You're telling me you're not going to be here for me? That you're leaving me because you can't face my family situation? Or you think I've gone nuts?" There was no good answer.

"Listen," he said, lowering his voice, trying to sound normal. "I want to see you. I've got to see Callum and Baxter. Are you in town?"

"Yes, Matt. I'm in town."

"Can we meet? Can you come over here to the house and bring the boys?"

"Let me think about it. It's already late. Why don't just sleep on things a bit and I'll give you a call in the morning?"

She wanted some time apart, she said, time to herself.

When he hung up he walked out of the bedroom and through the still house. It was nearly ten at night and still light outside. Rayner's car was gone from the driveway. There was a note beside the phone in the kitchen: "I'll call you later. R." He hoped that wasn't Rayner's idea of a joke. He crumpled it and threw it against the wall.

The next morning he paced the house from room to room, doing an inventory of its contents, deciding what he should take. Whether he went to Penticton right away or stayed behind, it was only fair that Amanda and the kids live in the house. So he went into the basement and emptied two large Rubbermaid containers of tools and Christmas decorations and took them upstairs, filling them with his books, his files and clothes. He tossed in a couple of bottles of wine from the fridge.

He had called Amanda when he woke at seven; she had agreed to meet him at the house at ten. He also called Rayner to keep him company until she arrived.

"I can't believe she's nearly an hour late." Matt and Rayner sat on the concrete steps outside the front door, watching Amanda drive up the road.

Rayner took a long pull off his second beer. "It's probably better that way," he said. "At least it gave you time to do inventory."

Matt's eyes didn't leave the black Infiniti SUV coming toward them. *Who the hell's car is that?* The heat rose up his neck as he watched her approach, her face coming into focus through the windshield. Even from a distance he saw the serious look etched into her features: all business.

He tried to focus on the backseat, to get a glimpse of the boys. Every moment of every day for more than six months he had thought of them. Knowing he would be back to see the kids had been enough to get him through the worst of times, to make sure he wasn't stupid enough to go off and get killed.

When he saw them waving and smiling in the backseat, it seemed as though he would erupt in pure joy. If he could run to the curb he would have, but he still managed to be there before the car stopped, his hand on the back door, reaching in and hauling out Callum, who squirmed with excitement.

"Hey, you little worm," he said as he hugged him on the sidewalk. "Are you trying to squiggle away from me?" Callum giggled as he wrapped both arms around Matt's legs and squeezed hard.

"Hey, Baxter," he said, extending his arm to embrace the older boy, who stood by smiling, almost shyly it seemed. Baxter let himself be drawn into Matt's side, keeping his hands in his pockets. He was always the more reserved one, but for a second Matt felt disconnected, as if he wasn't sure he could read his own son any longer.

"What happened, Dad?" Baxter asked, pointing at Matt's crutch.

"Oh, a little injury, that's all. I'll be good in no time."

Amanda had descended from the car and stood on the sidewalk watching them, her arms crossed rigidly in front of her. She had let her hair grow while he was away and had lightened it to a sandy shade of blonde. It was nearly to her shoulders now, every strand obediently in place like she'd just been to the salon. She looked great, and part of him wanted to walk over and hold her, wishing it was like it had been the last time when she was so excited, so relieved to see him.

"What took you so long?" he asked, unable to hide his frustration. It wasn't a great way to start off, but how was he supposed to open a conversation like this? Talk about the weather? About how he missed her and the boys every day when he was over there?

"Hello to you too," she replied, walking past him and up the steps to the front door. Her jeans could hardly be tighter. Or sexier. He was an idiot.

"Hey, guys," he said to the boys, resting a hand on their heads. Baxter had become noticeably lankier since he'd been gone. "Why don't you go for a little walk with your uncle Jeremy here while Dad takes care of some stuff with your mom?"

Baxter turned to walk toward Rayner, but Callum stood looking up at Matt as he clung to his thigh, not saying a word.

Matt took a deep breath and swallowed the lump rising in his throat. He kneeled slowly toward Callum, supporting himself on his crutch on his way down, and pulled him in close. "Look, buddy," he said. "Your mom and I need to talk about some stuff, okay? We'll just go in the house and get our business done, and then I'll come back out and play with you guys, all right? Did you bring the soccer ball?"

Callum's head bobbed slowly, but he still didn't look at Matt.

"Well, this might give me a bit of trouble kicking it around to you," he said, jiggling his crutch as Callum grinned back at him. "Go catch up with your brother and I'll be out in a minute." He bent forward and brushed his lips on the top of Callum's fine hair, resting his chin on the boy's head while he squeezed him hard, inhaling Callum's scent. His hair smelled of honey, the same shampoo Amanda used. Matt had to will his fingers to release their grip on the boy.

Matt finally stood and turned around, walking up the steps and through the door, imagining this could be his last time in his house. This time he didn't hesitate when he opened the door to enter.

Amanda was already in the kitchen, sitting on the black vinyl bar stool by the counter, one heel wedged over the circular metal footrest, her other leg crossed over her knee. Her free foot bounced up and down, her arms crossed firmly over her chest, one hand holding a burning cigarette from which she took a short drag. He couldn't believe she had started smoking again. How could he still find her so damn attractive?

"I hope you don't do that in front of the boys," Matt said, pointing to her cigarette.

Her foot started doing double time, but the rest of her stayed still as she stared at a point on the floor.

"I don't know what you look so upset about," he said. His heartbeat was rising, trying to keep time with her drumming foot. He couldn't help spitting his words out. "I'm not the one who did this. *You* wanted this. *You* left *me*. That's right, isn't it? You're leaving me. How can you sit there and look so goddamn smug?"

"Matt, let's try to keep this civilized," she said. Her voice was jagged sharp, the sound of ice forming. With her long crimson fingernails she scratched her upper arm, grazing the surface of her skin just enough to make a rasping sound, an old nervous habit. "I don't want to make this any harder. We just need some time apart, and I just want to get on with my life." She lifted her head and locked eyes with his, probably the first time she had looked straight at him since she'd arrived.

"Is that it? So there's no explanation? No attempt to even talk about this?" He waited for an answer. None came. "Is there another guy?" The question hung in the kitchen like the smell of fried fish.

Amanda looked away from him. "It is what it is, Matt."

"What's that supposed to mean? Come on, Amanda. Why are you doing this?" His voice was rising.

"Keep it down Matt," she said looking toward the door.

"Don't tell me what to do!" He slammed his fist on the counter. The force of it blew any remaining sound out of the room, and they sat in a silent vacuum. Amanda stood frozen, her eyes fixed on the counter where his fist had landed. He rotated suddenly on his crutch, jamming one hand into his pocket and turning his back on her.

"What are you going to do, put your fist through the door again?" she asked, her voice rising to match his. "Or this time are you going to hit *me*? Eh? How long do I have to be with you before *that* happens?"

Matt's face was flushed; the tops of his ears tingled with warm blood. He clenched his fist in his jeans and walked into the living room toward the sofa. He let his body collapse into the seat, his shoulders rising as he inhaled deeply, an attempt to calm himself.

Amanda walked to the living room's entrance but didn't go in, leaning instead against the door frame. "Look, maybe we should do this some other time. Like when you've had a chance to come to terms with things and do this, you know, more calmly." Her voice had softened.

Matt looked out the window, somewhere far away. "Forget it." His voice cracked slightly. He slowly shook his head. He suddenly felt tired. "Everything I want I've got in that pile by the door, and it's only clothes and books. Have a look if you like. The only other thing I want is the boys, so don't think you can run off with them too. If you want some time apart that's fine, but I'm not leaving for Penticton until we've figured out what we're doing with the boys."

"You're in no shape to take them, Matt. You can't even care for yourself."

He shot her a look. The boys would be better off with *him*, even if he *was* a little raw.

"Take what you want, but just stay away from me and the kids, at least until you get yourself sorted out. You think you're so goddamn innocent in all this, but take another look. I can tell just by looking at you that you're already worse than the last time you were home. Even the army thinks so, for god's sake. Everybody knows what happened over there anyway, but you're too goddamn tough to even admit you have a problem, let alone do anything about it. You didn't even tell *me* what happened!" She waited for a response, but there was none.

"I know what's going to happen. You and Rayner and your buddies are just going to get drunk every night and sit around and tell war stories to each other and exclude everybody else. If you think I'm leaving my kids with you, you're out of your fucking mind. God knows what you might do to them in your state, Matty. There's no way I'm taking that chance."

She was wrong; she didn't understand a thing, and he wanted to argue with her, to walk right across the room and confront her, but he couldn't. Even though she stood there regarding him as though he was a monster, the fight had slipped out of him. He was spent. He looked down at the carpet as he took slow steps toward her, toward the front door. Amanda glanced over her shoulder, inching backward.

"For god's sake Amanda, I'm not going to hit you. I've *never* done that. I never *would* do that." He stopped two arms' lengths away. How had she come to be so scared of him? "Just let me go out and play a little with the kids, would you?" He looked out the window at the boys. "I'm not going to hurt them. I can't believe you would think that."

She looked out the door toward the boys on the street. Her bottom lip was trembling. Slowly she nodded.

As he walked by her to the door, she suddenly said, "I'm sorry about Gwen, Matty." Her voice was barely a whisper, but the force of her words stopped him. He turned to face her, looking at her close up. Her eyes danced back and forth on his, nervous and tired.

"Thanks," he said quietly. "We're going to have her memorial service when I get back to Penticton." A question hung in his eyes as he looked at her. She looked away, toward the street.

"I'm sorry, but I can't go." She shifted her weight. "You'll say hello to Lizzie for me? Please give her a hug for me." It was the sudden tenderness in her voice that got to him. He wanted to take a step toward her, put his head on her chest, hold her while she told him that everything would be all right. Wasn't there some way he could just go back to how it was before?

"Yeah." He sighed, as if all the breath was leaving his body with one word. "Lizzie and Gwen always liked you. And the boys. Hey," he said, sensing she was softening. "What if I took the boys with me to Penticton, even for a week or so? You know how much they love it there. I haven't spent any time with them at all."

"You know I can't let you do that. How do you think you could manage them *and* your mother at the same time? What are you going to do with *her*?"

"I've handled a lot more in my life, you know. I'll find a way."

"But you don't even know what you're up against there."

"Maybe, but I've got no choice. I have to get there to figure it out, and I don't want to leave the boys behind."

Amanda ignored the last sentence. "Can't you just put her in a home?"

"You know we don't have the money to do that. Maybe if I sell the farm. I don't know."

He looked at her, trying to read anything behind her eyes. He hated this, feeling like a dog at her feet, begging for morsels while she stood there barely tossing him a crumb. If he could get beyond this, if they could only unravel all the complicated stuff, he knew he could still love her. That he still did.

"You look good, you know," he said. The muscle under his left eye started to twitch. His testicle groaned.

"Oh, Matty." She exhaled, his name gliding out on barely a whisper. "Please don't."

He wished he hadn't said it. He didn't know where it would go, a trial balloon he had simply released without thinking about it. "Listen, I gotta go. I guess I'm taking the Grand Am, eh? I'm just going to spend a little time with the boys before I leave."

He bent down to pick up a suitcase then opened the screen door with his elbow. "See? No fist through the door. I *can* be gentle, you know." He winked at her with half a smile and then hopped down the steps to the driveway and the dusty Grand Am, throwing his suitcase into the trunk. He had come expecting respite from war, and now here he was engaged in a new battle, and all he could think about was getting as far away from here as he could.

He could only hope that what faced him in Penticton was easier than this. But he doubted it.

April 29, 2006, Kandahar Air Field

It's Baxter's 8th birthday today. I was trying my best to keep it light and happy on the phone, but I almost started blubbering while I was talking to the little guy. It breaks my heart to be away for his birthday, or to leave them behind at all. I'm sure he'll forgive me when he gets older and understands better. Even now he's such a cool kid, really level headed and seems to think it's his responsibility to be the new man in the family while I'm away. He told me he didn't want a birthday party because it was "what kids do," but Amanda threw him one anyway. It's a good thing they keep us busy here because whenever I get a break I ache for Amanda and the kids.

We went on a familiarization trip to Kandahar City today, about 15 km from the base, our first outing with the troop rotation. The outgoing guys take you as part of your orientation and download a transfer of information. The field trips are something the troops do frequently anyway to show our presence, even if we're just passing through on the way to a mission in some gawd-forsaken place. It was my first experience of the landscape around here, outside the wire of our KAF base. We're going to be dusty for the next six months. No wonder we were laughed at when our troops were first deployed to Afghanistan in our green camouflage gear. If you're anything but dusty beige here, you stand out like hot pants in a mosque. Whoever designated green as the colour of Islam 1,000 years ago knew what they were doing; green looks alive and refreshing in the middle of this dustbowl.

I'm stunned you still don't see one woman out of a burka except for the occasional old grandmother and little girls. It's such an otherworldly sight, those ghostlike creatures wrapped in blue tents floating across the dusty roads, like solitary raindrops in the desert. There's no more than a little mesh screen to see through, and even their hands are covered. I thought things were supposed to have changed here since the Taliban were ousted. Most men are dressed in their traditional shalwar kameez, a loose smock that drapes from their shoulders to their knees. Both the men's and the women's outfits are perfect hiding places for suicide bombs.

The kids often run after us in our vehicle with their hands out for little gifts they've come to expect us to toss their way. It's better than when the troops first arrived and the kids would throw rocks at the LAVs—the Light Armoured Vehicles. We keep a supply of pencils and candies all the time; one of the guy's moms has taken to sending him cartons of pencils with a little Canadian maple leaf on them. I'm sure most of the kids who run after us are pre-teen (we're supposed to keep a suspicious eye out for FAMs—fighting-age males—pretty much anyone old enough to shave), but even the youngest ones' faces look like they've already lived a full lifetime. What girls you see are always prepubescent, otherwise they'd be covered up, and the boys are constantly shoving them out of the way. If one of the girls does manage to get a candy, coin, or a pencil, she runs with it as fast as she can (it's amazing how fast these kids can run without shoes), most often with the boys in hot pursuit. She knows if they catch her she'll have to give it up to a 'superior' male. I've managed to get some pictures of some of the kids who smile up at me as I aim the camera at them, which melts me into a puddle of Jell-O thinking of Baxter and Callum.

When I leave this place, if I forget everything else I will never forget the smell. I thought KAF had its own memorable aroma, where it seems no matter where you are you're downwind of the sewage treatment plant. But Kandahar City is one big assault on the senses: diesel fumes, ripe fruit and chai tea, meat hanging in market shops that's buzzing with flies and suspended there for who knows how long, often while streams of human and animal waste flow by in gutters. The guys have told me this is nothing compared to the smells I'm yet to experience, of burnt corpses and human flesh left to rot roadside in makeshift graves.

They say an Afghan is never in a hurry to get anywhere unless he's driving, and if the chaos on the KC roads is any indication, then I'm a believer. Donkey-led carts full of watermelons, mixed with cars, trucks and pedestrians, all seemingly oblivious to being millimetres away from death by traffic. And the 'jingle trucks', these big transports that look like an ice cream truck in drag—one even had a tiara on top of the cab—remind you you've dropped into a different world. They have little metallic tassels that dangle from the bottom of the truck's frame that 'jingle' as they ride along, and every inch of the vehicle is painted (no naked ladies on mud flaps here in Allah's territory), beaded or embroidered in reds, blues and yellows and topped off with flashing lights and neon running boards. If Callum were here, I can just hear the kind of wide-eyed questions he'd be asking: *Why do they decorate their trucks like that? Do they sell ice cream on them? Why do all the women have to be covered like that?*

We watched the Afghan police stopping vehicles and searching male passengers (I'm not sure how they would have handled searching a female) for weapons. It's a dodgy job; anyone could be the next potential suicide bomber. We're told always to be on the lookout for suspicious-looking people or vehicles, especially white Toyotas for some reason, but it seems every other car here is a white Toyota, and every man wearing a turban or a tunic looks suspicious. You want to think of these people as fellow human beings, the civilians we're here to free and protect, but you wonder what they think of you, if they'd rather blow you up than look at you. It's not a job for compassion, only for suspicion.

We heard that one of our guys shot a suicide bomber in a white Toyota who was speeding directly toward one of our convoys. Picked him off right through the windshield not 100 feet away. It's a good thing he did because the guy was wired and his package detonated right there, blowing him out of the windshield of his car into a ditch a few metres away. The guys called him "Ronald" because he looked like some circus clown being propelled out of a cannon. There wasn't much left of him.

On our way back we passed dozens of Koochis, tribal nomads herding sheep and goats. Their convoy is a little more primitive than ours—it's on foot for one thing, and there are no vehicles except for camels. What's really striking is that the Koochi women are not covered up like other Afghan women; they dress in flowing, colourful skirts in those typical deep Afghan reds, blues and oranges, the kind of clothing that we most often associate with belly dancers except not that provocative, at least not here in the open. (I remember when I was a kid hearing that little sung rhyme, "Oh they don't wear pants in the hoochie koochi dance" [nyah nyah nyah nyah ...]. I wonder if its origins have anything to do with these people. I'll have to check it out.)

Our interpreter, Kareem, is a wiry little Pashtun, couldn't be much older than 20. He's a handsome kid, brown as a chestnut with big green eyes and hair so thick and wavy you could surf on it, but he's always got this worried look on his face, so we do our best to try to make him laugh because it's amazing to see him smile. Hutch does a good job of it cause Kareem can barely understand a thing he's saying, and he teaches him all these Newfie expressions about fucking and fishing.

Kareem says nobody respected the Taliban before they were in power; they were just a bunch of religious fanatics from poor families who sent their boys away to the madrassas (Koran school) because they couldn't afford to keep them at home, so they're raised as lunatic radicals. They're taught to hate women—kissing in public would be unpardonable—so he says they're all a bunch of sodomites. He hates them but fears them at the same time. What they did in this country is almost unspeakable, but he knows they're still a force. Kareem says no one knows he works for us, because if he was betrayed to the Taliban he'd be flogged, his skin flayed from his body before being publicly hanged. He actually cowers a little when he tells you that, and you get the impression he's not being overly dramatic.

There's been some whispering around that maybe Kareem is a spy, but that's the current thinking about any of the 'terps' since one of them was found out just recently. They way Kareem talks I can't imagine it, but we watch what we say, and we keep a close eye on him and the others.

I'm writing this in my little 'room' in our Big Ass Tent sleeping quarters. There's not much privacy with 200 other guys around but we manage to drape spare sheets or plastic bags around our beds to create our own little rooms, which leaves us enough space to stand up and put on our uniforms. It gives the boys a bit of privacy, at least from sight if not sound. Some of the slaps and moans I could do without hearing, but the guys joke about it. Somebody told Rayner the other day they were sure they heard him calling out "Kareem!" while he was 'relieving' himself. Rayner threw his boot at the guy and cracked his lip open. No secrets here.

I keep a worn paperback copy of the Koran beside my bed that I bought in a used bookshop before I got deployed. I try to read a little of it every day. I can imagine my mother's horror if she knew I had anything beside the bed but a Bible, but it seems to me that it must be the key to understanding these people. Know your enemy. Sometimes I wonder if it's religion that's kept things so primitive. The Koran was written 1,400 years ago, so to interpret it literally seems about as crazy as a literal interpretation of the Bible. If North Americans were as fanatically Christian as these people are Muslim, I wonder how advanced our society would have become, although you don't have to scratch the surface too deep to find our own share of fanatics. Then again, if we prayed five times a day, maybe we'd be a little more tolerant of each other. It strikes me that Allah must be an awfully needy god for him to require people to pray to him so often.

I'm amazed how closely some of the Koran tracks the Bible—they believe in Mary, Jesus, Noah, Abraham—and there is a lot there, like any religion I suppose, that makes good guidelines for living. The trouble always seems to start when anyone buys this stuff lock, stock and particularly (smoking) barrel.

I had been talking to Kareem about it, about how fanatical their religion appears to us in the West. Yet Islam is bred into them and everything they do. "Inshallah" is what you hear all the time: "If Allah is willing." I think they truly believe it, as though all their actions were governed by Allah, that their destiny is decided in a simple dance of action and reaction. I envy them in a way, relying on a god the way they do as if he had a little roadmap for each and every Muslim creature, with everything preordained, leaving yourself in god's hands so completely.

I wonder what would happen if you took a kid like Kareem out of here and transplanted him in North America. Would he keep the same idealism, or would he succumb to our materialistic culture where life is determined more by how much money you make, with a deity only there to ask to keep on *increasing your abundance (if you believe in a god at all)? How long would it take him to be seduced by our malls, our cars, our advertising?*

When I got back from Kandahar City I looked at the pictures I took of the kids in the streets, the big smiles on their dirty faces, their tattered clothes. There was one I'd taken of a young girl whose legs were blown off in a landmine, who drags herself begging through the streets. I felt a bit guilty taking the picture, but these are the realities of this country, and something I need to remind myself of. It almost makes me feel sick when I think of the able-bodied panhandlers at home whose lives are a miracle by comparison. Then I clicked on the pictures of Baxter and Callum and Amanda, their lives seemingly perfect by comparison, and if I were a religious man I would thank god they were born there and not here. Perhaps a Buddhist would attribute it to karma, a Muslim would say it's god's will, but I think it's just pure damn luck.

I posted some pictures on Facebook for the kids of all these mangy dogs that I keep snapping pictures of. They had been bugging me like crazy before I left to get them a puppy, and how could I possibly say no? I figured it would be great company for them and a distraction while I'm gone, so we brought home an eight week-old golden retriever the kids named Bosley. I'm hoping that when they see the pictures of the mutts here that struggle to survive, they'll feel lucky and take good care of the little guy.

Lying here last night about 2:00 a.m. a rocket screamed past our tent and landed with a rumbling boom just outside the base. Sirens started going off, but no one had briefed us yet on what the various sirens mean. We just knew it was serious, so you had a bunch of guys running around in their underwear wondering where the hell they should go. I made sure we got briefed today, but they told me that after a while you just ignore the sirens like a false fire alarm in a condo. Still, it makes it all seem pretty real when it dawns on you that somebody just outside that razor wire tried to kill you.

CHAPTER 4

"Earth to Graydon." Rayner cupped his hands around his mouth like a megaphone, aimed across the car's armrest.

Matt jumped in his seat and clenched the steering wheel tighter. He moaned as the pain shot back through his groin.

Matt's eyes had been traveling from the blacktop to the odometer and back, for how long he didn't know. Even with his injury he had insisted on driving; he found it calmed him, especially through the long stretches of the uninhabited Rockies, and as long as he didn't suddenly move his leg he forgot about the ache. He'd barely said a word to Rayner since their last pit stop near Calgary, and they were already in the mountains, just outside Banff.

Driving through the Rockies had made him think about the first time, flying into Afghanistan, he saw the spectacular Hindu Kush range; his thoughts had daisy-chained from there, one onto the other until he was back in the dusty hills, trying to peer around ridges and boulders, waiting for the enemy to pop up on the horizon so they could pick them off like some fucked up whack-a-mole game. He felt the tension squeezing his shoulders together as he drove over the road, knowing no one would possibly plant an IED – an improvised explosive device – on this highway, but he couldn't convince the nerve endings all over his body that tingled on alert.

He looked back to the odometer again, annoyed as he watched the kilometres click by, each a measure of how far behind he was leaving the kids, a reminder that Amanda had won this round if only by default; she knew Matt was the only one who could go and do something about Shirley. Instead of the mountains lifting his spirits as they once did, he felt claustrophobic, as though life as he knew it was being squeezed through a funnel and he was about to be shot out the other side, in what form he wasn't sure.

He wondered how long it would be before he felt like himself again. Before Afghanistan he would surrender to the simple awe that the mountains had always evoked in him, but instead he felt the pressure pushing against his chest, trying to escape in a shout or a punch, something physical that would pacify his demons if only for a moment. Any physical action he took only fed the monster; this much he knew, the hook of adrenalin just like in battle, only there it doesn't release you until you've killed what you're fighting. A thought about driving off the road kept on worming its way into his head, a way of ending the waking nightmares. Thank god Rayner was with him; he'd never do that to him.

"You okay, Matty?"

"Yeah, yeah. Just lost in thought, that's all." The pressure in his chest tightened like a wrung towel.

"Back with the kids?" Rayner asked.

Matt looked in the rear-view mirror, as though it might have some clue to what was disappearing behind him.

"No," Matt said. A half lie. "Back in Afghanistan, unfortunately." He opened his window and the air drum-rolled into the car. He extended his forearm across the window frame, the wind ruffling the sleeve of his T-shirt and tickling the hair on his arm. Maybe he was just a little hung over from the night before, his brain muddy from overindulging with Rayner. "Sorry I haven't been very good company."

Rayner expelled a long breath. "Man, you gotta let it go. I mean what happened back there." He brought his hands down to his knees with a *slap* and looked out the window. "We were doing our *job*, Matty, that's all. You can't knock yourself out forever about that stuff."

Matt snorted deridingly. "I wish I was more like you, Rayner. I really do. You're a better soldier than I am. Just get in and get out, do your job and don't think about it again. I used to figure I was built that way too."

"It's not that I don't think about it, man," Rayner said. "But it's what I signed up for. You can't make the mistake of letting yourself think of them as people with families Matt. They're the enemy. They're different than we are. They're fanatics and terrorists and would blow us away in a second in the name of Allah. They want to annihilate us. So tit for freakin' tat is what I say."

Cumulus clouds to the west were building a head of flint-coloured steam over the mountains. A curtain of rain in the distance paced toward them, a cold front moving in.

"You can't tell me the Taliban aren't evil." Rayner apparently was not getting the argument he wanted. "Look at how they treat women, and how they torture or kill anyone who doesn't want to think like they do. The minute we're out of there they'll swoop in to fill that vacuum again. We all know that. And things will go back to exactly the way they were."

"Don't you think you're oversimplifying?" Matt couldn't help but engage. "How much has changed in the seven years since they were overthrown? Women are still walking around completely covered from head to toe and will never be equal citizens. We're fighting a war of culture, of religion"—he hit the steering wheel with his fist—"of something that has been ingrained over centuries that we don't understand and never will be able to relate to. Unless the Afghan people do it for themselves, nothing will change."

Matt stared at the road ahead. He was sure the argument was lost on Rayner. "I just don't think we're doing any good over there. They have to want things to change before we can be effective, and there's only a handful of people who really do want that. Afghans are pragmatic. They've survived being invaded for their entire history, and they've always prevailed."

Rayner shifted in his seat.

Matt continued. "I'm not saying what North Americans think is wrong, but maybe it's just not right for them. Maybe we should let them sort themselves out."

Rayner pushed his frame into the door and looked at Matt—mockingly, Matt thought—with an expression of shock. "Shit, Matty, you almost sound like a fucking pacifist. So tell me, if we pull out, what happens to all the terrorists? Do we just let them run all over the place?"

"If we're going to take out terrorists, then we should be in Pakistan too, and in Iran," Matt said. "As long as they feel suppressed or that we're trying to impose our will on them, there will always be people who want to fight us. Maybe we'd be better off staying at home and finding better ways of defending ourselves against attacks here that are bound to happen. And I'm not a fucking pacifist, Private. Only a realist. Maybe we're just wasting our time out there."

"I don't know, man. You're a lot smarter than me, Matty but I think there are guys further up the chain who know more about this than you and I ever will. I gotta believe we should get those fuckers before they get us. You know how it goes. This is war, and the minute you start thinking in shades of grey is the minute you get gunned down. Kill or be killed."

Matt straightened his elbows, pushing his weight harder into his seat. The sky was darker now, and large raindrops had begun to ping and bead on the hood of the car. He pulled his arm back in and rolled up the window, listening to the clouds unload on the roof. He tried not to think of the irony of wanting to be back in Afghanistan more than where he was headed.

Rayner switched on the radio. "Let's stop soon for something to eat, all right?" he asked, looking out at the downpour. "Are you going to want me to drive soon, or are you going to let me have a beer when we stop?"

Matt chuckled. "I'm good to keep driving Rayner, and I'm still recovering from last night. Just keep me awake and talk to me about something other than Afghanistan."

Rayner considered this for a moment. "Okay. Let's see. Why don't you tell me what you're going to do when you get to Penticton? Like what are you going to do with your mother?"

"Boy, you sure pick the easy topics, don't you?" Matt grinned. The tires hissed through the water on the asphalt. "I really wish I knew. Some of it will depend on how bad she is. I won't know that till I get there."

"Does this stuff have a chance to get any better?"

"Apparently not, and it's not going to get any easier for either one of us unless I eventually put her into permanent care, and we can't afford that. I think I might have to put the farm on the market and use the money to get her into a home. She would fucking hate that though. I could get her into a small apartment in Penticton and use the money left over to get her some home care, assuming she's not too bad and doesn't need to be put in a home right away."

His groin started to bother him again.

"I don't know how long any of this is going to take. I just want to get out of there as fast as I can." His future was playing out before his eyes, and he didn't like what he saw. He felt like a fox in a leg-hold snare, and would have gnawed off a limb if he felt it would free him.

"I don't even know what I'm talking about, Rayner. I'm going to have to make it up as I go along. I haven't even seen her for years, and as much as I hate to say this about my own mother, she's been a real bitch about it."

"Yeah, but you haven't exactly reached out yourself."

"Okay. I suppose it's hard to say who has been more stubborn."

Rayner gave him a "Who, you?" face.

Matt laughed. "Well, I guess my stubbornness will have to get me through this as well."

They were approaching a large sign hewn out of timber on the side of the road that announced their arrival in 'Golden, Town of Opportunity'. What he would have given to stay put right there, to find whatever opportunity Golden promised, away from Edmonton and away from the farm and his mother, in this place, where he knew no one and could start his life fresh. Instead he was living between everything now, between his marriage and bachelorhood, between caring about the kids and caring for his mother, between his military career and whatever his future held. It was choking him. Once he had been a child living with his mother, then a bachelor, and then married with children. Now he was on the wheel going backward: a bachelor again, without children, going back to live with his mother, even if it was only a short while. He glanced in the rear-view mirror again.

He pulled off the road at a PetroCanada station, shifted into Park and then lifted himself out of the car and into the fresh air. He leaned his crutch against the car and raised his hands above his head, stretching and inhaling deeply. The storm had left the air rich with the smell of pine trees and nitrogen, and with each long inhalation his lungs expanded with the lightness of it all, the crisp Rocky Mountain air.

Matt twisted off the gas cap and placed it on top of the trunk, where it rolled in a semi-circle. A small puddle just beside his right foot had remained from the earlier rain; a rainbow gas slick had formed on top of the water, glistening like snakeskin on the pavement. He reached into the back pocket of his jeans for his credit card, noticing the speckled brown leather of his wallet had begun to separate; a stray thread dangled from its corner. He extracted his Visa card and slipped it into the pump's card slot and then reached for the nozzle, pondering it as he held it in his right hand. The nozzle was heavy and cold, and the sun's reflection in it flashed in his eyes. He lowered the end of the nozzle into his left hand, balancing the silver metal there, cradling it, the sight of his hands and the nozzle fading to a blur. Something had registered in his peripheral vision but also in the dark back of his brain, tugging at him and making his finger twitch on the trigger of the nozzle. He could see in the reflection of the pump's glass a man in a dark turban standing just behind him at the next pump. The man held a similar metal nozzle as the one Matt held, waving it absentmindedly in Matt's direction.

Matt heard the sounds around him, but they were muffled, as though through a wall—the crow that cawed overhead, the children who had climbed noisily out of the car in the next lane, running toward the station's store, even the sound of the nozzle that dropped out of his hands clanging to the pavement. All his senses had recessed into a slow-motion silence, every nerve ending tingling on alert. He had become perfectly still, barely breathing while he dropped his right hand to his side in a trancelike silence, reaching instinctively for his firearm.

Suddenly he screamed and charged the man, bounding around the Grand Am, forgetting about his injury. In three long strides Matt was on top of him, and with one punch sent him backward into the pump and sprawling to the ground. Matt grabbed the nozzle from the man and threw it behind him, striking the turbaned man's white Subaru, creating a puddle of gas where the nozzle hit the pavement. He seized the prone man's collar with one hand and the man's belt with his other hand, flipping him over on his stomach and yanking his arms behind his back.

"Stay the fuck down!" he yelled at him. "Don't fucking move, you bastard!" A spray of spit shot involuntarily out of his mouth and landed foaming on the man's turban. Matt ground his right knee harder into the man's back and held his hands together while he searched for a cord to bind them with.

A small ring of people had formed in the periphery of Matt's vision. He looked up at them, his chest pumping hard with each breath, his eyes defying them to come nearer.

"Matt! Matt, what the fuck are you doing?" Rayner jumped on him from behind, wrapping an arm around his neck and pulling him hard away from the man. "Get off of him, man!" he said, pulling him backward and up to his feet.

"It's okay, Matty, it's okay." Rayner had a hold of Matt's arm and threw him over to their car, pushing his back up against the Grand Am's door. "Matty," he said, standing in front of him, looking directly into his eyes. "Matty, listen to me. It's okay. You're here with me. You're back home. You're in Canada. He's not Taliban, Matty. He's a Sikh. It's okay." He pushed Matt up against the car door and shook him, forcing Matt to look in his eyes. "Look at me, man. He's a Sikh Matty. He's Indian, not Taliban. It's okay. You're okay."

Matt leaned back into the door, staring somewhere far beyond Rayner's shoulder, 10,000 kilometres away. The coiled spring inside him that had been wound so taut now just as quickly unravelled, so when Rayner shook him by the shoulders his body responded like a gelatin sack, his arms dangling limply by his sides, his head weaving back and forth.

Rayner stood directly in front of him and placed both his hands around the back of Matt's neck, pulling his face forward so he could look straight into his eyes. "Matt, come on, buddy. You're going to be fine. Here, let's get into the car." He held on to Matt's arm and guided him around the Grand Am to the passenger door. He gently lowered Matt into the car where he sank without resistance, and shut the door. Matt sat staring straight ahead, the only movement coming from his heaving chest.

Rayner walked around the front of the car to the group of people who had gathered around the Sikh man. They had rolled the man over and were coaxing him to his feet. Blood was dripping from the man's nose as he staggered forward, supported by a man on either side.

"I'm sorry, sir," Rayner said, clasping his hands in front of himself. He looked toward Matt as he talked. "My buddy just got back from Afghanistan. We're in the military. He's a sergeant, a really good guy, and a great soldier. He was in direct combat there, and this has absolutely nothing to do with you, but ..." He paused for a minute, groping for the correct words. "He must have caught sight of your turban and something triggered inside him."

He was quivering. He was trying to protect Matt in a way no one else could ever understand, not if they hadn't been there. "Some really awful things happened over there," Rayner said to the man, pointing backward with his thumb toward a far-off place. "I couldn't even begin to try to explain it to you. But things get in your system and it's like you're programmed to react." He couldn't help babbling. "I know he's sorry. You've gotta believe that. *I'm* sorry too." All he could hope for was a little sympathy at this point, that the man wouldn't call the cops. He needed to get Matt out of there.

The bleariness in the Sikh man's eyes had been replaced by anger as he looked at Rayner face to face. He reached up with his sleeve and wiped the dark blood dripping from his nose. "You think anyone is the enemy, people like you," he said. "Anyone with different colour skin than you, or different kind of dress. People like you look at me every day because of my beliefs, because of my customs, the way I dress." His shoulders were tense around his neck.

Rayner looked away toward the mountains.

"This kind of maniac should be taken off the streets," the man said, jabbing a finger in Matt's direction.

They stood for a moment in silence, the only sound between them from the bloody bubbles being blown from the man's nostrils with each exhalation.

After a moment, Rayner reached into his pocket and took out a piece of paper. "Here, I'll give you my number. You can take down my driver's licence too. I'll pay for any damages, for anything at all. Please, you've gotta believe me that my friend got a little fucked up over there but I'm going to get him taken care of, I promise you. We're on our way out of here anyway, and we won't bother you or anyone else." He held out his hand to the man. "Please," he said looking directly into the man's dark eyes.

The man shook his head and looked down at the ground, refusing Rayner's extended hand. "I don't know," he said slowly. "I will take your details and I will think about it."

With Golden nearly two hours behind them they had yet to see any sign of the police, but Rayner still glanced frequently into the rear-view mirror. Finally, at Revelstoke, he pulled into a gas station. "I'm just gonna go inside and scare up some food, buddy," he said to Matt. "Stay away from the gas pumps. I'll be right back."

Matt heard Rayner's voice but paid no attention to the words. He had not spoken since they left Golden.

Minutes later Rayner returned to the car and tossed a foil-wrapped burger through the window into Matt's lap. Matt flinched.

"Shit, Matty, I'm sorry. I forgot about your nuts. Did you hurt yourself again back there?"

Matt shook his head almost imperceptibly.

Rayner climbed back in the car and reached his right arm around the passenger's seat as he backed up, giving Matt's head a quick reassuring rub as he did. "Don't worry, man. You'll be okay."

Matt's thighs were warm from the burger's imprint. The haze that had descended on him after Golden had partially lifted. He had returned from wherever it was he went in those moments, but he felt shameful, drained of energy and still couldn't bring himself to speak. Whatever had risen from inside him seemed to have left him, along with his pride.

Now he stared straight ahead, afraid to speak and afraid to move, as if the slightest action might tip the demons that danced on his shoulders from one side to the other. The same thing had happened in the past, with a sudden burst of the crazies leaving him drained once the damage was done. His body seemed to almost crave the moment, releasing the escalating tension so that when it was finally spent he could sit there like a sack, useless and no longer dangerous.

So he remained quiet in the passenger seat of the Grand Am while Rayner drove, the numbness flowing through Matt like a low-voltage current while the mountains and trees passed in a blurred backdrop.

He wouldn't allow himself to acknowledge how feeble this all was, to feel sorry for himself. But how pathetic was it that he couldn't control this thing that had burrowed into his head, overpowering him both physically and mentally like a man possessed? As best he could he held back any emotion like a dam against a flooded river, afraid that if he let go for a minute he would be swept away, losing whatever remained of himself, uncertain if he would find his way back to something he could command.

When he was a boy there were incidents like this, although not violent, not where he would physically lash out at anyone else. Some things would just provoke him unpredictably, light a fuse inside him and he would explode, raging as though possessed, the demon only extinguished when he became physically exhausted. A bad temper was how his mother had put it to his schoolteachers.

The incidents were long gone, buried in his childhood, at least until Afghanistan. Combat has a way of teasing the demons out of you, harnessing them for its own use. For an infantry soldier in battle, all life is refined and distilled to the tiny endings of every nerve, each fibre focused on constant high alert. Well-directed anger is a positive thing, the soldiers were told. All else drops away except this: stay alive, and kill the enemy. Like so many others, Matt found it intoxicating, hooked on the drug of combat, scared of what he was becoming.

When you come back to Canada, a country that has never known modern warfare on its soil, where only the tiniest percentage of men or women have ever experienced battle, you keep searching for the switch to turn it off, to stop the reactor that's generating that unnecessary fuel because it serves no purpose in this place that now seems so dull. The guys ended up feeling like tourists at the ends of the earth where no one speaks the same language, where no one would understand your story, even if you wanted to tell them.

He knew Rayner understood, but talking to him about what was eating him made him feel weak. Rayner wasn't affected in the same way, for god knows what reason; Matt wished he had drunk from that same fountain.

When he returned from his first tour of Afghanistan, Matt understood there was no magic way to disengage, that hunting for that little switch was futile. The feeling becomes constant and engrained, imbedded under your skin like a microchip sensor injected into a pet, in a place you can't reach. He knew that for a few of the guys the feelings, if not the memories, simply eroded with time, and with a little luck, in the meantime, you stayed out of trouble.

But for Matt, time was an enemy, not a luxury; there was just too much that lay ahead of him, and he needed his head straight now, to sort it all out.

He rolled down his window and vomited.

May 4, 2006, Forward Operating Base (FOB)
Martello, near Gumbad

Through some small miracle we made it to FOB Martello after three of the most intense days I've ever lived. I only wish we could have made it back intact.

Kandahar province is known for its concentration of insurgents—that's why we're here, but the city of Kandahar itself seems like kindergarten compared to the outlying areas where you might as well be on the moon—the landscape even looks the same—surrounded by alien beings whose intentions are unknown but assumed unfriendly.

We set out on an operation from KAF three days ago for the FOB, one of the farthest outposts in our area of responsibility, near Gumbad in Kandahar province's northern region. We were a large convoy, nearly 40 vehicles led by Light Armoured Vehicles in front with the less protected, more vulnerable G-Wagons interspersed. A LAV can take a hit from an IED or a mortar and often survive intact. The boys inside get shaken up and go half-deaf for a while, but our track record for low injury is good. The problem often occurs with the exposed gunner sitting in the turret, the most dangerous position in the vehicles. He's a prime target and you've got to have nerves of steel or be totally fucking nuts to sit up there. The rest of us track what's going on from inside the LAV with video monitors.

You know your chances of an ambush or hitting an IED are high on just about any road leading out of Kandahar, and the closer up the road we got to Shah Wali Kot the nearer we moved into insurgent country. You're on high alert, your nerves are vibrating like a tuning fork and your finger is never far away from the trigger of your weapon. We try to lighten things up in the LAV, so even while we're keeping one ear glued to the communications from the other vehicles, the guys are usually joking around to take the pressure off. As you can imagine, we bump along in pretty close quarters. Rayner let go this rancid fart in the vehicle that nearly flattened us all; I'm sure we would have glowed hot red on an infrared scan. As sergeant in charge I decreed that anyone in my section who pulled that again would be cleaning toilets with their tongue for a week. Hutch handed Kareem his chemical mask, which made Kareem laugh.

Kareem's a pretty good sport about it all. If we feel like strangers in a strange place in his country, imagine how he must feel in this rolling hi-tech fortress, our little Canadian microcosm. The body armour he wears must add another 20 pounds to his slim frame and makes him look younger than he is, like a kid dressing up in his dad's clothes. His English is good, but the smile on his face doesn't mask that he misses a lot of our humour. I think his dad must be a dentist; he has such perfect white teeth. He looks like the cover of an Afghan Tourist Bureau magazine, with his green eyes, thick hair and dimpled chin.

You don't cover a whole lot of ground in a convoy over desert roads, and we stopped for the night off the road not far from Tangay. We were pretty exposed out in the middle of a wadi but far enough away from any sheltered area where someone might be hiding, waiting to use us for target practice.

I'll never forget the sight of the sun going down behind the mountains as the muezzin called the faithful to prayers over a distant loudspeaker. It is a haunting sound, a singsong, seductive refrain that builds into a crescendo like a siren, both an announcement that something is happening and a warning to watch out and heed it. I will always associate that sound with this place, with its mystery and its trouble.

We hauled out our sleeping bags and lay them on the sandy ground while one of the guys stayed up as sentry, scanning the horizon with his Sophie, a thermal viewer that picks up anything in the dark. We had set out at 0500 that morning and were pretty tired, so sleep comes easy but is light, with your body on subconscious alert. The sand fleas and ants that want to share your sleeping bag are no help, nor is sleeping clothed, but it's a necessary precaution.

I watched Kareem spread out his sleeping bag and bow toward Mecca, saying his prayers as he did so often during the day. Once he was finished he stood up and looked like he wasn't quite sure what to do. I got the sense he was nervous sleeping out in the open and so exposed, so I spent a bit of time talking to him about other things to see if I could take his mind off our situation. He's only nineteen, the oldest of six kids. His father is a butcher just like my dad, George, and while he doesn't say his family is poor, I know his salary with us is enormous compared to what most Afghans make. It's danger pay, and he knows it. He told me that when he was a kid he dreamed of being a doctor so he could do some good for people. It's still his dream, but you can see in those deep eyes (too old for his face) a far-off look that tells you he knows it is only a dream. He uses the money he earns with us to look after his family.

He says we are fighting against history, that no invader has ever successfully conquered Afghanistan, but even so he hopes it will be different this time. That's why he's involved. Not that he wants outsiders to conquer them, only free them from the radical noose the Taliban had around their necks. According to Kareem we don't understand his people; we North Americans only think of the freedom of the individual, whereas they think of the survival and solidarity of their tribe. They view themselves as governed by god, not man, and that

Islamic Imperialism is all about the spread of the religion itself, a divine and rightful goal and duty. As much as I like the kid, that little speech left me with some nagging doubt about his loyalties.

I was the last to fall asleep, wanting to make sure the boys were down for the duration and everything under control. Sometime later I woke with a start when I felt something bump against my leg. Kareem had laid there beside me, his sleeping bag perpendicular to mine with his head pressed up against my thigh; I guess it gave him a sense of security to be close. Even though I felt a little self-conscious I didn't bother moving him but reached down instead and tousled his hair, just to let him know it was okay and that I was right there. I couldn't help thinking he was somebody's kid, just like Baxter and Callum. I had to take a bit of ribbing from the boys in the morning when they woke up and found us like that, but fuck 'em. Hutch kept looking back and forth between me and Kareem later in the LAV and winking at me with this stupid grin on his Newfie face. Always the joker.

We scarfed down our individual meal packs—wretched stuff—and were on the road, if you can call it that, before sunrise, our convoy rumbling along at a breakneck 15 kph over rocks and sand. I rode in the turret for a while so I could take pictures to send home to Amanda and the kids and to catch some of the crisp air as the sun came up. The slowly brightening sky had started to reveal the colours and contrasts of this land: dry clay wadis butting up against rich green fields and rugged sandstone mountains. It smells fresher in the morning out here, away from the urban areas, none of that heavy odour of kerosene, diesel, cooking meat and spices you get traveling through cities and villages. You could be forgiven for being deluded into how peaceful it all feels, bathed in orange and pink dawn light like a little Shangri La nestled in the hills and lost to the rest of the world. Still, I had this stupid feeling that something was wrong, a bad foreboding about the day, but I tried to write it off, telling myself that whenever you're out on patrol, your nerves are on heightened alert.

And sure enough, that's when all hell broke loose.

Out of nowhere came a massive explosion in front of us, and I was thrown back against the side of the turret from the impact. The boys pulled me back in, and Corporal Wilson, our gunner, shot up there into position. A LAV had been hit by an IED not 100 metres ahead of us, most likely remotely detonated by the insurgents who then began firing on us from a position behind the squat mud buildings off to our left.

My side felt a little fucked up where I hit the turret, but I couldn't think about it. Everybody was at their stations in a second, waiting to hear on the radio where the contact was coming from, ready to engage. Within seconds we heard bullets striking the metal vehicles like a hailstorm, and rocket-propelled grenades going off around us. Our captain pulled up in his G-Wagon alongside us and we heard him yelling for a situation report on the LAV up front to see if everyone was okay.

"Out of the vehicle! Out of the vehicle!" I was yelling at my men to get out while Wilson covered us to take position on the ground. Black smoke spewed from the LAV ahead of us, and you could hear rounds 'cooking' inside; you just prayed no one was in there with all that ammo igniting.

One of the guys was bent over the side of the turret struggling to get out.

"Cover me!" I yelled at my guys while I ran to him. He was screaming so loud as I pulled him out that it practically drowned out the sounds of the rounds going off around us and inside the vehicle. I was choking from the black smoke that was pouring out of the turret. His legs were dangling behind him as I edged him over the top of the vehicle, and one leg ripped open and gushed blood like a geyser.

"Get a medic!" I tried to shout over the sounds of all the fucking chaos as I got him down to the ground at the side of the LAV.

I applied a tourniquet to his upper leg while he was tearing at my shirt with his hands and screaming. I figured his femoral artery must have been hit, and without quick attention he'd die unless I could slow the bleeding. I kept talking to him, calling him by his name—Dawson—and tightening and then loosening the tourniquet, waiting for the medic. I noticed other parts of him—his back and butt—were bleeding too but not nearly as much as his leg.

We needed to evacuate the guy as quickly as possible, but I realized how exposed we were. We were being engaged not just from the buildings on the left but from the field ahead of us as well, and the Company has started to *move into a defensive U position. As soon as the medic, McAdam, arrived I told him to get in there and cover him and Dawson while I went back and rejoined the rest of my section. I heard the medic already calling in a Priority One casualty even while he was struggling with bags of QuickClot to pour on the downed corporal. Not a good sign.*

By now the dust was swirling around us from the rounds going off, while we watched black turbans darting silently like prairie dogs between the buildings in front of us, all of it surreal in the low morning light. Later we estimated there must have been 200 of the enemy in a well-planned ambush. They were as prepared as any fighting unit in any army I've ever seen. These were not unsophisticated warriors.

Our CO called in air support, but by the time it got there we had been fighting well into the afternoon and the sun baked the sweat and mud on us into clay. By then we had sustained nearly a dozen casualties, one I noticed fatal for sure, lying on his back with his mouth and eyes open, a puddle of blood surrounding his head.

They say war has a smell all its own, and I don't think I'll ever get the stench of it out of my nostrils. It's the smell of cordite from the rounds going off around you, the heavy smoke of burning metal and plastic, of body odour and blood mixed with dirt as it seeps into the ground from downed men, of soldiers shitting themselves out of fear. It must be what hell smells like. They say that dogs smell fear and react to it, but so do men, and it either sends them running from a fight or straight into one. All your senses become acutely fixated as your brain shuts down every other part of you, both physically and mentally, that isn't necessary for combat. Tunnel vision takes over so you become focused only on what's in front of you while your hearing stands guard on the periphery. And when you look straight ahead, into the eyes of one of your soldiers, you can see it there, that laser-sharp focus mixed with adrenalin, mania and fear that dances just this side of panic. Only a scrap of grey matter allows him to recognize that you're not the enemy, and you know as you stare into those black pupils floating in eyes stuck wide and white that if his instincts had not been honed for that very moment to reach out and kill the enemy, he would be running hard in the other direction.

We finally heard the screaming engines of the B-1 Lancer overhead followed shortly by Warthog chain guns aimed at the buildings and fields surrounding us, and then choppers descending to collect the wounded.

The Taliban who didn't flee fought to the last man standing, well into the early evening. We counted more than forty dead on their side.

You don't lose track of your men easily in combat; even if you can't see their faces you can feel when they're around you. So when I walked back to the LAV I already knew two of them were missing. When I checked out the vehicle, only two guys were left inside; one was Kareem, who hadn't set foot outside it and looked a lighter shade of brown when I saw him. One of the missing I knew was Rayner, and I was like a mad dog spinning around asking everyone if they had seen him, walking to every casualty still on the ground, checking each of them out and hoping I wouldn't see Rayner's face. I finally located him, and that's when I also found my man Hutch, lying beside a tree with Rayner and a medic squatting over him. He was bleeding out from a hole in his chest where the medic was putting pressure on a compress. We all knew he was dying; even Hutch himself knew it. Rayner was holding Hutch's hand and talking to him, telling him he'd make sure his wife and kid were taken care of. It didn't take long. I'll never forget the bubbling sound, the gurgle that emerged from his throat and then he was gone.

It took Rayner about five minutes before he would let go of Hutch's hand, and when he did he just collapsed back on his butt and sobbed. I wanted to step in, to somehow comfort him, but instead I turned my back and went and stood under the dark shade on the other side of the tree where no one could see me. I kneeled down and lost it. It wasn't only out of grief for Hutch. It was for his family, and for my family as well. What the fuck was I doing to them? What if I was the one dying and leaving them? The adrenalin of the battle had released its grip, and suddenly sadness and grief poured in to replace it.

Finally I got a grip and went back and stood with Rayner for a moment over Hutch's body, when the weirdest thing happened. A cloud of small white butterflies, each no bigger than a thumbnail, appeared suddenly and fell on the tree like a soft snowfall, their wings reflecting against the tree's dark leaves like spots on a pointillist painting. Then dozens of them floated down farther and lighted on and around Hutch's body where they remained for a few moments, their wings pulsating to the rhythm of a silent waltz—open, close, close, compressing together a little harder on the second close beat. A minute later, just as mysteriously as they came, they left again, back to the tree where the others seemed to await them, all of them then ascending to wherever it was they had come from.

Rayner and I stood silently watching as this happened, barely breathing, and when the butterflies had gone we looked at each other and said nothing, absorbed in a moment, wondering what we had just seen.

When we made it to the base and Kareem had finally regained some of his colour, he gave me the copy of the Koran that he carries with him. He knew I already had an English one, but he wanted me to have a copy in his own language, a book that was special to him. Inside he had inscribed it, "To Matt, Allah's soldier, my protector." I guess it's a matter of his own self-preservation or maybe a higher rationale of conscience that can dissociate himself from many of his countrymen. Still, I wonder how many kids just like him we killed today. And when I look at those eyes that have already seen a lifetime of violence and suffering, I can't help but wonder how many deaths of people like him I'm responsible for. Some might even be Kareem's relatives; who knows? We are trained to think of them only as targets, like shooting tin cans off a fencepost. If you stop and think about them as human then you yourself are also one, and that is not the machine the military wants. Yet once you turn your back and face the casualties on your own side, only the coldest of us would feel no remorse, would remain the robotic, non-thinking killing machine we are trained to be.

We lost four men in that battle. The man I pulled out of the turret, Corporal Terry Dawson, didn't make it, nor did the kid who was driving the LAV Dawson was in. I found out later that he—the driver—was still inside when the rounds were cooking in there and the smoke belching out of it, but I had no fucking idea at the time. And then I remembered the smell of it, the distinctive smell of seared flesh in that smoke and I figured I should have known. Fuck! It would have been too late anyway.

The dead and the wounded were evacuated, and the convoy gradually got itself together and continued the trek northbound. We had to move on, just like that, with no time to sit around contemplating what had happened. There was no turning back, just like Lot's wife at Sodom and Gomorrah, lest we freeze into pillars of ineptitude, longing for something we'd left behind. So on we went to the FOB.

I can't believe we won't even be back at KAF to say good-bye to Hutch at his ramp ceremony, as they march him up the plane for his final journey home. Godspeed, my dear Newfie, Hutch. Godspeed.

CHAPTER 5

SHIRLEY

Bob Andrechuk's curly hair looks like it has been shorn by a frantic sheep-shearer. Tight blond curls spiral out of the top of his head, but the sides have been shaved punk short with no regard for angle or artistry, or caution for that matter. Shirley notices this now about him, but it was his height that she remembered striking her when they first met at church. He is tall and lean, a runner's build on his young frame, and as he walks toward her leaning with his hand outstretched and smiling widely his stride broadens, allowing his legs to catch up to his tilting torso.

She stands and extends her hand firmly as he catches it. "Hello, Bob," she says. She feels she barely knows him well enough yet to call him by his first name. And it's not his friendship she wants right now, it's a ride home from the loony bin.

"Hello, Mrs. Graydon!" With both his hands he pumps Shirley's with such energy that she is forced to involve her full arm, bouncing in its socket. She smiles out of politeness but hopes he will notice the look on her face that says she doesn't share his enthusiasm. After a moment he releases her hand and tucks his own into his pockets, hunching his shoulders into a "What next?" look. His smile remains undiminished, though now it looks more puzzled than sincere.

"I'm sorry for your loss," he says awkwardly. Is he talking about her daughter, Gwen, or about her mind? The joke would be in poor taste and wasted on him anyway, so she decides not to pursue it.

"Thank you, Bob." She smiles. "Gwen was a good girl, in spite of some of her proclivities." She thinks the word is right. Damn her mind! Everything comes out so measured, so pondered before spoken. He'll know what she means. Shirley hopes she doesn't sound callous or pompous. They nod at each other, then cast their eyes downward, staring awkwardly at the grey floor. "Thank you for coming to pick me up," she says, changing the subject. "It has been a nice rest, but I'm ready to go now. I have to visit the ladies' room first. Then we can leave."

She retreats to the bathroom, the heels of her black leather shoes clicking on the cement floor as she pushes the bathroom door open. Something is rattling her, making her feel a little edgy, but she can't put her finger on it. Maybe too much tea after lunch, she thinks; it seems to affect her more these days. She stands in front of the mirror and smoothes her ash-coloured skirt, leaning in toward her reflection as she studies the part in her hair. Her dark roots have begun to show under the blonde strands, and she picks at the straight divide in her hair with her right pinkie in an attempt to weave the two colours together. She didn't come in here to relieve herself—she has no need to go—so she is quite certain she must have come to collect her thoughts, such as they are. She leans in closer to the mirror, examining the black flecks in her blue-grey irises for a moment, then leans back, thinking how her right eye has always looked so much more sympathetic and friendly, rounder and more open than her left, which appears much wiser, as though there was nothing it hasn't seen. It's the same with most people, she notes, as if half their being wanted to experience life and all its possibilities and the other half already knew what kind of crap was coming.

She remains there quietly, barely breathing, looking from one eye to the other as though they could unlock the code to her mind that has become such a tangled thicket. Her eyes start to well up. She was beautiful once, she thinks.

Does one ever get to the point where one stops looking in the mirror? She isn't sure what she is expecting to see—maybe some sign that the aging process has been arrested, that the deterioration of her mind and body had stopped for a moment, as if there were an anti-aging sweepstakes and she had the lucky ticket. Still, something remains there, enough to hold on to. Standing quietly, she takes a deep breath while a smile creeps across her face, thinking of how she always regarded herself as clever, that her own mind had always intrigued her—if she does say so herself—with its creativity, its daredevil twists and turns. But this new ride has become a roller coaster, and at this stage it just makes her nauseated.

It had taken her years to pull her life back together after George left her, to learn how to deal with raising two kids as a single mother. Then Matt left, and of course she felt herself a failure yet again. Was that it then? She wishes she could mark the beginning of her mental spiral. As time went on and Matt faded further into the distance, she developed a new peace with herself, and for the last ten years or so she had felt so strong; her job had finally started to pay off, at least a little, and she was immersed in a newfound confidence. But it's not like the gods to allow that to stay too long. There had to be some trial to test her.

When she returns to the waiting room the wretchedly cheerful Nurse Nightingale or whatever her name is, is sitting in a chair beside young Bob, leaning in close to him and speaking quietly. She can't make out what they're saying, but they stop talking when Shirley gets nearer.

"Hello, Mrs. Graydon," the nurse says as she stands, motioning to the seat she has just vacated.

Shirley remains standing with barely an arm's length between her and the nurse. The nurse takes a step backward and circles around her so she is no longer stuck between Shirley and the wall, her escape route down the hall now clear. *They must teach you this in Care 101 for Nutbars,* Shirley thinks, *just in case things get a little messy.*

"I was just having a chat with Mr. Andrechuk," the nurse says.

Shirley smells onions on the woman's breath and wonders if her own breath smells the same from lunch.

"He tells me he's come to pick you up and take you home."

Bob has risen from his chair and is no longer smiling. He doesn't take his eyes off the nurse, looking away from Shirley. His hands are in his pockets.

"Yes, that's right," Shirley replies. "Bob is from my church. He's been very kind to offer to take me back to the farm." The words come out tentatively, slow and staccato in spite of her attempt to sound determined. Her small suitcase sits beside the chair the nurse had just occupied, standing lengthwise on its casters with its handle extended. She turns casually and reaches for it but so does the nurse, their hands both grasping the handle, touching one another. Shirley, who was looking at the suitcase, now cranks her head toward the nurse, whose face is as tight with resolve as the grip she maintains on the handle.

"Mrs. Graydon, I thought you said your son, Matt, is going to come and pick you up. Didn't you?"

Shirley releases her hand from the suitcase's handle and stares into the nurse's face, one that seems to have transformed from cherubic to simply chubby, and mean. A pressure forms between Shirley's eyes as she feels her eyebrows reaching for each other, and then she lets out a sudden chuckle.

"My son, Matt?" she says. "I haven't seen Matt in years. He's in Afghanistan, killing people. Or something." She shakes her head as if the nurse is crazy and bends toward her suitcase. The nurse's hand remains firmly wrapped around the handle.

"Mrs. Graydon," Bob says, reaching out to pat the back of Shirley's arm. She remains motionless, like an alligator having its belly stroked. "I didn't realize your son was on his way back to come and get you." He is addressing her like a schoolgirl. "The nurse tells me he's called the hospital and is coming today or tomorrow. In any case, they tell me I can't discharge you because I'm not related to you. I'm very sorry."

The nurse stands silently by Shirley and Bob as they exchange looks.

Her chest becomes suddenly tight and she raises her hands quickly in front of her sternum, interlacing her fingers. She wrings her hands and feels the crease forming across her brow thicken; the heat rising in her body forces tears to boil in her eyes. She will not blink in case it squeezes out any teardrops, instead looking back and forth between Bob and the nurse and then at her trembling hands.

Bob uses the hand that remains on her arm to guide her over to the chair. She sits without resistance. "I'm so sorry, Mrs. Graydon."

She doesn't look at him. He lowers his tall frame into the chair beside her, bending his head next to hers so she will be forced to look at him if she raises her eyes. A tear falls and hits her skirt, starting a small dark stain that follows the fibrous tendrils in a quick-fizzling starburst. Her voice is feeble. "I don't know what to say."

Her mind bolts back to her room to do a mental inventory of its contents, wondering if there is anything there to help get her out of this predicament. She is desperate. Even suicide would be better. Her spirit floats for a quick moment on the whimsy, a way out of all of this.

The nurse's knees pop as she squats beside Shirley. "It's all right," she says. "Why don't I just take you back to your room? Maybe Mr. Andrechuk can wait there with you until Matt comes." She gives Shirley's knee a shake with her hand. "Eh? What do you think?"

Shirley nods her head slowly without lifting it, and as she rises, the nurse puts her arm around her back and leads her down the hall, Bob Andrechuk loping behind like a faithful greyhound.

MARK E. PRIOR

Shirley's Diary
January 2, 2006

Winter is such a productive time for me. There are fewer distractions, it seems, and certainly less temptations to go outdoors in the cold, not like in the summer when there is nothing better than to wander through the orchards ducking under branches heavy with cherries and peaches. It is beautiful though; looking out my study window at the sparseness of the landscape is like falling into a Lemieux painting in all its haunting bleakness. All I need is a family of three flat-faced, expressionless people staring blankly back at me and I could be on one of his rural Quebec farms. The ground outside is virgin white after last night's snowfall, and each frozen drop on the icy branches creates its own prism as it glistens in the sun.

I'm feeling so good these days. My nutritional counselling business is going well, giving me enough money to get by—just. The irony is that now that I'm feeling good about life, little things are starting to happen with age. My elbow has been aching from shovelling snow, and I find myself forgetting things more and more. The other day I didn't even realize until Cynthia called me that I had promised to meet her in Penticton for shopping, and there I was at home having a coffee. I find that even at church I don't have the recall for names I once did.

Although I never seem to forget the name of that Virginia Dyer (or Vagina Dryer as I like to call her, god forgive me). Such a prissy name, but she could probably be a stripper the way she dresses like such a tart. A woman in her late 30s should not wear clothes that tight even if she can fill them out well. I saw her on the street in her "casual" clothes the other day, those skin-tight jeans so low on her hips that when she bent over I could see clear to France. Since when did ass crack become the new cleavage? I guess that's the way they dress back in Toronto, where she's from. Everyone at our little country church seems so thrilled that we've got an injection of big-city sophistication. I think she should take those oversized peaches and go back to the big city that sprang those mutant things. How am I supposed to compete with that, or anyone my age compete with something so young and fresh? Age is not a beautiful thing, no matter what they say. The older you get the more you fade into the background, like old wallpaper that has yellowed and absorbed all the odiferous life that has passed in front of it. If anyone notices you at all, it seems it's always with a subtle quiver of distaste or condescension.

The episode with Cynthia got me thinking, so I went in to see Dr. Rosen about it. I felt a little better once he reassured me this is around the time that words or names start to slip beyond our grasp for a moment, but it certainly doesn't make me feel any younger. He's going to line up some cognitive tests for me in Kelowna, just to put my mind at rest.

Amanda came to visit with my darling grandkids a couple of weeks ago. Those children are so dear. I'm not sure who's more stubborn, Matty or me, but there is still no way I can bring myself to see him, even as he's about to leave for Afghanistan, and I'm sure he feels the same way. And I do feel the pangs of a mother; I'm not that evil. What if something were to happen to him over there? Could I ever forgive myself for not seeing him again? Amanda says he's happy to be going, to do the job he's been trained for. Besides everything else he's actually chosen to kill people for a living! How can I condone that? Thank god Amanda still brings the kids by from time to time. I really can't believe I've actually grown to like the girl given how much I detested the little heathen when Matt married her (I hadn't met her—shame on me!). How could I think any differently when my son had gone off and got the girl pregnant and then married her?

Oh, who am I to judge? Sometimes I think I'm just a selfish, horrible woman. Maybe if I were the one to reach out to Matty, to back down, then maybe things could be better. But how do you swim against a tide of your own making?

CHAPTER 6

MATT

"Matt!" Liz screamed his name into the phone. "Welcome back, brother! Where are you?"

Matt gathered from the tone of her voice that his little sister-in-law was back on her feet after Gwen's death, or at least she appeared to be. The last time he had spoken to her was from Afghanistan more than two weeks ago, after he'd finally returned to KAF from the worst mission of his life or anyone else's—a career stopper. He found out Gwen had died while he was recovering in hospital, and though he was relieved that her pain was over, his seemed to be just beginning.

What happened on the mission had turned his career inside out. When he got back to the base there was the surgery, and the stark reality of having to return home and face a litany of challenges: his sister's funeral, his wife's distance, his mother's care, his ruptured masculinity. If he believed in astrology he could at least blame the planets for aligning their outhouse right over his head. Or even karma—at least he could fault himself in a past life if not this one. He hadn't taken the time to analyze things and didn't care to.

He smiled through his hangover as he listened to Liz's voice on the phone. That was the thing about Liz; she was always infectiously upbeat. No wonder Gwen had been so crazy about her. Even with all Liz had been through lately—caring for Shirley, Gwen's death—her voice still managed to wrap around him like a warm blanket.

"I'm in Penticton Liz, down at one of the little motels on Lakeshore Drive," he said, his voice sounding like he had been dragged out of a swamp. "I got in last night but it was kind of late to call you, so my buddy Rayner and I just went out for a few beers. I figured I'd give you a call this morning." The greasy eggs and bacon he had eaten in the coffee shop had helped absorb some of the alcohol, and the coffee may have looked like creek water but at least it was caffeinated enough for a decent buzz.

He switched the phone from his left ear to his right and paced over the faded green carpet in his motel room, tracing the worn path between the nightstand at one end of the room and the mismatched dresser at the other. When he had last spoken to Lizzie from Kandahar, Gwen had already been dead for a few days, and he knew he had to get back as quickly as his doctors would allow. The trip back had seemed endless. At least his superiors had allowed him to skip the obligatory decompression stay in Cyprus which was usually a five-day drunken bust up where the men were expected to get the stress of war out of their systems, instead of letting it diffuse unpredictably back home.

After losing men on his first tour, he knew he was already feeling the symptoms of post-traumatic stress but managed to hide it well enough that they let him go back for a second tour. The thing is, the PTSD was much less likely to manifest itself in military life than in civilian, or so he thought until his last mission when he had blown away the unarmed Afghan civilian. Maybe he needed to go back to figure out what had gone wrong, to right the mistakes he had made, or maybe it was just that things now seemed more normal in Afghanistan, in a place where life seemed more black and white, and less emotional. Now after the second tour the signs were clear. The military had made him promise he would get counselling as soon as he could once he returned to Canada, and he had assured them he would. For now, at least while the court martial was pending, the military called it a medical discharge and characterized it as temporary. He wasn't so sure.

"You must be exhausted," Liz said. "I made an appointment with the lawyer this morning like you asked me to. Are you good to go?"

He looked out the window, sticking his fingers between the metal slats of the blinds, parting them into opposing chevrons. He watched the dust inside the room float lazily on the shaft of light he had let in. He looked out toward the Okanagan Lake, the ripples on the water sparkling like shattered glass.

"Yeah, I'm good to go, Lizzie. It'll be great to see you. What time do you want me there?"

"Eleven is when he's expecting us. Maybe we could meet for coffee half an hour before, and then if you're up to it we can have lunch afterward and talk about the arrangements for Gwen's memorial service."

She had always been a practical girl. Matt knew she was hurting but she wasn't about to show it, not when there was business to be done.

He agreed to meet her later, deciding to take a walk down to the beach in the meantime; maybe even walk around town to get reacquainted with the place. He had avoided Penticton since he left the farm in Summerland, and when he visited it was only to see Gwen and Liz and then for as short a time as he could, enough just to absorb what he could of their goodness. God how he'd miss the two of them together!

They were close when they were kids, he and Gwen. She always stood up for him, especially against Shirley, even though Gwen was the younger of them, probably not even aware that she seemed to be trying to compensate for their mother's indifference toward Matt.

He remembered when he was twelve and Shirley was in the hospital after her car accident. Matt could still visualize the accident report pictures, the driver's side of Shirley's car crumpled completely into the interior, pushing her into the passenger side of the vehicle where she stayed wedged for nearly two hours, sliding in and out of consciousness while the paramedics tried to keep her alive.

Uncle David—that's what they called him, even though he wasn't related—had come to look after them and took them to the hospital to see Shirley. Matt had expected to find her completely battered, but besides the tubes and wires attached to her unconscious body, she simply looked like she was sleeping, her face more placid than any time he saw her awake, the torment she normally wore on her face having deserted her.

Later the threesome stood just outside her hospital room, the doctor speaking to Uncle David with a look of professional grimness.

"There's been some internal damage," the doctor said. "Her hip was badly fractured"—something Matt hadn't been able to tell through the blankets—"as have some ribs. It appears her head was jarred enough that there is some swelling on the brain." The doctor took a deep breath. "We're not sure when she'll come out of the coma." Matt knew the only thing Gwen, just six at the time, could interpret was that their mom was probably dying, and he hugged her as she buried her head in his chest. Yet all Matt felt was embarrassment, ashamed that no other emotion seemed to register with him at all.

For nearly three weeks David stayed with them on the farm. In the mornings he would go to his day job at the Placid Hills Winery near Oliver and come by afterward to take Gwen and Matt to visit Shirley, and then back home to cook for them and spend the night.

One day when Matt and Gwen arrived home from school, David was already there waiting. "She's awake," was all he said.

When they arrived at the hospital, Shirley was sitting up in bed, leaning back against her crisp, white pillows. Her face was no longer peaceful as it had been when she was in a coma, the puckered tension around her eyes and mouth hinting at her pain. Her breathing was short and windy, like an asthmatic's, and he watched her hospital gown rise and fall in gallant puffs.

Shirley unfurled an arm with great exertion.

"Mommy!" Gwen ran over and wrapped herself in Shirley's arm.

Matt stood on the other side of the room making no effort to go to her uninvited.

Shirley knew he was there, but she wouldn't even look at him. It wasn't until his uncle David, standing behind him, practically shoved Matt that he went to her, looking at her without saying a word. Gwen had taken her hand out of Shirley's and replaced it with Matt's, and their hands sat there immobile, two dead pieces of meat that had fallen against each other by chance.

All the time David had stood to the side of the room staring at Shirley, his arms crossed over his chest. He jerked his head in a nervous tick, sending his unwashed bangs momentarily to the side of his face, and then tilted his head down again above sloped shoulders until his hair fell over his eyes again. Then he would start the whole hair cycle again: fall, flick, tilt, repeat.

Finally David approached Shirley's bed. "Come on, kids," he said. "Let's get home."

Shirley had turned away from David, never giving herself a chance to notice he hadn't looked up through his stringy hair once at her. No words had passed between them for the entire visit.

Matt sat on his bed in the hotel room, looking at the other bed opposite him with its leafy autumn-scene bedspread and sheets still rumpled from where Rayner had slept the night before. Suddenly Matt felt so alone that he had to fight from gasping, as though all the air had been sucked out of him. This was the first time he was alone, truly alone, in years it seemed, and now it felt like the solitude mocked him even physically. Whenever he felt lonely before he had always known there would be Amanda and the kids to see, to look forward to and that feeling had been enough to satisfy him, filling the dark vacuum whenever it had gripped him before. But now even Rayner had left—on his way back to Edmonton—and with him the bulwark of everything Matt had naturally relied on was crumbling, as worn and twisted as the bedspread across from him. His family, his friend, the camaraderie of his fighting unit—none of it was there any longer, and it hit him hard. The tawdry little hotel room felt like his only world now, that and the contents of the zippered canvas bag behind him on the bed and the boxes he had left outside in the car.

He had stupidly fantasized that his return home from Afghanistan would release him to the comfort and security of home and family, of streets where he would no longer need to look over his shoulder for someone who was gunning for him, of supermarkets brimming with foods and goods, of glittering car dealerships and cacophonous malls, the contentment of boredom that a night of watching bad TV would bring, or playing hockey on Friday nights with the boys and having too many beers after the game. But here, back in this country that he had always considered home, away from the open fields and jagged mountains of Afghanistan, from the monotonous food at KAF and the crowded sleeping quarters, from the silence of the cool mornings just before the unforgiving sun would levitate over the craggy hills, from the fateful call of the muezzin in the dusty minarets, he could not remember ever feeling so alone.

How could he step back into a yellowing, faded family album? The memories were like pictures on a disintegrating negative. It was no longer his life, no longer even real, yet he still felt an obligation, like a keeper of some sort of legacy, the guardian of all that past that had projected itself like an unexpected stray missile into his future. He could still look back at the pictures, reliving the memories as they played through his mind, but even when the experience was pleasant it left him feeling unnerved.

Why did the past tug so insistently on his heart? It was as though it were trying to pull him backward, seducing him downward with its soft memories, tricking him into thinking that maybe, once there, he would understand. He remembered certain days of placid innocence as a boy, meeting the world so blank and naïve. Those times when he would walk into the world with no protection and no thought of any danger that might lie lurking, ignorant of any threat. The memory of those days pushed a smile to his face, and he felt the lines beyond the corners of his eyes, etched like roadmaps to a severed past.

Matt stood up and turned his canvas bag upside down, shaking its contents onto the bed. He grabbed a pair of white jockeys and carefully refolded them into a small square. He rooted through the rest of his clothes until he had found each pair of underwear, which he then folded identically and stacked neatly, fly side up, one on top of the other. He took all of his socks—eighteen pairs—and arranged them on the bed in order by colour, descending from a dark-black pair on the left to a white pair of ankle gym socks on the right. He then took his five collared and buttoned shirts and refolded them with the collar facing up, stacking each on top of the other, from the darkest on the bottom to the lightest on top, doing the same with his T-shirts. Finally, with each item from the bag's contents arranged individually or grouped by kind, he lay flat the large canvas carryall and peeled back the sides then slowly—almost worshipfully—placing each item into the bag starting with the largest groupings: the pants, then sweaters, shirts, underwear, socks and toiletries. The material of each garment was alive in his hands, as though he could feel every fibre, every stitch and fold of his possessions, and only reluctantly, reverentially, did he lay them into their dark bunker, his concentration unwavering. This was his life now, the sum of his possessions, all that he was taking to the new life that awaited him.

He could not admit he was afraid, scared too that if he didn't feel fear then he might feel nothing at all.

He grasped the bag's zipper and drew it slowly and deliberately closed. When he finished he turned around the room, slowly scanning it for anything he might have left behind, getting down on his hands and knees to peek under the bed. Then he lifted the canvas bag from the mattress, placing it on the stained carpet beside the door, and stepped toward the bed where he threw back the covers and smoothed the bottom sheet, pulled the top sheet tight then flattened the bedspread over it. Everything was in its place; everything was in order, exactly as it should be.

He stepped toward the door, and grasping the handle he stooped slightly to look through the peephole. Seeing no one, he lifted his bag and turned the handle, wiped his hand on his jeans and stepped out into the crisp summer morning with no idea where he was headed.

The instant he walked out of the noon Okanagan heat and into the entrance of the Colonial Hotel, a blast of harsh air conditioning shot through him, enough to stop him for a second as he shivered involuntarily. He squinted to adjust to the low, incandescent lighting and quickly crossed the lobby to the hotel bar, hoping to see no one. The reception area seemed desperate to retain some of its original charm from the forties, green shaded brass bankers' lamps on the registration desk, and the old wooden pigeonhole board behind it to store room keys on long steel phallic-looking holders. Just the other side of the lobby, the bar was a venerable old drinking hole, a town staple for as long as he could remember. This was the same bar where, when he was seventeen, he had downed his first illegal beer, where he showed the female bartender what was obviously borrowed ID and she winked at him and served him anyway. Now it was just past noon, so he stepped into the bar as though by mistake, as though to say what the heck, now that he was here he might as well stay for a drink.

The fresh lake air from outdoors had been swallowed whole by a musty, beer-soaked stench, the smell of upholstery that had absorbed countless lagers spilled carelessly into banquettes, mixed with the stink of rancid butter and popcorn and cigarette smoke blown into worn fabric over the years.

Three tables of the dozen or so in the room already had patrons filling their seats. Two young Japanese women watched him as he came in, their elbows perched on white paper placemats between their utensils as they whispered and grinned at each other, pretending not to notice him. But he noticed them. It was his training to take note of everything in a room, to do a quick survey as he walked in, even as his eyes adjusted to the darker space. As much as he wanted to fade into the background, he knew he looked the definition of a military guy, except for perhaps the crutch.

He slid quickly onto a barstool.

The effects of his first vodka—a double, lots of ice, straight up—started to sink in just about halfway through the glass, and as he turned around on his barstool and scanned the room, he welcomed the dulling haze that had started to creep slowly down his brow, embracing the feeling like an old friend. He let out a long breath as he followed the course of alcohol that trickled through him as effortlessly as a clement river falling downstream. Its warmth tickled him inside, as though every droplet of cool alcohol enlivened each cell that it touched and then put them back into a soothing sleep. Alcohol was the only thing that seemed to work, to unravel the nerves that Afghanistan had twisted into a writhing pit of snakes. The counsellors had warned him about chasing out the memories by 'self-medicating', and even though they included alcohol in their list of cautions, he hardly thought a drink or two to relax could be considered harmful. He tried to ignore, on his walk around town, that he had passed in front of the liquor store twice, standing outside on the sidewalk wondering if he should go in. It seemed too desperate and cheap though, and too early in the morning. What would he do, go back and drink in his car? The bar at least seemed a little more civilized.

To kill time before his meeting with Liz he had walked first on the beach, shuffling his grey Nikes carefully through the sand while leaning most of his weight on his crutch, his mind drifting out over the lake's tiny waves that lapped at the shore's pebbles. He tried consciously to absorb the sunlight, hoping it would penetrate the darkness that seemed to have set up home from his chest to his bowels, hoping the light might extinguish the nightmares that lived with him even through the day.

He gazed out at the sandstone cliffs that bordered the lake to the west and then back at the sand beneath his feet, and instantly he was sucked into the familiar anxious vortex. The beach had suddenly become a dusty desert floor mined with explosives, and he staggered to keep himself upright.

He took a step, but he could not convince his brain that he wasn't about to explode like popcorn in a microwave, scattered in flesh and bone clear across the sand. He could see, literally see, his severed arm lying six feet away from his legless torso, the bloody flesh shredded and dangling, his body still seeping blood as his heart pumped in slowing beats. The sky had turned into black smoke from artillery discharge, oxygen replaced by the sulphurous smell of spent ammunition hanging heavily in the air, as though it had risen through a vent directly beneath him, from hell itself. His leg shook as he examined every small mound in the sand, stepping only in footprints where others had already stepped. He could see all the body parts strewn across the sand, an arm here, a head there, suddenly reanimated into twitching flesh looking for its owner. He screwed up his body, trying to contain a scream from the frustration and madness that rose inside him like a pressure gauge, begging him to explode if only to lessen the pressure of it all, to blow the visions right out of his head.

He found a bench and sat down, sweating. Minutes later, when he raised his head and looked across the sand, he saw two boys throwing a Frisbee back and forth. Four other kids screamed in unison as they ran into the lake's cold water, and farther down the beach the familiar giant peach refreshment stand stood where it had always been. It was as though the curtain had lifted in a darkened theatre to reveal himself impossibly back home, safe and away from the horror of the war, the nightmare just that.

Finally he reached the end of the beach and turned to walk up Main Street, imploring his limbs to keep moving, trying to distract himself by attempting to remember which businesses had been there before the new shops replaced them, trying to ignore his craving for a drink. The travel agency where he used to drop in as a kid, thumbing through coloured brochures and dreaming of faraway places, was now a women's lingerie store. He stood for a moment and stared at the cheeky displays of rosy satin bras and panties and pictures of luscious-lipped models pouting seductively. Half a block farther the old bookstore was still there but now abutted a Vietnamese restaurant. He stood outside the Elite Restaurant—eighty years old and still going strong—under the cockeyed crown perched atop its sign, looking across the street at the coffee shop where a young man with a red-dyed faux-hawk sat shirtless on a bench outside, rocking a baby stroller back and forth. A slim-hipped girl in flip flops strolled out of the café, handing the man an iced coffee drink overflowing with whipped cream.

Why did he always feel so compelled to return to the place where he grew up, needing a taste of whatever it was that formed him? And when he softened enough to allow the past to pull at his heart, it was like a tangible, physical tug that lured him backward, smothering him in those confusing memories. It was like reversing into a dream that he had never forgotten and never quite awakened from, trying to jam all the pieces of the puzzle together so it made sense of who he was now, of what he had become.

He turned the corner as though pulled, wanting to see if the old sporting goods store was still there, the place where his dad had taken him to load up on ammunition for his first deer hunt. But he checked his watch and saw that it was just past noon, so he decided it was a respectable enough time to head to the Colonial Hotel. Even though he wasn't meeting Liz until 12:30, it would give him time to settle in and have a drink first.

"And here you go." The bartender, her inky black hair swept back in a ponytail, startled him as he sat with his back to the bar scanning the room. He spun around in his seat, his feet thudding into the side of the bar beyond the foot rail. He winced. "Sorry." She smiled. "I didn't mean to scare you."

She set down a second highball glass of vodka on a stained cardboard coaster as he rested his forearms on the bar, hands clasped in front. His right elbow slid a few inches to the side on the wet wood, but he recovered quickly and pretended nothing happened.

"Finished with this one yet?" she asked with a wry smile as she reached for his glass of ice cubes. Her nails were buffed but not polished, trimmed neatly so just a sliver of white capped them off.

It took Matt a few seconds to realize she had said something. As she smiled and looked at him, he noticed the brown flecks in her green eyes, and then his eyes followed the inner edge of the neckline of her sleeveless white blouse down her tan cleavage, continuing his gaze quickly to the countertop and his second drink. He tried to convince himself she didn't notice the peek.

"Yeah, sure. Sorry," he said and smiled back weakly, realizing he had not responded to her question. "Just got lost there for a bit."

"Well, happy to help out," she said, removing his first drink. He wasn't sure what she meant.

She was alluring for sure, probably all of 28, but he told himself it might just be the alcohol, or him missing Amanda. Or maybe it was a rising inkling of revenge against his wife, whom he still had a hard time thinking of as an ex.

Matt had met Amanda in much the same way as this, back in Edmonton. Her nails, unlike the current bartender's, had been cartoonishly long, arching more than half an inch beyond the tops of her fingers and painted with sparkly coloured designs, and he remembered how they clinked against the beer glasses that she set in front of him and his friends at the table. It was one of the things his mother had commented on when she finally met her, "those hideous nails," in her words, not to Matt but to Gwen, who had relayed back the comments. "Trailer trash" Shirley had called her and the awful thing was that she wasn't far from the mark, at least then. Shirley had seen his future wife for barely half a day only once and managed to size her up in a way Matt grudgingly wished he'd paid attention to. But after puberty, what son ever believes his mother is wiser than he?

When Amanda got pregnant shortly after she and Matt met, he realized the pregnancy and the subsequent shotgun wedding only enhanced the trashy stereotype. Then Amanda miscarried in her seventh month, and they were devastated.

Matt watched the bartender now as she walked to the other end of the counter. How he missed the feel of a woman, of hugging softer flesh tightly against himself, his leg thrown over her smooth hips as they spooned in bed, his arm wrapped all the way over top of her, hand cupped between the bed and her breast lying heavily in his palm. To feel the rise and fall of her satiny stomach with his calloused hand as she breathed, her breaths slow but still faster than his own, his flat stomach pushing gently into her back with each of his inhalations. To have a night of making love and then sleep undisturbed by the nightmares he feared every time he closed his eyes.

"Do you want to order some lunch?" the bartender asked, returning from the other end of the bar. She leaned on her forearms with her hands clasped in front of her, mirroring his own pose. She was close enough that he could pick up a light trace of her perfume, maybe a skin moisturizer. She smelled like clover picked on a summer day, squeezed lazily between your fingers.

"No, not just yet," he said, pulling back slightly in what he hoped was an imperceptible motion. He didn't want to send the wrong signal. Not that he didn't find her attractive, but getting this close was a little uncomfortable. Giving in to her, or anyone's, charms right now was the last thing he needed to think about, which meant the thought quickly pushed itself up to the first thing on his mind, unable to be dismissed. He took a sip of his second drink.

"I'm meeting a friend here at 12:30," he said, glancing at his watch. "Looks like she's a little late."

The bartender pushed herself away and started clearing glasses from the dishwasher's conveyer belt, towelling the remaining spots dry and then jamming the glasses in the rack above her head. He watched her armpit as she stretched overhead, the concave burrow that glistened as smooth as the inside of an oyster shell against her bronzed skin.

"She's a friend," Matt said. Was he that obvious, explaining like this? He felt his swagger beginning to melt. "She's my sister's girlfriend. Wife really. Or partner, I guess you could call her. At least ex-partner. My sister just passed away." What a buffoon! Did he have to lay it all out on the bar like this?

The bartender's eyes widened as she took a step backward. Maybe he shouldn't have mentioned the lesbian thing; Penticton might not have grown as fast as he thought.

"Wait a minute," she said. "You mean Gwen?" It was *his* turn to look surprised.

"You know Gwen?" he asked.

"Gwen and Lizzie?" she said. "Oh man, I'm so sorry." She reached over the bar and rubbed his forearm. Her hand was warm and still a little wet from handling the washed glasses.

"Hey, that's okay. How do you know them? Or how *did* you know them?" He corrected himself.

She picked up the damp towel again, buffing and racking the glasses absentmindedly. "They used to come in here sometimes and shoot pool in the back," she said, nodding toward the back room with a smile on her face. "I know, I know; they used to laugh about it. It was such a lesbian stereotype. Gwen was pretty bad at pool but Lizzie's an awesome player, and she beats the crap out of most of the guys around here." She extended her hand over the bar. "You must be Matt."

He took her hand. The inside of her hand, her palm, was rough, but the outside, the part that his thumb rested against, was soft, lightly freckled like her chest. "I'm Sage."

"Pleased to meet you, Sage." He realized he had been hanging on to her hand without shaking it. He gave it one small pump then released it quickly, folding his hands into his lap and looking to the side of the room. He figured he'd been living with men for too long; at this point a mortar shell dropping beside him would be less intimidating.

"I was so sorry to hear about Gwen," Sage said. "I used to love it when they came in. This couple of hot chicks and none of the guys could take their eyes off them. And I really liked Gwen. I was having a bit of a tough time financially a while ago and she used to invite me over for dinner with her and Liz, and they even babysat my dog for me and then would send him home with all this food." A sudden look of regret appeared on her face. "Oh god," she said. "I'm sorry. Maybe I shouldn't be talking about her like this."

"No. It's okay." He felt odd, as though she was burrowing under his skin, and it raised his hackles if only a little. Even so it felt reassuring, remembering his sister, who he never saw enough of.

Sage broke his reverie with a laugh. "I remember once when this cowboy was coming on to Lizzie at the bar while Gwen had gone to the washroom. When Gwen got back she stood on the other side of the guy, smiling at him, all kind of sexy and seductive. You could just see in his face that he thought he was going to get lucky with a couple of girls, like this fantasy every man has of watching some chicks get it on and then doing him. So Gwen was flirting right back with him until he asked them point blank if they'd come back to his place for some fun. Gwen kept on smiling at him while she reached down and grabbed his balls and squeezed so hard I thought the guy's head would blow. He was in so much pain his face was turning red but he wouldn't say a thing; he didn't want to look like a sissy in front of all his buddies. Then she said to him, 'From what I can feel, you haven't got the equipment to satisfy *one* of us, let alone two.' Then she let go of his nuts and she and Lizzie went off and played pool while his friends, who stood around watching, laughed their asses off. It was hysterical."

Matt laughed. "I hope you're not going to tell that story at her memorial service," he said. He sighed. "I guess I missed a lot of good times with her. I just couldn't stand the thought of being back here."

Sage raised an eyebrow in agreement. "Yeah, I understand. This place can get to you. It's not some people's thing, but it's home to me. I tried living in Vancouver for a while but just couldn't do it. Too big of a city. You get lost, and you don't know anyone. I think even Penticton is getting a little too big for me sometimes."

"As big as it is, it's always been too small a place for my mother and me. Did Gwen ever tell you anything about that?" He couldn't believe he was he opening the door to this woman he had known for only a few minutes. He felt nervous but excited at the same time.

She smiled back at him with what he thought was real compassion in her eyes, that aloofness he first noticed in her suddenly gone. "Gwen talked about you; sure. She missed you. She told me how you'd gone into the military and were off in Afghanistan. She even introduced me to your mother once when I ran into the two of them shopping." She was wiping the counter with her rag as she spoke, chasing small islands of water. "I guess it's pretty hard for you to be back."

Matt sensed a shadow of someone moving from the door. He turned and jumped up from his stool. "Lizzie!" he yelled.

She broke into a trot while he stood with his arms open. He grabbed her and pulled her into him, hugging her tightly as he rocked her from side to side.

"Man, it has been way too long since I've seen you," he said, putting his hands on her hips as he leaned back to look her up and down. "Here, sit. Pull up a stool and let's have a drink before lunch." He sat back on his stool and patted the one next to him. She looked at the almost-empty glass on the bar.

"Starting early?" she asked, smiling at him. "Not that I'm judging or anything."

"Just something to take the edge off." He fidgeted with the neck of his shirt. "You have no idea."

She remained standing in front of him, her smile eating up her face. She looked like a classic rodeo cowgirl, the kind you see in movies, curves in all the right places and the tight jeans and shirt to show it off, all of it topped off with dark undulating hair and a sideways smile as if she knew she was always one step ahead of you.

"It's so good to see you, Matty. You look amazing," she said, sinking her fingers into his bicep. "The army's done good work on you."

"Well, they did a number on me, that's for sure," he said, looking down at his crutch.

She reached up and put both arms around his neck, pulling him toward her and planting a loud kiss on his cheek.

"Do you want me to get you guys a room?" Sage had been standing behind the bar, silently watching the mutual admiration fest.

Liz turned and slapped the bar with her hand, sending the little puddles flying. "Oh my god, Sage, I didn't even see you there!" She stood up on the bar rail and leaned across the counter, reaching for Sage's shoulders. They kissed each other. "How are you, girl?"

Sage smiled broadly. "I'm doing great, Liz. I guess the better question is, how are you keeping?"

"Well." Liz had her hands on the counter, fingers spread wide. "It's been a bit tough I guess, but it's not as though we didn't know it was coming." She smiled even though she looked somewhere far away. "Gwen was incredibly strong and insisted on being at home until she just couldn't do it anymore. She wanted to be close to Shirley, and she knew I had to be caregiver to both of them, so it was easier if they were both at home. Not that Shirley's all that bad. I mean sometimes, a lot of the time, she's still pretty lucid, but you have to keep an eye on her." She gave a nearly imperceptible glance in Matt's direction. "It hasn't been easy on my job though."

"Are you still at the law firm?" he asked, deciding not to pick up on the report on Shirley.

"Yeah, I'm still clerking there and they've been incredibly understanding, but I want to go to law school as soon as possible now. I really didn't have the time before, obviously. Not that I regretted any of my time over the last couple of years. But with you here Matt to take care of Shirley, things will get a little easier."

He had hoped she would offer to help him out, a fantasy he had probably concocted to make coming home easier.

Sage opened a Sprite and poured it fizzling into a glass of ice for Liz. "I'm going to give you guys some time to catch up. Can I get you a table?"

"Sure, sure," Matt said. "Sorry, Sage, I didn't mean to be rude but you're right, we've got a lot to talk about."

Sage reached under the counter and pulled out a couple of menus for them. "Take any seat you want."

Matt followed Liz to the table, pulling out the curved wooden chair for her with a small bow. She smiled and shifted her gaze toward the floor with a bashful, mock giggle and reciprocated with a dainty curtsey.

He slumped back in his chair, feeling looser now, and folded his hands across his lap, looking beyond Liz as he spoke to her. "I'm really sorry I missed the lawyer this morning. I just couldn't do it. It feels like I'm not ready to face any of this yet."

"No sweat, soldier," she said. "Thanks for calling me to let me know. You'll have to see him at some point, but it will take a while for Gwen's estate to be settled. In the meantime though, your mother had signed over power of attorney to Gwen, and you'll have to figure out what to do with that." He was fascinated by the little plastic butterfly she wore anchored on top of her thick chestnut hair. Here she was so pragmatic, so damn bright and he knew she dialled it down so others wouldn't find her pretentious. "Does it feel good to be back? We never really talked much about how it was over there."

"It was a job," he said, almost forcing the words out. "Like anything, sometimes it's hard and other times you enjoy it." His response was automatic, but she wasn't accepting it. She sat looking straight at him, waiting. She would make a good lawyer, or poker player. "You know, Lizzie, I honestly don't want to talk about it. Things happened there that I don't even want to think about ever again. And sure, I'm glad to be out of there in a way, so in that sense I'm okay being back. But I don't know where home is anymore, so I can't really say where I'm back *to*. It's so damn confusing, and this whole thing of taking care of Shirley turns my guts inside out."

His throat was beginning to feel a little dry even while sweat was rising on his forehead. He became acutely conscious of the sensation, so aware of the pressure that he almost felt each bead of perspiration pressing its way through his pores, sprouting like a plant through clay soil. He couldn't talk about any of it. Not now. He cleared his throat and looked back up. "What about you, Liz? How are you doing?" He hoped she would ride along with the intentional deflection in conversation.

"I'm okay I guess." She responded to his detour, consciously, he knew. "You know me. I'm tough on these bigger things. It's probably something small and insignificant like losing my keys that'll take me down later." As she spoke she stared sightlessly beyond his left shoulder, somewhere in the recent past he guessed, and a smile rose slowly, warmly, on her face. "I wish I could have done more for Gwen. I wish I could have done more *with* her. It seemed like we had so little time together, even though it was seven years. Stupid luck of the draw, I guess. Why would it have taken her and not me? I always had this fantasy that we'd have this graceful exit together. Not like *Thelma and Louise* exactly, but kind of." She squeezed her bottom lip between her teeth. "Okay, maybe it's *not* the little stuff that'll get to me. I haven't let my guard down, or really stopped to think about much of our lives since she died. I'll be glad when the memorial service is over."

He reached across the table, smothering her small hands with his. "I'm sorry I couldn't be around much near the end, but it almost seemed like she didn't want me to be."

"She knew how hard it would be for you, and she figured it wasn't going to help anyone really. She knew you'd have to face your mother if you came home to be with Gwen, and besides, she really didn't want you to see the condition that she was in. The last few months were pretty fast for her."

She pulled one of her hands free and patted his. "But what about you? What are your plans?" Time for her own deflection, skilled as a prize goalie.

He wasn't expecting the question. He tilted his head back, his eyes frozen on a corner of a greying acoustical tile halfway down the room. He realized he had been trying to contain tears, and he was clenching his teeth.

"Well, it's time for me to face the music, I guess," he said slowly. "I've got some issues to deal with back in Edmonton, but Shirley needs someone to take care of her. I just need to get things wrapped up here as fast as I can." He felt like he was pushing the words out of his mouth, straining with each word and letter, like forcing alphabet soup through a sieve. He took another sip of his vodka. "Gwen was pretty conniving about the whole thing. I know she figured she could force a sort of reconciliation by making sure I was the one to step in. Not that there was anyone else. But having Shirley live with us—with me—would be insanity right now."

"She's actually pretty good you know," Liz said. Matt knew she was trying to be reassuring. "She got all confused when Gwen died, and I felt awful but there was nothing I could do but eventually put her in the hospital. Her doctor, Dr. Rosen, and I have become pretty close, and he agreed to take her for a prolonged assessment, I think as much to take her off my hands while I dealt with the funeral arrangements and all the other details. Other than that there have been a couple of scares, and she's awfully forgetful, you know, repeats herself a lot and is always wondering where she left *this* or if she did *that* already. But she's still feisty, and you can still have a decent conversation with her some of the time."

She looked away for a minute, toward the door. "And you know that one day you might *have* to institutionalize her. I'm just telling it like it is, Matty. This isn't going to get any better. It will be a lot of responsibility. I don't know what your plans are for work, but you're going to have a full-time job on your hands until you get this sorted out."

Her words were turning in his head, burrowing into the back of his brain, while a different voice rising to the foreground. *Why had he come home? How was he ever going to get away from this?* Just then the room's walls faded from his peripheral vision; he was looking down a dark tunnel. *No,* he thought, *don't lose it; just hang on.* His heart pushed against his shirt, its pace rising with each quickened breath. He reached for his glass and drained what he could out of it, sucking back a few of the melting ice cubes to chew on, the sound echoing inside his head. The ringing in his ears that had been troubling him for the last few weeks was back, gripping the side of his skull, blocking out ambient sound. Liz was still speaking but he looked and listened as though through a spongy membrane, seeing nothing but her face, her mouth moving but her words floating off unintelligibly.

Matt jumped up from the table, nearly knocking it over while he fumbled for his crutch. He saw the sign for the washrooms, and without a word to Liz hopped in quick leveraged strides to the bathroom, bumping into the bar as he passed.

Sage stopped wiping the glass in her hand, turning her head as he hurried past her. "Are you okay Matt?" she called after him, but he had already pushed open the bathroom door, stumbling over the tiled floor.

He braced himself against the cool tiled wall with his hand, feeling the slickness of the porcelain under his sweating palm. He turned and leaned back, bending his legs involuntarily as he slid slowly down the wall until he was sitting on the floor. He folded his head onto his knees and couldn't contain a loud sob. His body convulsed as he exhaled in a long moan that ricocheted off the room's hard surfaces. It didn't matter if anyone walked in on him, if anyone was in the stalls. He didn't care about anything, about Gwen, or his kids, or Liz, who stood waiting outside the door, calling his name.

So he waited, hoping this time the attack would pass as it had before, even though he knew the beast was stalking him like a skilled predator, stronger than he was, with no sign of letting up.

※

Matt had been physically wounded before. Severely. He had taken a bullet in the shoulder at close range during a firefight but kept on fighting, his assailant practically on top of him before he shot him literally single-handedly. Shrapnel in the nuts. He knew you keep fighting, even through your pain, because if you're feeling pain then you know you're not dead, you're still alive and you've got a job to do. You go into battle knowing things could get messy but the job has to be done, so you face down your fear. If you don't, if you allow it to worm its way into your brain, then it will destroy you.

Back there, in Afghanistan, he knew how to deal with it. But this was different. This was a new person, a man he didn't recognize, wanting to run instead of face what was ahead. And it was this fear of the unknown—the worst kind of fear—that stalked him. The body was mostly the same but something he didn't know and couldn't fight had taken up living in it. Matt didn't have the tools, the training or the backup of a battalion to deal with something that threatened to ambush him at any moment.

And there was no way to go back and undo everything that had led to this.

CHAPTER 7

SHIRLEY

No sooner has Shirley dismissed the notion of suicide, only a bothersome wisp of a thought remains, a remnant of an idea she can no longer wholly identify. It lingers disturbingly in her brain like the smell of something unrecognizable but unpleasant that long ago left the room.

Now she contemplates this new presence, a man who stares back at her. There is something familiar about his face, but she isn't quite sure she can place it. She stands in the hallway, just outside her room, cocks her head slightly to the side, as though seeing him from a different angle might trigger a memory, or perhaps the motion might allow her mental ball bearings roll into a hole like a pinball target, the success of her aim producing a mental cacophony of ringing bells and flashing lights in celebration. But there is none of that.

She folds her arms across her chest—the hallway feels cold and disagreeable—and lets her head come back to level, scanning him from the top of his short-cropped blond hair down over the hills and ridges of the baby-blue T-shirt that contains his tight torso, the shirt untucked from his jeans. He supports himself on a crutch but his posture is perfect, his legs rigid, feet spread and firmly planted in well worn but clean grey running shoes. She is quite certain, as certain as she can be, that he is not from her church.

The doctor must recognize her confusion, her inability to connect the face with a name or memory. He takes a step toward her and reaches for her hand, cradling it gently in his soft palms. He is just a baby himself, she thinks, not even mid-thirties. He looks like George Clooney on *ER*.

"Mrs. Graydon," Dr. Clooney says. "Matt is here to pick you up." Her eyes tighten. She blinks but says nothing. "Your son," the doctor says.

Certainly, if he has said what she thinks he has, he is mistaken. This is not Matt. The man in front of her has full stubble on his face and neck, is taller and older than Matt, even though she admits there is some resemblance. There is a vertical dimple carved into his chin like a baguette diamond, and his blue eyes—like Matt's—are intensely piercing, almost dangerous. He shows no expression on his face.

She feels herself smiling, politely at first so as not to make the doctor feel stupid or the stranger uncomfortable, but something chinks away at her composure. She senses her lips crinkle into a less-certain grin, still hoping that if she appears amused it will distract them from her increasing uncertainty.

She attempts a volley just to see where it will go, hoping it leads somewhere familiar. "I think you've made a mistake," she says to the man in jeans. She practically squirms as she says it, squeezing the words out of her mouth like old toothpaste out of a tube. Her eyes are propped open wide as she looks around for Nurse Comfort, feeling unsettled, as though the room pressure is starting to increase around her, crushing her from the outside. Even listening to the nurse's annoying voice, like air being expelled from a balloon's sphincter, would be a relief. She sees a chair a few feet away and moves toward it, sitting down.

Yes, she is in the hospital. A flicker or a memory says she has been waiting for her son. They are saying this is Matt, and he does look something like him. Has she been wrong about this?

Oh good grief.

She gazes down at her knees, contrite, feeling suddenly like she did when she got her first period, cheap and ridiculous. She shakes her head, not looking up at the doctor nor at Matt, her son, and mumbles quietly. "I'm sorry," she says, a clumped porridge of words. "I'm a little confused."

If someone would hold her, just put an arm around her, she knows she would feel better, but even as she thinks this she senses a current surrounding her like an electric eel, knowing she'll zap anyone who tries to get closer.

The doctor says nothing but watches as Matt sits in the chair next to Shirley and lays his large, tan hand on hers, sheltering them like a warm tea cozy. At the first touch of his skin against hers she flinches but then is surprised—relieved almost—that the tension starts to unravel inside her, the voltage now moderating to a tingle. She wants to lift her head and look at him, but it seems held in place by an invisible force, the force of her pride, she acknowledges tacitly, and her shame. How strange that her emotions can be so strong, even while her thoughts are fleeing her like rats on a sinking ship.

But somehow, having Matt here seems oddly right. Her son is finally home.

***

Shirley was still a beautiful woman, and it surprised Matt. The pictures Gwen had sent him years ago until he asked her to stop showed a still elegant, composed woman, but he had painted a different picture of her, especially now with her slide into dementia, imagining a wild-haired wizened hag, all mumble and drool.

He looked at her now with intentional reticence, studying her as he would a portrait in a museum, pushing down on any emotion that attempted to rise from his gut. She sat in her grey, tailored suit, every hair impeccably cut and combed, still an elegant, pretty woman but diminished, as though someone had taken a fire hose to that feral blaze that had once raged in her belly. Part of what had always made her attractive, he realized, was her fierceness, her composure in the face of any situation. Her coldness, as he had come to know it. Still, he approached her now as he would an apparently good-natured hyena, doubtful that the look matched the intent. She was now his responsibility as he was once hers, this woman whom he no longer knew, whom he had never really known to begin with. And now it appeared she didn't know who he was either, and it surprised him how it twisted his insides.

The doctor had warned him about this when they spoke in his office before seeing Shirley. "She'll slip in and out of current time and reality," the doctor said, "but she's a long way off from losing her grip totally."

Matt sat silently in the chair, fighting the pressure in his torso, his legs twitching to bolt for the door.

"She is still an intelligent woman with a sharp sense of humour," the doctor said. "You'll find that a little frustrating though, because in her lucid moments she'll often seem fine, but then she'll trip on a thought and lose it. She'll become very frustrated, as will you. The recent memories are what fail first. She's showing signs even now of regressing to her past, where the mind only retains memories of where it was at a certain age or time."

The doctor must have noticed Matt was sweating, his eyes welling. "Are you all right?"

Matt took a couple of shallow breaths. "I don't know. I'm feeling a little claustrophobic."

"Just sit back and take some deep breaths. Does this happen frequently?"

He couldn't look toward the doctor. Matt finally broke the silence. "I've been having some weird things happen to me since Afghanistan. The military doctors have wanted me to get some treatment for post-traumatic stress. On top of everything else, I've been having these panic attacks."

"And have you seen anyone about it yet?"

"I just got back from Afghanistan. This is driving me crazy. How is one nut supposed to take care of another?" he had asked, resting his hand on his crotch.

"I'm going to refer you to someone Matt. From what you've told me, there is little choice but for you to take care of your mother right now, and it's not going to be a stress-free job. You should get some counselling as soon as you can if this is PTSD. You might want to consider getting some help with your mother as well."

~

Now Matt stood looking down at her, her hands folded in her lap. He sat beside her and did what he thought would be the right thing, allowing his hands to descend softly, completely covering her cold hands with his. Matt felt the doctor's eyes on them. Shirley flinched slightly as he touched her but otherwise remained still, her hands not moving underneath his.

How many times had he held these same hands as a child? The touch to him felt foreign and strange, like cupping his fingers over a captured exotic bird that might fly away if he relaxed his hold. He remembered once when he was five years old, getting lost in the Eaton Centre in Toronto. It was Christmastime and they had been visiting their big-city relatives. He had never seen anything like it, the mall filled with colours and crowds and Christmas carols, the Santa whose knee he was forbidden to sit on so he wouldn't believe any lies, the suspended geese that seemed in flight over one end of the mall. He was craning his neck, trying to peer above the overcoats and parkas and hats of the frenetic crowd. He stopped for a second to stare at the pictures in the lingerie shop, and a minute later when he turned around, his mother and sister were gone. He never would have admitted how afraid he was; he couldn't have imagined how alone he could feel in the midst of that crush of people. But later, when the sweet young lady at the Lost & Found handed him over to his mother, Shirley had effortlessly reached down and taken his hand in hers, giving him a little smile before she guided him back through the crowds again. He would have got lost every day for a year if he had known how good it felt, that rare touch of her hand.

"Mom," he whispered, his eyes remaining on his hand in her lap. "It's me, Matty." He gave her hands a little squeeze and looked across at her, her hair still hiding the profile of her drooping head. He shook her hands gently. "Hey," he whispered.

Shirley slowly raised her head and turned to face him, her neck pivoting in tiny increments. He wasn't sure what to expect when her eyes followed to meet his.

"Take me home, Matty," she said quietly. "Please." Her eyes were wide but wet, and he could see she sat unblinking in case a tear rolled down her cheek that would defy the tigress she once was, that she so wanted to be.

He had visualized this scenario so many times, had run it through his head over and over, how he would feel on seeing her again, and each time it had ended in conflict and anger. But now she turned her hand up to grasp his, just as he had with her that Christmas in the mall, and he hadn't expected this twinge in his heart.

July 2003, Shirley's Diary

I had to go to Naramata today for a new client, a woman who couldn't get herself to come to my office for counselling because she was afraid someone would see her at a nutritionist's office. I don't often make house calls, but she sounded so nervous and needy on the phone, so off I went after my other appointments. Good lord that woman would have barely fit through my door if she'd made it to the office. Her house smelled like old grease, and she was baking a mincemeat pie. Sometimes I just want to tell someone like her that if she doesn't stop eating pies and cookies she'll have to attach blinking lights to her ass for when she backs up. But it's kindness she needs—that and a whole lot of willpower.

It's hard to admit, but I find it lonely these days. Chances of finding a like-minded husband in this community are slim to none. Not that I'd get married again anyway, if the last one was any indication of my chances at success.

Amanda brought the kids down to the farm a few weeks ago so I could meet Callum, her and Matty's littlest one. He's so darn cute; looks just like his dad. The first time she visited she caught me by surprise—I didn't even know who she was—showing up without any warning at all with Baxter in tow. I have to admit I had thought of her as a tart before without even knowing her, I suppose due to the fact that she got pregnant before they were married. But then who am I to talk? Even though that was totally different.

If I thought stubbornness was unique to my family, then Amanda certainly joined that circle quickly enough—as inhospitable as I was, she dug in her heels and insisted on staying until I talked to her and acknowledged my grandson. I'm grateful now that she did and that she's started to make these regular summer visits. Matty won't come and it's just as well because he's not welcome. Every year that goes by puts more distance between us, and it gets harder for either of us to reach out. I don't think it's going to happen.

At least I'm getting to know my grandchildren. Honestly, why couldn't my relationship with Matty have been as easy as that, or as my relationship with Gwen? I suppose I'm as guilty as he is. But he doesn't seem to care a lick for me or for this beautiful farm he used to love so much. I swear I should leave the farm to the grandkids when I die.

CHAPTER 8

"Why did you wait so long to come and get me?"

Her question made him jump, grip the steering wheel harder. She hadn't said a word since Matt picked her up, and it was her tone that startled him out of his daydream as much as the fact that she had said something. This was the old Shirley, and her voice pierced him with the efficiency of a dentist's drill. The mother he knew was still kicking, and she had fired her first salvo.

He steadied his hands on the wheel. It was true: he had left her at the hospital for three days beyond the time he was originally to have collected her, and each of those days had been a drunken binge, an exercise in evasion. He called the hospital every day with another excuse, telling them he would pick her up first thing the next day. Liz finally tracked him down, catching him on a morning when he was sober but hung over, guilting him into finally going to get his mother.

In the meantime, though, in those three days, it was as though he was hanging in limbo between his old life and his new, uncertain whether taking a step forward would free him from the stubborn chokehold he found himself in, even while knowing that he was unable to turn back.

He did not respond to her question, unsure if speech or silence would lead down the least confrontational road.

"Every day I was ready Matt, sitting there in my suit waiting for you." She was not going to let this go. She spoke tentatively, as if contemplating each word, trying on every syllable before letting it slide from her mouth. Her patterns of speech had always been literate, spoken in complete, well-formed sentences. Even when he was a child he didn't recall her ever speaking baby talk to him, always addressing him as though he were an adult. But now, while there was determination in her tone, the old confidence didn't seem there.

She spoke wistfully, as though retelling a dream she had recently had. "I was excited in the beginning that you were coming. Then they would tell me you hadn't shown up, and that you would be there the next day." She paused and looked out the window at the sparkling water of the Okanagan Lake, diamond chips on black velvet. "You think I don't know. Everyone just humours me. They assume I really don't understand what's going on anyway. But I'm not an idiot. I may not be what I once was Matt, but I'm not an idiot. Not completely." She looked out the window. "Not yet."

He let her go on, mostly out of not knowing how to respond.

"You think this is easy. Everyone thinks I'm just quietly slipping away, that I don't matter anymore or don't have the brain left to know what's going on." Her hands were clenched into little white fists on her skirt, puckering the soft material of her skirt into grey flannel whirlpools. "But I do know, Matt. I may have to keep reminding myself, when I can, who you are, that you're my son, and I might not be there 100 percent of the time, but when I am, I *know*. I am there ... maddeningly intact, even if it's only for minutes or hours at a time, and it's awful. But I'm not going gentle into that ..."—she struggled for the words—"that fucking night, just like that poet, what's his name, said.

"Goddamn it Matt." Her voice cracked a little. "Sometimes I just want to wither away and be done with it. I hate this. I hate everything about this!"

Himself included, he was sure.

And since when had she started talking like this? *Fucking? Goddamn it?* He understood how her predicament was eating her up, but did she think this was easy for him? But tables had turned, and now it seemed he would need to be a better parent to her than she had been to him, to make her fading as comfortable as possible, however long that might take.

He saw an exit ramp and suddenly pulled off, following the small road to the provincial park, spinning around the first corner and jolting to a stop. He got out of the car and slammed the door behind him while Shirley sat rigidly still, following him with just her eyes.

The breeze from the lake was warm on his face as he stood facing the water, his back to the car and to her, watching the whitecaps peak like meringue. He took a few deep breaths then turned around and hobbled back to the car, the dust rising in little clouds behind his shoes and crutch.

Her window was still rolled up, so he pulled the door open instead. "We need to talk." His sergeant's voice. "Come on." He nodded toward the lake. "Let's go for a walk."

He noticed her face and suddenly felt a small pang inside. She was looking back at him, her eyes large and questioning. She was scared, and he had made her feel that way.

He shook his head, upset for being so harsh. He squatted beside her. "I'm sorry, Shirley," he said, supporting himself on the open door. "I didn't mean to scare you." He tried to make his voice sound soothing, non-threatening. "Can we just go for a walk, maybe talk a little?"

She stared back at the windshield, and without saying a word reached for the buckle of her seatbelt and unclasped it, guiding the grey strap as it retracted to her side. She unfolded an elegant leg from in front of her, allowing it to rest on the ground outside the door.

Matt extended his hand to assist her, and she gazed up at him for a moment, the fear from her face suddenly gone, her countenance sphinx-like and unreadable. As she reached for his hand she gently angled her other leg out of the car and then stood at his side, one hand now looped through his arm while she looked out toward the lake, clutching her purse to her chest. She was the picture of incongruity and defiance, the coiffed matron in her grey-flannel suit and black heels come to the beach, determined to participate if she must, but on her own terms. He couldn't help but find it mildly comical, even as the wind courageously challenged her lacquered hair that floated above her shoulders like a small hydrofoil.

Matt guided her slowly down the road toward the water. He inhaled—the warm scent of cedar filled his lungs—about to speak, but then held his breath for a few seconds.

"Look," he finally said. "We've really got to try to make this different." He glanced over to make sure he had her attention, but he couldn't be certain. He decided to continue anyway; he was calmer now. "You and I hardly know each other anymore, so maybe this is a good time to start fresh. I know this must frustrate the hell out of you, and you don't like these circumstances, but we're going to have to make the best of it for a while until we get it all figured out. I haven't got a clue what I'm doing, and at the risk of sounding selfish, I have issues of my own to sort out."

He was stopped suddenly by her tugging on his arm, forcing him to retract a step. She continued to look straight ahead, out toward the lake, saying nothing.

He unlocked her arm from his and grasped her gently by the elbows. "Please, Shirley, talk to me," he said. "Mom."

He looked from one eye to the other, trying to read what was behind them. "I'm not shrugging this off. I wouldn't be here if I wasn't going to do this, but I really don't know what I'm doing, and if you're capable, it sure would be nice for you to let me know what I need to do."

She bent forward a little and brushed some invisible lint from her skirt. Then she straightened up and looked directly at him. He saw the small vertical wrinkles that had started to carve their way out from the contour of her lips, deeper near her mouth where they were etched scarlet from her lipstick like small tributaries. She examined him as though she had just accidentally spilled grape juice on a new white carpet, disgusted with herself that she could have produced such a thing, and equally resigned that it wasn't going away. She blinked once, deliberately, as though she might change the scene in front of her like a frame in a slideshow, and then, blinking again, resolved she could not.

"I didn't ask for this." Her voice was soft, tentative. "I didn't ask for Alzheimer's or for you to come home or for Gwen to die. I just wanted to go on quietly living my life. But it seems I'm incapable of any of that or of taking care of myself, according to the doctors." She stood absolutely straight. "We should try to make this the least amount of hardship for either of us. And frankly, I don't really want to start over between us, even though you say you'd like to try. I'm too old, and I wouldn't know how anyway, besides which I just might forget tomorrow that I was supposed to be starting all over again."

She had been looking away from him, her eyes searching the birch trees to her left for the proper words, but now she looked back at him, managing a small laugh as she shook her head. She walked on ahead, guiding him in a wide circle to a wooden bench that faced the lake. Small waves clawed at the pebbles on the beach, their sound a susurrant reply to the hissing birch trees behind Matt and Shirley. A few chips of green paint came off on Shirley's fingers as she turned and brushed off the bench, and after a little cluck with her tongue she sat, indicating with a nod that he should sit next to her.

Shirley perched her black bag on her knees that were pressed together like two popsicle wedges, snapping open the purse's brass clasp and then digging through its contents. Her hand combed through the bag like a backhoe, exhuming a detritus of clinking coins and crinkling wrappers and raising the smell of cinnamon gum and Chanel perfume, each scoop coming up quicker than the last, her exasperation rising with every repetition.

"Where is my ... oh ... where is it?" she said.

He could see the frustration on her face.

"You know, my waxy thing. The coloured thing." She took her hand out and shook it as though something in her purse had just nipped at her fingers, looking at him for a second, her eyes indicating her confusion. "You know. Not my shoe polish. My ... my ..." She puckered her lips and took one more dive into her purse, finally pulling out a small white cylinder.

"You mean your lipstick?" he asked.

"Oh." She sighed, letting her head go limp. "Yes, my lipstick." She pulled the top off the case and then clicked it back on, watching her hands as she repeated the action noisily, compulsively. She shook her head. "I feel so stupid sometimes, Matt."

How could he respond? She had done some stupid things in her life, but he had never thought of her as an idiot. Yet she could be so damn mean.

He reached over abruptly and covered her hands with his to stop her from clicking the lipstick tube. "It's okay," he said, not really buying it. Then he gave her hands an awkward squeeze. "We all do stupid things."

She withdrew her purse—her hands with it—to her side, resting the bag on the bench.

"Where's Amanda?" she asked, obviously changing the subject. He was grateful for the diversion and figured a straight-on answer was probably his best approach.

"She left me."

"She what?"

"I got home last week from Kandahar and she had moved out with the kids. I don't really know much more than that."

"So what does that mean for me then? I was afraid you were here to take me back to Alberta with you."

"I don't really know," he said. "I'm taking you back to the farm until I get my next plans sorted out and figure out what the best thing is for you. So you're going to have some company for a little while."

"Well, thank god you're not going to try to take me to Edmonton. I want to stay on the farm Matt until my very last day, whenever that is. You've got to promise me that."

"I can't promise you anything right now. I don't know anything about you, about your finances, what you need. I certainly don't have the financial means to look after you, so you're going to have to let me sort that out. And I need to try to plot things out for myself right now. I just don't know what that involves. So let's just be patient with each other while we're ploughing through all this, okay?"

She stood up suddenly—her heels crunching into the pebbles—and pressed the unseen wrinkles from her skirt. "I'm not leaving the farm. I don't care what you say. That's my life and my home, and it's all I know anymore. So you can carry me out of there in a box because that's the only way I'm leaving."

If she only knew how tempting it was, he thought, but not knowing how intact her sense of humour was, he let it go.

"And here's something else." She was like a stunt logger on a barrel roll; she might as well keep going until she fell off. "We may as well have some rules while you're staying with me."

How is it that she could make him so quickly feel like a child again, pushing buttons quicker than anyone else? He bit his tongue.

"No smoking in the house."

"I don't smoke, Shirley."

"I know, but I'm just saying, in case you took it up or something. And no women."

"How about my inflatable doll?" He couldn't help himself.

Shirley glared straight ahead.

"I'm not the least bit interested in women right now," Matt said, "and in case you forgot, I'm still married."

"I didn't forget," she snapped. "But you never know. I won't have my house run through with fornicators, whether you're my son or not. So suck it up."

"I guess we're going to have to sort this thing out sooner than I had imagined, or I'm just going to go back to Afghanistan to get my head shot off."

"That's another thing. I don't want to hear anything about your war, about your job or whatever it is you did over there. It's against my beliefs for anyone to go there and shoot people. So let's just not talk about it. All right?"

Hang on to it, old boy, he thought, *just control yourself.* He wished Gwen were here to run interference between them the way she used to. Why was it that Shirley and her fellow zealots were right and everyone else wrong? She couldn't buy that he might be doing something good for the world.

Even if he succeeded in pulling her away from her little Christian world, it would be like taking a heroin addict away from her fix. The withdrawal would be too harsh and the world far too real to cope with. Her planet was already small enough and getting smaller, so why mess with things at this point?

Shirley was facing him now, but the fierceness had been replaced by a faraway gaze. She looked like she might cry. Her eyes darted over his left shoulder, back toward the highway, and then pleadingly but indecipherably back to him.

"I wish," she started, her eyes filling with tears. "I wish …" but then her voice trailed off.

How could she be so infuriatingly intransigent one moment and then stand there in front of him so helpless and frightened the next? And how could he be so angry with her and then in an instant feel like he had been shot through the heart, bleeding the same blood?

"Come on, Mom," he said, taking her by the arm. "Let's get back to Summerland." He led her to the car and folded her into the seat, the same seat Rayner had lowered Matt into back in Golden, and gently clicked the door shut.

He got in the driver's side and started the engine. "We'll figure this all out when we get you back home."

He wasn't so sure they would.

⸻

January 10, 1983, Shirley's Diary

George left me today. I might say that I left him, except I'm the one still sitting here in the house, and he's the one who drove away. But it was my instigation all along, I know. I pushed him, without ever acknowledging to myself that that's exactly what I was doing. Of course I knew I was being belligerent (is that the opposite of distant, my other state with George?), but I never thought I was giving something he couldn't take. That's what you get when someone marries you out of charity; you just carry on thinking those same saint-like qualities that compelled him to commit to you in the first place will always prevail.

We had a long talk—okay, argument—last night that brought out anger in him I have rarely seen. Rage in George is so interesting to watch; it's never explosive, always contained, but you can see it simmer just under the surface while his face turns red, contorting and sweating like a wrung-out chamois. It's hard for him to articulate his feelings; he stammers and gets all muddled. And me, sitting there like a virgin princess barely acknowledging that he is in the room, hardly a response to his pleas and accusations—no argument from me. How could I argue? Most of what he was saying was right: I do pay less attention to him than I do the dog; it has been years since we had sex.

When we first got married we screwed like crazy. It was like I wanted to be joined to him, that if we stopped having sex we would become decoupled like a train in a switching yard, his freight car from my caboose. We kept at it as long as we could through my pregnancy with Matt and then picked up again as soon as we could after Matt was delivered. I was desperate to get pregnant again, to have my own child, conceived in wedlock this time. Then when Gwen came along we stopped having sex completely, just like that. It felt like I had my child; she completed my little family and everyone else be damned. I couldn't help myself.

He says I drink too much, which really is a load of crap. I enjoy the occasional little tipple, my gin and my wine. I often catch him staring at me with that self-righteous little look on his face while he sips his soda. He thinks too many of my friends drink, that all the people down at the church are a bunch of lushes. I admit that sometimes the thought has crossed my mind too, but how else would we loosen up? He says they're all a bunch of phonies. It's just that he can't understand that they're not putting it on, that they really are that nice. Most of them anyway.

I slept on the couch last night, and this morning he came around the corner with his coat and boots on and his suitcase packed and in the hall as I just sat there. I barely looked up as he told me he was going. I did manage to ask him where, and he said he was going to go off to his brother's in Calgary for a while, that we should have some time apart to figure things out. Both of us know we're not putting any stock in that. I asked if he was driving and he said yes, so I told him (sincerely) to be careful as it was a treacherous trip through the mountains.

What did we ever have in common to begin with? He's a sweet man—way too sweet for me. I needed someone who was strong enough to shake some sense into me, to stand up to me, otherwise I'd walk all over him. And where I'd rather stay home and cook, he wants me to come out hunting with him, camping and fishing and hiking. Nothing gives him more pleasure than downing a deer. I went with him once, and you could see the excitement light up his face like a dog with a new squeaky toy when he shot the poor thing. I swear he sees every animal in cuts of meat, like a cartoon X-ray of filets and rump roasts. He's taken Matt hunting since then, even though I thought Matt might be too young to go, but it's saved me from the agony of going myself and given George some company.

Financially I'm not sure what we'll do if he stays away. Money trickles in from my work, and George barely makes enough to keep us all. I might have to put my pride and anger aside and hit up David for support money for Matt. God knows he owes me big.

I kind of wish George would have taken Matt with him today too and just left me and Gwen here to ourselves. Poor Matty. I'm so hard on him. He doesn't get that he's a constant reminder of the terrible act that resulted in him. I try to love him but I can't, I just can't. But now with only the three of us left I'll have to try a little harder, I suppose.

CHAPTER 9

"Are you ready?" Matt crossed the kitchen to Shirley's closed bedroom door and knocked. "Shirley? Everything okay in there?" He grasped the handle and waited, gradually pushing the door open.

Shirley stood in front of the mirror in just her slip, looking at herself. She ignored Matt, continuing to gaze at her reflection.

"Mom, are you all right?" He treaded into the room. Shirley inched her head around, her body following slowly to face him. "Are you almost ready?" Matt asked.

"Matt?" She seemed confused. "Where are we going?" The words came out as though she didn't even know she was the one speaking.

He had been moving toward her, but now he stopped and pondered her instead. "Don't you remember?" He softened his tone, hoping to sound nonchalant so she wouldn't interpret the question as an accusation. "We're going to the funeral."

Shirley's eyes squinted as he watched her trying to retrieve the information. She shook her head. "What funeral?"

Her moments of clarity sometimes surprised him, they were so sharp, but then they vanished with no warning or signal, as though thoughts were escaping her head like tufts of down through a worn pillowcase, falling gently, as if to feather her coffin.

He braced himself for her reaction. "Gwen's funeral, Mom."

She searched his eyes as if she were trying to decipher a mystery, a child that had lost her way. "Gwen's funeral?" The question filled the room. "Gwen died?"

Matt watched the memory leach into her body, the weight of the recollection forcing her down onto the bed.

She started to cry.

"Oh, Mom." Matt sat beside her, putting his arm around her. He couldn't remember the last time he had let himself get this close to her. "It's all right."

She shook her head. "No it's not." She sniffed. "My daughter is dead? Why didn't anyone tell me?" She tried to catch her breath. "Oh my god."

"It's okay," he said, patting her hand. He tried to think of what to do, what to say. He had no training in this. There was no map to follow, nothing that could chart the detours and dead ends of her mind.

"Here, why don't I help you get ready? What were you going to wear?"

Shirley turned and looked at him through red eyes. "I don't know. I've never been to my daughter's funeral before." She pushed herself off the bed, toward the closet. "I can do this," she said. "Give me a few minutes."

But he didn't leave. He went to her side as she shuffled through the hangers. At first she tried to ignore him, throwing back her shoulders as if to dismiss him, but he stayed. He reached into her closet and pulled out her grey flannel suit, the one she had worn home from the hospital.

"Here," he said. "You looked beautiful in this when I picked you up."

She took the hanger from him, holding on to it as though he had just given her a precious gift. Something in his heart moved as he looked at her, a feeling so unfamiliar it made him squirm. But as he turned to leave he smiled quickly back at her, hoping she didn't notice the quivering that had started to press through his chin.

Liz and Matt stood in the late-morning sun on the steps of the church, greeting people as they walked inside. Matt peeked through the doorway to see if Shirley was all right where he'd left her in the front row, fidgeting with her purse.

"How's she doing?" Liz asked.

"I'd say today she's having a rough day."

"And what about you? How are *you* doing?"

"I'd say I was having a rough day too." A little smile rose to the corner of his mouth. He gave her a hug. "I don't know how you and Gwen did it."

"Gwen was a pretty remarkable chick. And she just had a way with Shirley."

He couldn't help feeling envious, and missing Gwen. "How about you, Liz?"

She grabbed his hand and squeezed. "I'll just be glad when today's over," she said, then turned to smile at the people climbing the stone steps.

Matt looked through the archway toward the front of the church, watching as a man approached Shirley and put his hand on her shoulder, bending down to talk to her. He saw Shirley recoil, a frightened look on her face. The man turned and Matt recognized him; a man he once called "Uncle" David.

"How the hell did that scumbag sneak by me?" Matt asked.

"Isn't that David Estridge?" Liz asked.

"Yeah. I can't believe he's taken time from counting his money to come here. I don't even know why he thinks he's welcome." Matt felt the blood rushing to his ears.

Matt hardly heard a word through the service. When it ended he put his hand behind Shirley's back and helped her up, feeling a heaviness inside him but also relief that it was over, the formal beginning of a good-bye he knew would never be complete. Liz took one side of Shirley and Matt the other, and they escorted her to the back of the church, nodding at the sombre well-wishers as they passed. Matt's eyes followed the stone tiles, watching Shirley's steps. Near the back of the church, just inside the entrance, his lowered gaze fell on three sets of feet, two smaller pairs on either side of a woman's heels. His heart stopped as he looked up.

"Amanda?" he said incredulously. Without thinking he let go of Shirley's arm, Liz taking over like a seasoned diplomat and escorting Shirley out the door.

"I never expected you." His mouth was dry, his voice thin.

"She was my friend too, Matt," Amanda said, looking away. "I loved her too."

She wore a dark linen suit, one he had never seen before, appropriate for the occasion but still provocative, at least to him. He couldn't believe how much his heart was pounding.

"It's good to see you," he said, pausing for a second before looking down, his face stretching into a broad grin. "And you too, munchkins." He squatted on his haunches and grabbed them in a bear hug. "And what about you guys, eh?"

The delicate smell of Amanda's perfumed wrists sent a small tremor through him. The boys smiled tentatively back at him, overwhelmed he was sure by their first funeral, by the surroundings, by seeing their father, who was once again separated from their mother, but this time not by his job.

"Come on, boys, let's get some fresh air." He guided them down the steps, holding their hands. He heard Amanda's heels following.

He turned to her. "I'm glad you came. You didn't have to. It's a long way."

"I wanted to be here. And the boys wanted to see you too."

He always thought she was at her best when minding the boys. It hurt to know how bad she thought he was for them. Maybe being here was a sign of her softening.

He took a moment, not wanting to seem too anxious. "Can you stay for a while?"

"No. I've got to head back tomorrow morning."

He suddenly felt like the air had been sucked out of him. "I miss you, you know. I miss the boys too, like you wouldn't believe." He couldn't help blurting it out.

"I know, Matty, I know. It's just, well, I think it's going to take a while for us to get things sorted out, you know?"

He tried to read her face, but she was giving him nothing. "Was there even a small part of you that came here to see me?" As awkward as it felt, he had to put it out there. He thought maybe it was just his imagination, but he was sure he caught a smile rising even though the rest of her face gave away nothing.

Callum, who had been playing on the lawn, ran over and hugged his dad's leg. "You're the good dad today, right?" he said. "Not the mean one."

Matt glanced over at Amanda. With Callum's comment she had turned to face the street. He squatted down and drew Callum between his legs, looking back and forth in the boy's eyes. He didn't want Callum to see how much the question hurt.

"Of course, sweetie. And I'm always going to be the good dad. You don't have to worry about that." He squeezed his son tight, trying to contain the emotion that felt like it might spring through his chest. "I love you, you know. You and your brother. Don't you ever forget that." Amanda was still gazing down the road. "And I'll be home soon."

"Come on," Matt said. "Let's go get your brother. Maybe your mother will let me buy you some lunch." He winked at Amanda, who at first hesitated and then nodded her consent.

He wondered if they served vodka at Denny's.

August 15, 2006
Kandahar Air Field

I've been trying to make sense of the events of the last few weeks, to give myself time to digest the emotions that keep rising from my gut before writing in this journal again. I'm not sure time has contributed any clarity. But I'm writing anyway, under my own personal duress, hoping it will help tame the madness that has been battering my brain punch-drunk.

They say that battle turns even the staunchest atheist into a believer in god. I know now that there is some inkling of truth in that as even I have found myself holding a wounded man, praying for him to live as he lies bleeding to death in my arms, hoping impossibly (isn't that what prayer is about?) that a miracle will happen to snatch him from death's grasp. And then, in my more sane moments, I realize that religion, a belief in god, is mostly what this war has to do with in the first place, of men being brazen and arrogant enough to imagine speaking for god. When I stop to think about it (which I've been doing too much of, the curse and sure sign of a failing soldier), I ran from my mother's Christian beliefs for that very reason, figuring the military would take me far away from her fanatical heavenly musings.

I can just imagine the Taliban praying to Allah for the same outcome our chaplains pray to their own god for: to be victorious, that their ways will triumph over ours, that they'll slaughter us or chase us from their country forever. Yet who couldn't have compassion for a mother who prays as she cradles her daughter who has been killed by one of our jets that's just bombed her village; an inevitable civilian casualty we call it, collateral damage. Still you know that, were the tables turned, if this war were on our own soil back home with an outsider trying to take over our country, we would be as fierce and determined and as bloody-minded to get them—the enemy—out of there, to wipe them off the face of the earth if that's what it took. Turning the tables only makes your head spin.

Why are we doing this? They say we're fighting a war against terrorism, so that it doesn't creep across borders and eventually into our own country, but the fact is most of their warriors have never even heard the word 'Canada' let alone know where it is. These are a tribal people, fiercely proud and protective of their land, their culture, which has developed over centuries. But we would eliminate that, blow them straight from here to Armageddon for the sake of homogenization. Sure we're fighting for democracy and personal freedom and *all that stuff we're told to cherish in our 'free world,' but how much of a right do we have to determine their destiny, to mould them in our image? So while we tell them they're wrong, that their interpretation of the divine is misguided and evil, we ourselves choose to play god.*

I talked to Kareem about it a lot and came to realize that his people's religion and their culture are inextricable. I tried to explain that we started that way ourselves in North America back in the days of the pilgrims, but freedom of choice trumps just about everything else now for us, and for any thinking man, science surpasses religion in its credibility, its ability to explain things that before seemed supernatural or divine, or just a great mystery that only god understood. Yet I still catch myself praying. It's as though I fight myself. I want to stomp on any compassionate notion that I was raised to respect, as though I fault myself for having a conscience. It's laughable that I even try to understand the people I am trying to kill.

None of that matters now. No matter how hard I try to understand the enemy, no matter how much I try to reason over how right or wrong each side could be, I will never forgive them, these fanatics, and the harsh reality of what they have done instantly slays any Christian Cinderella-like delusions. They are savages. And no amount of reason will overcome that.

And what has made me so bitter, so full of anger? This is what happened.

We stopped in a small village while on patrol to hold a 'shura', or consultation, with the elders, a meeting where we sit in a circle and talk about their challenges and see if there is anything we can do for them in exchange for blowing up their country. These are mostly led by the Canadian CIMIC (Civil-Military Cooperation) guys, soldiers or reservists who you could say are usually more gifted in the humanity department than the rest of us. Mostly we try to get information out of the elders and their lackeys about the Taliban: who is and who isn't, where we can find them and (of course this is implied, not spoken) put some bullets into them. They're quick to tell us how we can throw money at their villages to replace a building, dig a ditch or a well to water their poppies or to make clear what other misfortune we have rained on their heads, but when it comes to revealing anything about the Taliban, they are suddenly struck dumb as donkeys.

We were in the godforsaken dustbowl of Kacha, a small town in the Helmand province west of Kandahar. Captain Gordon Melmund, one of the CIMIC guys, was leading our little delegation in the tribal council, and I had been assigned with a couple of guys from my unit, Rayner and Stenner, to accompany Melmund and his posse for protection. I took Kareem along to be our interpreter if we needed him, even though Melmund had his own.

These things are usually pretty peaceful, not much more than civilized bitch sessions, but you never know what's going on in their heads as they sit across from you, eyeing you as they would the town latrine, knowing you're useful but holding their noses as they sit down with you. You never know if they're really cooperating or if some of them are actually Taliban. That's the thing about most Afghans. They can go either way, depending on how deep the pockets are of whomever is engaging them. He who pays the most—or in some cases threatens the most convincingly—wins. But only until a better offer comes in.

The shura was assembled in the town square, a dusty piece of earth off the main road that runs through Kacha. A handful of large grey boulders lie around the outside of the square under the spotty shade of a pathetic-looking tree, the boulders usually used as benches by men who sit and shoot the shit, whiling away the hot afternoon or observing the proceedings in the middle of the square a couple of metres beyond their feet. Two adjacent sides of this wannabe piazza are flanked by low-lying mud buildings that look like they rose organically from the soil below, like someone had just added water and stirred then put it in this Easy-Bake Oven we call Afghanistan.

We knew out of respect (whatever) not to sit on the boulder/benches as we didn't want to be higher than our Afghan hosts, nor would we allow them to take the alpha-dog position, so Captain Melmund gestured to the brown pebbly ground in front of him, inviting the elders to join him in the middle of the square. One of the Afghans came along and spread out a blanket, and three of the elders held their robes as they sank nimbly to the ground, and Melmund sat cross-legged across from them with his interpreter between him and Lt. Pete Schofield.

When they were all seated I motioned for Kareem to sit on one of the boulders and I remained standing beside him, just behind the Afghans. Rayner and Stenner went around to the other side of the circle and stood behind Melmund's threesome where they could keep an eye directly on the Afghans. It was all pretty much standard procedure and formation.

It was midafternoon and hot, one of those days the air is so heavy it descends on you like someone had thrown a dusty horse blanket over your head. I remember thinking how quiet it was. No barking dogs, no chirping birds, as though everything had come to a standstill, afraid to move in case the heat killed them. Of course the Afghans brought out steaming-hot tea and offered it around, Melmund politely taking his and placing it just to the side of the blanket.

The oldest of the Afghans led the conversation from his side, speaking slowly and softly in a fluty nasal voice, smacking his lips every few words and then pausing for a sip of his tea. His eyes were small and black, gooey in the corners, partly covered by the skin that sagged over them, two black marbles embedded in tanned elephant hide. Like so many Afghans it was impossible to determine how old he was.

I didn't pay much attention to the conversation, but at one point Melmund threw his head back and laughed, so I leaned down to Kareem to have him repeat what the elder had said. Kareem had a smile on his face as he lifted his head toward me, and then suddenly from around the corner of the mud building behind us I heard a man scream as he ran in our direction.

I was still bent over listening to Kareem and had barely raised my head to look at the man running toward us when I saw the glint of steel come into view. Before I could move, the man swung a massive sword through the air. It came down and hit the top of Kareem's spine with a crack as it connected with bone and flesh, slicing cleanly two-thirds of the way through Kareem's neck, partially severing his head from his shoulders.

I jumped back as Kareem's blood spurted up at my face, and I stood there, frozen, watching as he teetered forward for a moment on his seat, his head hanging limply to one side attached only by sinew, his body belching blood like a volcano from the hole where his head had been.

I remember everything else around me going black except for what was directly in front of me: Kareem, now lying on the ground with the eyes in his partially severed head still open and his blood turning the earth beneath him to a dark puddle of mud, his heart pumping ignorantly, trying hopelessly to fill the rest of his body with life.

I'm not sure if I reached for my weapon at that point, but I heard nothing, everything disappearing into complete stillness, like I was stone-cold deaf and everything in front of me was taking place in a vacuum. I know there must have been more going on around me, but the only thing I remember hearing, the only thing that pierced the silence was the sound of automatic gunfire. I heard the bullets leaving their weapon and whizzing by me, all in slow motion, and I knew instinctively that the gunfire was coming from two different weapons. It snapped me out of whatever trance I had entered, and as the darkness started to open up I saw Rayner standing over a Taliban attacker who was now dead, his torso stretched face down over the top of Kareem's legs, the blood from his bullet wounds soaking through his tunic and mixing into the dust with my Afghan friend's.

Stenner had run past us along with Lieutenant Schofield around the corner of the building where the killer had emerged from to see if anyone else was there, and our other troops were starting to run from the LAVs and wagons into the square.

I don't know how long I stood staring at Kareem's body. It was as though I thought that somehow, if I stared long enough, his head would be reattached to his torso and he would get up and walk.

It seemed like half a day had passed, but they told me all of this had happened in about six seconds, and then I started barking orders at my men, sending a few of them after Stenner, with the rest making sure the perimeter was secure while screaming for a medic. Rayner and I took a few steps back and trained our weapons on the elders in front of us. No one knew if they were involved, and no one was going to take any chances.

I barely remember getting out of there. Later during the debriefing I discovered I was not the one to pull the trigger and kill Kareem's murderer. I apparently stood there dumfounded as Kareem slumped over the boulder and his assailant raised his sword to take another swipe. That's when Rayner and Stenner opened fire on the guy. They had been reluctant to say anything about me not taking a shot, and I'm sure they would have tried to convince my superiors afterward that I had been the one to pull the trigger if they could get away with it.

The fact is, I froze. Rayner and Stenner didn't say it in the debriefing, but I froze, pure and simple. I heard the guy coming. I saw him lift his sword as if it was happening in slow motion. I could have had time to take out my weapon and cut him down instead. But I didn't. It might have been only seconds, but I stood there like an idiot, my training gone out the window. A lifeless, plastic, store-bought GI Joe could have done a better job.

And I watched my friend, the too-young Kareem with the thick dark hair, the emerald eyes too old for his age, the boy who counted on me, who trusted me enough to lay his head on my legs that night convinced I would protect him, bleed out in front of my stony eyes.

PART 2

CHAPTER 10

DAVID

You have to be an idiot to open a restaurant. At least that's what David Estridge's boss had told him twenty years ago, back at the Placid Hills Estate Winery. At the time David had been unsure if Mr. Cleghorn was saying that David was stupid simply for wanting to start Dave's Grill, or if the boss's comment was a blanket indictment on David's general intellect, period. May as well throw your money right on the grill and watch it burn, Cleghorn said.

David realized Cleghorn wasn't the only one who questioned what kind of business a high school dropout had opening a restaurant, even though David had woken one morning two million bucks richer from a lucky 6/49 ticket. "It's an evil business," Cleghorn had said, God's way of tempting you with meringue dreams and then making you eat crow instead, and restaurant ownership should be classified right up there with pride and greed among the mortal sins. Then there were the other friends and acquaintances with whom he had excitedly shared his plan, who had told him that many a rich man had been made a fool by starting his own restaurant. Well, twenty-three (and counting) Dave's Grills later across western Canada, David Estridge hoped they now knew his business had instead made a rich man out of a fool.

Yet as he stood surveying this new location—with its honey-coloured, wide plank floors, the plush chairs still covered in plastic pushed up against the high-gloss, yet-to-be-used pressed-fibre tables—he felt the slightest twitch of anxiety, that perhaps he had overextended his reach. He quickly dismissed the thought. This would be his twenty-fourth restaurant and his piece de resistance, a temple of gastronomy and payback time for those who thought he would never amount to anything more than a burger flipper. Sure he was taking a risk by his unusual choice of location on the outskirts of Vancouver's Gastown, in some people's opinion extending a little too far into the grime of the city's downtown east side. But it wasn't the first time he had pushed the envelope, and it wouldn't be the last where he succeeded while the city's money stood by in the safety of their Shaughnessy and West Vancouver estates, waiting to see if the new Estridge's caught fire—figuratively, he hoped—while they none-too-secretly forecast not just the restaurant's doom but his own demise as well. After all, what was a man like David Estridge doing opening a high-end dining establishment when his other restaurants catered to value-oriented diners, young men and women who thought a Gamay was the cousin of an ostrich?

But here he was the day before a trial run opening, looking out on his creation and smiling on it like God must have smiled on his, although it had taken David a few more than six days to fulfill his vision. All was good, he thought, and even though he knew that pride was not the most desirable of qualities, he couldn't help thinking even old man Cleghorn would have been impressed by how far he had come, God rest his Catholic soul.

Things in the front of house were shaping up just fine: the towering interior walls were freshly painted in cream and burgundy, large impasto abstracts and encaustic landscapes by local up-and-coming artists hung, lighting skillfully focused; all that was left was for the tables to be set and the plastic unwrapped from the chairs. But as for the kitchen, the beating heart to this goliath, he wasn't as sure. And while he knew his new star chef, the explosive but extraordinary culinary master he had lured from Montreal's venerable La Colombine restaurant, would call him when the sample morsels he was preparing were ready, he decided to risk the man's wrath anyway and wander over casually to the open kitchen to check on his progress.

As David turned to walk toward the kitchen at the back of the restaurant, he saw a jet of orange flame shoot up like a flare from behind the gleaming stainless steel counter. "*Hosti d'calisse d'tabarnac!*" cursed François, the diminutive Quebecois chef who was slapping wildly at his beard with a white tea towel. The smell of burnt hair wafted up David's crinkled nose while telling himself it was too late to fire the caustic little fucker. François threw a lid over the offending pan's contents, the flare up. He cast a colicky smile in David's direction that told him François would have preferred if they were both in different places.

"How's it going, François?" David asked. It was a loaded question. He had learned in the last two months of working with François that the little man was never satisfied unless there was something to grumble about. Even the day of his interview, when David had flown François in from Montreal for three days, he complained about the height of the counters in the kitchen (too high unless he wore stilettos, he said), the placement of the shelf where prepared dinners were laid for pick up by the servers (it obscured his vertically challenged sight lines to the dining room) and the too-casual attitude of all the wait staff in Vancouver ("*Has anyone been trained anywhere but The Keg?*"). So David did not expect the most light-hearted response from his little star chef but knew the reply would at least tell him what the *worst* of it was.

"It's going perfectly well, thank you." *Thank* you came out sounding like *tank* you, delivered with a soupçon of a sneer. "I am a magician, sir, did you not know? A Merlin in the kitchen. Just a twinkle of my wand and 'poof!' all is *parfait.*" The 'poof' was emphasized with a flick of the wrist over François's steaming stock pot. David made a mental note to check for eye of newt in the ingredients. Still, François *had* demonstrated the occasional sense of humour under all the attitude. Nonetheless, David figured it would be the wrong time to call him Cyrano; François had a beak like a toucan that threatened to topple the rest of his small frame off balance.

"Well, Monsieur Calbaut," David said, rolling up the sleeves to his white dress shirt. "I'm glad to see you're up to the task. May I?" He reached with his fingers for the tiny bird on the plate above François's head on the serving counter.

"Yes, of course. I made it for you. It's crab-apple squab on a nest of saffron fettuccine. An unusual taste pairing but delightful, I think."

David picked up the dark leg and took a small nibble, looking for a fork to twirl the pasta as he chewed on the tender brown meat.

François handed him some silverware.

"Mmm ... you're absolutely right, François." The taste was sublime, a friendly competition of flavours vying for attention on his palate. He took a second mouthful of fettuccine. "Where does a French chef learn to make such exquisite pasta?"

François rolled his eyes. "I am not French, Mr. Estridge. I am Quebecois. And my cooking pedigree is international. Here," he said, pushing another plate toward him, this time managing a little smile that David hoped was sincere. "Try this."

A crusty halibut floating in a curry beurre blanc garnished with carmine seaweed. Exquisite. How could he not gush? But he didn't want François to see him orgasm over the food; it would be a disaster if the volatile little egomaniac thought he had the upper hand.

The chef looked at him as though he was mulling his own private joke. David caught the sardonic grin but wouldn't be baited, simply nodding instead in François's direction.

"Very well done, my friend. Now let's see how you can handle a full restaurant." David walked toward the bar where he pretended to examine the wine list, feeling the burning eyes of the little chef follow him.

David had intentionally invited some of the most influential people he could think of to tomorrow night's dinner, even some of his would-be competition, the bright lights in Vancouver's culinary scene. He knew a lot of them would be naysayers, sceptical at first, but he was sure he could turn them around. And instead of asking them to pay for their meals, he had forewarned them they would be invited to make a donation to the Children's Charities Foundation; the table raising the most money would have a private dinner for ten cooked in their own home by none other than his star chef, François Calbaut. He had debated whether to gather their contributions *before* the meal, just in case things got messy in the kitchen, but really, how could anything go wrong? Still, when he glanced back at the kitchen where François was bawling out his sous chef, he did feel just the slightest pang of indigestion.

Other thoughts were nagging David though, a negative feeling that had been riding him since the morning. An e-mail had caught his eye when he scanned his incoming messages on his phone at 5:30 that morning, a short note from his nephew, Matt, whom he had not heard from in years. It said he was in B.C. and asked to meet.

At first the sight of the e-mail precipitated some blood loss from his head, leaving him feeling woozy enough to grope for a chair, which he sank slowly into, his eyes still fixated on the phone. He scrolled up and down the message, looking for more content that he already knew wasn't there, trying to read meaning into the message. David knew going to the funeral was probably a stupid idea, that likely Matt would be there, but it was an action he couldn't resist, like a perpetrator returning to the scene of the crime. And he had to admit, even if the e-mail worried him, there was a small twinge of excitement, another challenge tossed his way.

So he dismissed any sinking feeling almost immediately and fortified himself instead by drawing on his vast stores of optimism. It was what he did when he was called to any challenge, a shot of adrenalin that caused him to puff out his toned muscles, still looking buff for his late 50s, thank you very much, his positivity like a suit of armour, making him feel near impervious to the outside. It was the inside threats that he should be worried about, but there was little he could do about that other than stifle the negative thoughts.

His interaction with Matt in the last twenty years or so had been minimal, usually a terse, businesslike nod of acknowledgement from across the room at some family affair, a minimal gesture on David's part never reciprocated by Matt. They had not spoken since he was nearly a teenager, when Shirley was in the hospital.

That was a time he didn't care to think about, a whole different era when David had been a very different person, a man he didn't even know anymore. When he was forced to think about that time, when someone or something reminded him of the way he once was, like Matt's e-mail had done that morning, his stomach went into knots. Those demons had been hard to wrestle to the ground, and even though for the most part he had managed it, every now and then those ghosts would poke their heads through some wormhole in time, opening up a wound he hoped had long been healed.

The thing was, he didn't know what had caused him to be such an ass when he was younger, and once he had made up his mind to turn himself around, he never really cared to find out. Even now he was occasionally told (by anyone who dared to) that he had issues with power and control, and when he cared to contemplate such things, he supposed those qualities (or maybe they were merely attributes) might have something to do with the way he had acted in the past. He was angry then at Matt, at Shirley and at just about everyone. But once he started to channel his energies into business, everything seemed to click into place, like someone had thrown a switch in his brain. The more money he made, the more satisfied he felt, as though the cash itself would give him some degree of control. And he used his money for good things too, like the Children's Charity Foundation he had endowed, which now had influence in some of the most needy parts of the world. The whole Matt thing, along with everything else he had stupidly done during that part of his life, was behind him.

David had even converted to Catholicism, part of his efforts to turn himself around. He had been particularly attracted to the idea of confession, that you could simply atone for your sins by baring your soul to your priest. What a load for a priest to carry, he thought at the time, having to keep the strict sanctity and confidentiality of the confessional. *But better the burden should be on him than on me,* David reasoned.

On his path to renewal, and on the recommendation of his priest, David had tried a few times to get in touch with Matt. He needed to say he was sorry, that he wanted Matt to forgive him, and, as odd as it must have seemed to Matt, he wanted to have a proper relationship with him. He had called once, leaving a message that was never returned. He had even written Matt a letter, never referring to the incident (he wouldn't put anything on paper that might end up in court or in the press) but assuring Matt he was sorry for any trouble he may have caused him as a boy, and pointing to all his good works as an example of how he had changed. There had been no response.

Back at the restaurant, David watched the shadows of figures pass outside in front of the papered-up windows, still contemplating the message from Matt that morning. David absentmindedly ran his fingers lightly over the puckered pink tissue on the back of his right hand. The skin where they had removed the melanoma in April had healed but left a patch that was different from the rest, like a tiny stretched red balloon had been embedded just below the surface where the metacarpal bones funnel into the wrist. The scar tissue was surprisingly smoother than the rest of his dry hands and lighter than the brown spots that had begun to form on his hands and arms and even his face, like mould on neglected wood. Even if he had known as a kid that overexposure to the sun could kill him one day, he doubted he would have stayed out of it, drunk with the invincibility of youth and the vain appeal of a suntan. He had insisted on aggressive chemotherapy even though he was told it wasn't necessarily prescribed at this stage, and now his hair had started to grow back, although finer than before and lighter, almost white if he was really honest about it. His doctor had told him they were 99 percent certain they had eradicated the cancer. And although David thought of himself as a pragmatic, sensible man, he could not help but feel a sense of dreary fatalism about this, a constant low-grade awareness that felt like living in a chamber that the oxygen was slowly being sucked out of.

He always found it helped if he compartmentalized his problems, dealing with each one in isolation, not allowing one to seep in and contaminate the other, only making it worse. So when he thought of Matt as he stood leaning against the bar, he tried to convince himself that maybe his nephew had undergone a change of heart about him, and perhaps that was why Matt had sent him the e-mail asking to get together. And as he allowed himself to contemplate this positive idea, David felt as though some light was cast into the darker corners of his heart, which he noticed fluttered just with the cheerfulness of the idea, the chance of reconciling with the man he had always thought of as a son.

CHAPTER 11

In the weeks since the funeral, Matt had not seen or heard from his father, George. Matt had thought of contacting him, but the fewer people Matt needed to see right now, the fewer obligations, the better. This way he could avoid all the nauseating questions about his mother, his wife, Afghanistan, how many people he had killed. The isolation of the farm had started to suit him just fine; he would rather have not come into town at all. He knew it was all evasion; his psychiatrist had ordered him to get out and confront the crowds and his fears as a part of facing the PTSD.

Matt sat near the front of the OK Café in Penticton, his father's favourite meeting place for as long as Matt could remember. George was sure to grumble when he got there about how much better it would be if they'd left the restaurant a diner. Why did they have to go and change every place into a fancy café where they served you some coffee and foamy milk with fancy names and mark it up to some big-assed price? But deriding the current fluffed-up state of the café was a tradition for George when they got together, just like how he loved to tell stories about what happened when he was a teenager in this dark corner or that worn banquette.

Matt slid along the vinyl and rested his back against the wall, extending his leg out for more comfort. His groin was feeling better in the last few weeks to the point where he was no longer popping painkillers like Tic Tacs. He stared out the picture window in the front of the café, flipping his phone over and over in his hand, listening distractedly to a fly buzz angrily as it attacked the bottom corner of the window. He tried to tamp down his thoughts as they drifted toward Amanda—wondering if divorce ran in the family—attempting to sever the mental tug of war between his parents' divorce and his own separation from Amanda. It was hard not to wonder if there was an imprinting, a family pattern that gets established, even though it was Amanda who left him, not the other way around. To think he might have pushed her away in the same manner Shirley had done to both him and George was too much to swallow.

Matt had stayed close to George, bonding over their mutual alienation from Shirley, whose affection for them seemed to pulse like an arrhythmic heart, surging or withdrawing unpredictably. Looking back, George seemed to always do his best to compensate, making sure he got home from his butcher shop by 4:15 every day to play with Matt and take over from Shirley, a routine he kept religiously. Even now as Matt waited in the café, he knew George would show up on time.

Matt ran his hand along a seam in the dark oak table, rolling his fingers over some crumbs that had lodged in the rift. He didn't need the latte he'd ordered; his leg was bouncing up and down like a jackhammer. Just then two meaty paws descended with a slam on the table, and Matt jumped back in his seat. He looked up at the beaming face of his father, the ceiling lights reflecting off George's shaved, pale head. Matt stood to greet George, who was laughing at his little fright.

"Glad to see your trigger is still working, buddy," George said. "Maybe you should cut back on the caffeine."

He wrapped his arms around Matt, hugging him hard, and then stood back and looked him up and down, whistling. "Man, you're looking good, Matty. I see they've been keeping you in decent shape."

He gave Matt's stomach a couple of taps with the back of his hand and then pointed to the crutch. "Except for maybe that." George gave himself a pat on his bald head. "Hey, your hair's almost as short as mine right now."

Matt smiled as he stroked back the stubble on his own head. "It's good to see you, George. You scared the shit out of me. I guess I was off in another world. Here," he said, pointing to the bench opposite him, "what'll you have?"

George picked up the drinks menu, turned it over quickly, and then placed it back on the table. "How about a double-double?" he asked, smiling at Matt. "Maybe I should have brought my own Timmy's."

"Hey, don't start. You know you like this place."

"I like it because it reminds me of how we used to come here when you were a kid. Remember?" he said, winking at Matt and giving the air a little nudge with his nose, pointing to some time in the past. "It was our little escape, and I used to buy you ice cream and Coke and not tell your mother, until that time we got home and you threw it all up and we had to confess. Then when you were a teenager you got all healthy and self-righteous and wouldn't eat any of the stuff they served here anymore."

How many times had Matt heard that story?

"Well I've relaxed a little about it now, George. You have to learn to be flexible, especially in the middle of Afghanistan. Even camel shit starts to look appetizing."

He searched his father's face for a snapshot of his health. George always avoided the subject, especially the heart attack that he seemed to view as a personal failure. Matt was sure George's face was looking paler, almost a waxy grey. The wrinkles around his eyes were now deep and permanent, etched like petroglyphs in granite, each line telling its own story. He had always seemed so robust before, but age had apparently discovered him after the infarction.

"Hey, let me see your dog tag." It was an obvious deflection; George must have noticed Matt was examining his face like a patient's chart.

Matt fished out the chain and held the tag in front of him while George rubbed his thumb across the metal surface.

"You should wear these on the outside, you know. You should be proud of what you did over there."

"You know I am, Dad," he said, watching George fondle the metal. "I just don't like to call attention to myself. I wear them partly out of habit but also because it reminds me of being there, of my buddies." He smiled, searching George's eyes for an indication he was sympathetic to any of this. "I do know that I really wish I was back there right now. Life was simpler there. Get up in the morning, eat, hunt the enemy, sleep and repeat. Life is a bit more complicated back here."

"Maybe it is, but you shouldn't let it take away from what you did there. God," he said, examining smoke-stained fingernails, "what I would have given to be in your position. When I was in the military I didn't have a chance to see any real combat, so it never felt like I made much of a difference. I'm glad at least one of our family got to do something useful there."

He let go of the tag, which dangled from its chain over Matt's coffee cup. They were both quiet as they looked down at the table, waiting for the inevitable conversation to come up.

George waded in. "What happened over there, Matty? You know I talk to Amanda, and she's told me something was wrong, that something happened, but she hasn't said what." George had always had a relaxed, soothing way of talking. Not a twang exactly, but paced like a plough horse tilling the rich Okanagan earth.

His voice calmed Matt, but Matt couldn't look at him. He started instead to rearrange crumbs on the table. "I don't know, Dad." Matt spoke slowly. "Things just got out of hand. I guess I didn't realize what kind of pressure I was under and I snapped."

He leaned back and spread his legs under the table, looking back out the window. "I killed someone over there, a civilian, and I don't even remember doing it at the time, I just kind of went crazy." He pulled a paper napkin from the metal holder and tore off the corners. "They say I've got post-traumatic stress disorder and I need to take some time to get better. I'm not going to be allowed anywhere near battle until they've given me the okay."

He swirled the remainder of his coffee in the cup and then drank it in one swallow, examining the froth in the bottom of the cup as he put it down. "I've started seeing someone about it, but to tell you the truth, I feel like a damn disgrace. I don't want to be away from the military, and I don't want to be here. I've been thinking that maybe I should just get another job entirely."

George reached across the table and squeezed Matt's shoulders. "Hey, look at me Matty." Matt did. "We all screw up sometimes. You know that and so do they. Over there you're living in a pressure cooker and shit happens, but I'm sure whatever it is, it doesn't take away from you being a great soldier."

"I'm feeling kind of stuck, to tell you the truth. I don't know what I'm doing here; I feel like I should be back home trying to sort out things with Amanda. I miss the kids so much. I tell you, I can't get this sorted out fast enough so I can get home and see them. The boys and I chat, but instead of making me feel better, it just makes it harder, like a big hole opening up inside me. I've put the farm on the market, so as soon as I get that sold I can get some care for Shirley and then get back to Edmonton and figure out the rest of my life."

"You're selling the farm?"

Matt knew the news would surprise him. "It's all I can do. It's her only source of money anymore."

"But she loves that place. Does she know you're doing it?"

"I haven't broken it to her yet. I could tell her, but it would just get her more upset and confused."

"How's she doing Matty?" That was something Matt loved about George, that no matter what, he had never stopped caring for Shirley.

"It's hit or miss. She's still so stubborn and wants to be independent but it's just not possible anymore. We've had to put up little sticky notes all over the place to remind her what things are, like the fridge or stove, or to turn off the burner. I can't take any of her good spells for granted because it seems the minute I turn my back, she gets into trouble."

"Have her church friends been any help?"

"They've tried. The other day Janet Markdale showed up at the farm with her teenage granddaughter. I'm pretty sure I recognized the same dress from thirty years ago. I swear to god she tried to cover up the mothball smell with Febreze. She was all pleasant and sweet and wanted to see Shirley. I tried to say no but she was practically in the door already."

"Sounds like Janet."

"Yeah, and the teenage girl didn't say a thing. Just kept staring at me like I was a hamburger and she was a vegetarian who had a sudden craving for meat."

"How was Shirley with them?"

"She didn't even recognize them. She'd been gardening and still had her gloves and hat on and just stood in the hallway with an empty look on her face. After a few minutes she warmed to them a bit, but you could still see she didn't have a clue who they were. Then her hospitality got the better of her so she pulled down a bottle of vodka from the kitchen cupboard and offered them a drink at 10:30 in the morning."

George laughed. "Maybe she's better than you think."

"Do you talk to her at all?"

George coiled his sausage-like fingers together. "I've tried to, but you know how it is. When I called her recently to see if she needed anything, it was like opening the entrance to an igloo. And then a couple of times she picked up the phone when I called, and for all she knew I could have been the Amway salesman."

He popped a piece of gum out of the foil blister pack he had been playing with. Nicotine gum. Matt raised an eyebrow. "Yeah, trying to quit. And this talk about women makes me nervous."

They both laughed. He pushed another piece through the foil and stuck both grey rectangles in his mouth.

"It's hard you know. We haven't been together for more than twenty years, but I still think about her." George seemed to surprise himself by the admission. "That's not to say I don't love Jilly, or that I think of your mother the way I used to."

The odd thing was, when George remarried, everyone thought he was caught in some sort of masochistic groove, this time marrying a born-again Christian. If George had any religion himself it was hockey followed closely by football and then golf, and some people had speculated that he married churchgoing women to get time to himself to watch or play sports while they went to church. But even though Jilly was a lot of things his mother wasn't—outgoing, generous, playful—he was sure George's innate goodness would trump the pious churchgoers any time. Some people just didn't need religion.

"I still feel a little responsibility for your mother though, but there's nothing I can do. First of all I'm not in any position to help her financially, and she just pushes me away, even if I try to be there for any kind of support."

George took a breath and stared at the ceiling, clearly wanting to change the subject. "Speaking of money, did you see your uncle David at the funeral? Man that guy is loaded."

"George, I haven't called him 'uncle' in years. I never got that anyway, why we were supposed to call him uncle. What the hell was he doing at the service? As far as I'm concerned, the further he stays away from our family the better."

"I never understood why you're so hostile against the guy. He used to be a hellion when we were growing up but he's changed, got religion and all." George shook his head. "He gives a ton of money to charity. My theory is he's trying to redeem what a shit he was in his young days. He's got a couple dozen Dave's Grills in B.C. and Alberta now. I don't think anyone ever would have guessed he would do so well. Now he's got the winery and his son, Adam, is working there."

Matt felt his ears throbbing. "Yeah, I know. I've heard all the success stories, even though I try not to listen. As far as I'm concerned he's still a prick. The thing is, you have no idea what he's like. You think you do, but you don't. And I don't care if it looks like he's changed, a cobra doesn't suddenly become a fluffy puppy." Matt felt the latte curdling.

"I don't know. I don't like the way he used to be either, not a bit, but I've cut him some slack." He looked straight at Matt. "What's up with you? Every time he's reached out to you, you never so much as acknowledge him. Hell, maybe he's even got a job for you if you want out of the military."

Matt slammed his fists into the table and stood up. The café was suddenly silent. He stood at the end of the table, his face hot, looking at George, who stared back at him, eyes wide.

"Matt," he said in almost a whisper. "What is it? Did I say something wrong?"

Matt turned toward the cash register. The young woman behind the counter looked to the back of the room, away from his gaze. He took deep breaths, holding them for a few beats and then letting them go slowly, like he'd been taught to do to calm himself. He squeezed his eyes shut for a few seconds then turned around slowly to face George again.

"Matt, please sit down," George said, nodding to the seat across from him. "Tell me what's going on."

Matt sank into the seat and continued counting his breath: *inhale*, one, two, three, four. *Hold*, one, two, three, four. *Exhale*, one, two three, four. After a few sequences he let his arms down on the table, weaving his fingers in front of him.

"George," Matt started slowly. "David molested me when I was a kid." He let the words hang in the air. He watched the muscles in George's face slacken with disbelief, threatening to unhinge his jaw.

"What?" George said quietly, staring at Matt.

"It happened when Mom was in the hospital from her car accident, when I was twelve and he was taking care of us." He bit down on his lips and then took a deep breath. "I didn't really get it at the time. I mean, I knew what happened, but I don't think I could really believe it. And then he threatened me, and said if I ever told anyone he'd kill me. I believed him." Matt wasn't sure where to look. "He kept on doing it for the whole time she was in the hospital. It started just a few days after she went in and then continued for the next three weeks. I didn't know how to make it stop and I couldn't say anything." He paused, unable to look at George.

George sat completely still, his face frozen. Finally he lifted his hands and covered his face, shaking his head from side to side. "Matty, I'm sorry," he said through his hands. "I'm so, so sorry." He lifted his head. His complexion looked paler than when he had arrived. "I can't believe this. I mean, I know what you're telling me is true and all, but I just can't believe it happened. This is not good, Matty, not at all."

"Dad, it's okay." Matt could see his father's blood pressure rising. "It was a long time ago. I've just done everything I could to avoid him since then."

"It's *not* okay. Why didn't you tell me before? Shit, I could have done something about it. I'm so sorry."

"It wasn't your fault. You were living in Calgary then, and I couldn't have told you anyway."

"Well sure you could have told me. You *should* have told me. I would have looked after you. I would have locked him up."

"The thing is that I wasn't only terrified of what he'd do to me if I told anyone, or if I didn't let him. I was also scared as hell that maybe it was me, maybe I'd put some sort of signal out there that attracted him, that said I wanted it."

"And that's why you never told anyone? You were too afraid? The tough soldier?"

"Yeah that's me. No, I never told a soul. It wasn't exactly my brightest moment. I was so embarrassed by the whole thing and scared at the same time. It's funny, you know, when I finally started to get sexually attracted to women it was such a relief. He screwed me up for years."

"Did he ever try anything with you again?"

"No, never. I avoided him like crazy, and as you know Shirley didn't exactly like the guy anyway."

George ran his hand over his bald head and started massaging his temples with his fingers. There was a long silence between them, punctured eventually by George's sigh.

He reached over the table and put his hands on Matt's forearms. "Matty, I'm sorry. I'm so sorry."

"It's okay, Dad. Really. You had no way of knowing. I know you would have done something if you'd been around. Are you kidding? Do you remember how often I used to come and see you once you moved back to Penticton? Thank god you weren't gone for very long. I felt safe with you."

George blew a breath through vibrating lips. "Shit, the thing is, I still should have known better. David and I were best friends growing up, until your mother and I got married. He was a sadistic little bastard. Once he even put a firecracker in my sister's pet rat's mouth and let the thing blow. It was incredible what he used to do. But a lot of the time I hung out with him just for the adventure, you know, the stupid things boys do, because he was everything I couldn't be. He was constantly getting us both into trouble, and I just thought that was cool, the way it was supposed to be. It wasn't until later that I realized how twisted he was. I shouldn't have been so blind. He should have been in jail." George's eyes had welled up.

"Hey, don't sweat it Dad," Matt said, giving George's hand a little shimmy on the table. "I'm okay now. I'm seeing this therapist for the PTSD, and she's helping me with it."

Something stuck in his throat. He wanted to say more, to tell him how much it hurt him still, but he couldn't. George already felt bad enough and was blaming himself for something that wasn't his fault.

George's eyes narrowed into a squint, his chest rising and falling faster. Matt worried about another heart attack.

"You've never talked to David about this?" George's speech had become very deliberate. "You've never confronted him?"

"No, and I don't want to dig up those old bodies. Enough is enough. And I don't want you talking about it to anyone either. Besides, I thought you said he'd reformed?"

Rivulets of sweat had formed in the creases around George's neck. He dabbed at his nonexistent hairline with his fingers.

"George, let it go." Matt lowered his voice, trying to bring the pressure in the room down a notch.

"I'll deal with it, Matty. Fuck," he said, a little too loudly for Matt. Some customers' heads turned. "Do you believe that bastard is a big supporter of Kids Help Line and Big Brothers?"

"You're shittin' me," Matt said.

"I kinda wish I was. Must be his way of payback. I thought he was sincere about it."

"You're blowing kinda hot and cold on him, you know that."

It was George's turn to study the cracks in the table. "This stuff that you're telling me, it's all new information and … I don't know. I had started a long time ago to think of David differently." He smiled feebly. "I think I could use some air," he said, sliding his weight out of the booth.

Matt perched his sunglasses on top of his head, grabbing his keys and phone off the table. He smacked his tongue against the roof of his mouth, walking toward the register. "Coffee breath. I've gotta get some gum."

A mother in her 30s stood at the counter in front of George and Matt, giving her drink order, a non-fat, half sweet something or other, to the barista. A girl slightly younger than Callum, around six, wearing a turquoise sunhat and little blue running shoes festooned with comic decals, stood next to her mother,. She looked up at Matt, who was reaching by her to get some gum from the shelf.

"Excuse me there, little missy," he said, smiling at the girl.

The girl, standing with her legs crossed like she had to pee, pointed up to him. "Hey, mister," she said, her green eyes sparkling. Her mother turned around from the cash and looked Matt up and down. "What's that hanging from your neck?" the girl asked.

Matt's hand went to his dog tag that he had left dangling outside his shirt. "You mean this?" he said.

"Yeah, what *is* that?" the girl asked.

Matt chuckled and then crouched down so he could speak to her face to face. "That's my dog tag. I'm in the army and I just got back from Afghanistan where I was fighting the bad guys."

Her eyes were chasing Matt's as she stopped her little pee dance and stood perfectly still. It seemed like she was trying to take in what he had just said. Then suddenly she wrapped her small arms around Matt's neck and gave him a kiss on the cheek. She pulled back and looked at him solemnly. "Thank you, mister," she said.

Matt remained crouched for a moment, slightly stunned. He glanced over his shoulder at George and the girl's mother, who were looking quietly down at them, and then looked away again as his eyes welled up. He took the girl's hands in his and said, "You're welcome," probably the most sincere thanks he had ever given anyone, and then he smiled at her and tousled her curly hair. It was the simplicity of what she had done that overwhelmed him, this uncomplicated gratitude that he so rarely heard from anyone.

"I can't believe this little girl is going to make me cry," he said, his voice trembling, not knowing if the emotion he was holding back was pride, joy or relief. But for the rest of the day, even in spite of too much talk about David, he could barely keep the smile off his face.

The next morning Matt lay in bed past sunrise, hovering between wake and sleep. When he drifted into consciousness he had a lingering feeling of something warm and good, like a kid waking up the day after his birthday, still half-asleep but knowing there was something new, a gift he would rediscover once he leapt out of bed. Then he recalled the little girl in the café, and he bunched the pillow up to the side of his head, a small smile rising across his placid face. He drew his knees up around his chest and dug down further into the blankets, allowing the moment to wrap around him, clinging to it so it wouldn't disappear. His eyes weren't yet open but he could sense the warmth of the morning, the sun poking through the window and taking the chill out of the air, warming the thick foliage outside his second-floor window so the smell of cedar floated gently inside. It was the first time in months he had been able to sleep through the night or wake up peacefully.

Then, as he became more alert, the memory of the little girl that had soothed him like an opiate was pushed slowly but steadfastly from him, replaced as though by transfusion with a grating anxiety that had begun sprinting through his veins. He remembered the conversation he'd had with George about David, and the memory came down on him like an imploding edifice. He had never talked about the incident before. He knew if he did the floodgates would open, feeling a lot like it suddenly did now, a battle between guilt and anger that had begun to fill his head, one or both surely aiming to drown him.

It was as though a dividing wedge had been hammered into his life with one powerful blow when he was twelve, and everything took place on one side of it or the other, a gaping chasm between childhood and whatever came after that. He looked at his life before twelve as if through a long, soft lens watching a harmless dream. Everything after was denial. Finally talking about it, admitting it to George, felt scary but surprisingly liberating.

So often in the past he had become overwhelmed with questions. What if Shirley had never had the accident at all? What if George and Jilly hadn't moved away to Calgary? Had he just been proving a point, so anxious to get married, to fuck around, to get Amanda pregnant when they were still kids?

What if he'd known how to shoot a gun when he was twelve?

And would he have blown that man's brains out back in Afghanistan?

Matt rolled his legs over the edge of the bed and sat up, staring at the peeling, yellowed wallpaper in the tiny bedroom.

It was time to see David.

June 2008
Second Afghanistan Tour—Near the Pakistan Border

I'm near the end of my second tour here, and it probably won't be my last. After the incident with Kareem, they figured we should stay in Canada for a while for counselling, and I could have begged out of another tour, but I wanted to get back here as quickly as I could, like getting back up on a horse again after falling off. One or two deaths doesn't mean the job stops.

Amanda has been weird on the phone. Distant. Ten thousand kilometres can do that, I guess. I know I was a bit of a prick when I was last there, but I don't think she did anything to try and understand. She and all the other wives hear the stories but don't live this madness, they don't feel it like we do. The kids are usually a lot better about it; they're just glad to have their dad home, but even they seem to notice all this turbulence in my head that I try so hard to keep to myself. And then when we were playing soccer, Bax asked me out of the blue if I'd killed anyone. I was caught completely off guard. I lied to him. What else could I do?

I've got to try harder though when I get back, really concentrate on Amanda and the kids no matter how I feel. It's my resolution coming out of this tour, to not be so self-centered.

It's always unnerving when you're this close to going home. You try not to talk about it or consciously count down the days in case you jinx yourself. How many guys were so close to going home and got blown away within days of getting on that plane? I think everyone gets to this raw emotional state about this time in their tour, where it feels like something foreboding is hanging over your head. I'm sure it's just nerves.

CHAPTER 12

Shirley and Matt had fallen into a rhythm of taking daily walks through the orchard. It surprised him that she seemed to look forward to them, and so did he. That afternoon the shade of the Summerland trees provided a respite from the valley heat, the air under the branches fresh, the musty breath of the soil rising to mix with the scent of the warm leaves. Where he was once on heightened alert walking through the orchard, subconsciously vigilant of what might be hiding behind a tree, he now only felt a low-grade buzz, making for a much more pleasant walk.

Shirley had crooked her hand through Matt's arm, part of their walk's routine. Suddenly she tugged so tightly that it spun him toward her. Her eyes locked on him, and then, with what appeared to be a great effort, she pushed the words out of her mouth. "I want you to witness my will," she said as though she had been rehearsing the sentence in her mind until the words finally sprang free.

The sudden interruption of their quiet walk surprised him. She had become increasingly unravelled over the time Matt had been on the farm, far from the prickly sharpness of the mind he remembered. She seemed to be retreating, just like the doctors said she would, to a time and place that was clear only to her. He stopped reminding her that he was her son, as much to relieve her frustration as his own. He didn't disavow the fact that they really *were* strangers after so many years of being apart, but even still there was a familiar pattern to the two of them, a chasm of absence bridged he supposed by the psychic familiarity of family that didn't need to be spoken or rehearsed.

It was clear to him when she was not entirely present simply from the look on her face, as though she had misplaced something that she had in her hand only minutes ago. She would look at him with a pleading sadness, like a child who had broken something and didn't know how to put it back together. Most often she would alternate between seeming catatonia and near-hysteria, but then again, he laughingly admitted he could relate. It was harder for him to say who was more screwed up.

He tried to regress with her, to find the moment in time in which she found herself. He would piece together the clues from her speech as best he could so he could step back in time with her and give her the comfort of a traveling companion. Other times she would be lucid, almost shockingly so, like a high-powered searchlight that had been pointed into a cold, dark cave, and it was always accompanied by an urgency, as though she must set things straight while still coherent, while there was still light. Yet even in these largely aware moments she was distant, although it took on a different shape: polite repulsion rather than the awkward distance of strangers, borne perhaps of too much familiarity and too much history.

A windstorm was working its way through the valley; grey cumulus clouds towered over the trees, pushing heavenward. Matt smiled as he observed the determined look on Shirley's face, her eagerness to make a point. She was still a beautiful woman, although the strain had started to erode her features. He observed the dappled light that filtered through the blowing leaves, crossing her pale face and the dark roots of her honeyed hair, her brow etched with squiggled horizontal lines. How he wished he had the key to that puzzle, the maze her mind had become.

"Gwen is gone, so I changed the will." The words sputtered haltingly from her mouth. She was holding a piece of paper from her printer, folded in quarters, tapping it in the palm of her hand.

She stood looking at him, eyebrows raised, saying nothing. If she wanted him to ask her what the will contained he wasn't going to take the bait, lucid moment or not. There was nothing of hers he could imagine he wanted, not even the farm, and he suspected she would leave it all to the church anyway.

"Sure, whatever you want, Mom." He wasn't about to argue with her about how valid a will would be of someone who was suffering from dementia. He wasn't even sure if she recalled that she had signed over Power of Attorney to him.

Shirley unfolded the piece of paper and handed it to him, nodding to indicate he should read it. He had been wondering what she was working on at her computer, amazed she was sometimes still able to use it at all.

> *Dear Matty,*
>
> *I've kept a diary for most of my life. I've only ever kept it for myself. I want you to make sure that it is never given to anyone else.*
>
> *I saved these memories because I want you to read them, or at least as much of them as you can stomach. We've never been very open with each other, and it's too late to start now, but maybe you can get to know me a little better after I'm gone.*
>
> *I would have liked things to be different between us, Matty, but it seems it's too late and I can't get my poor brain to function coherently most of the time. It seems I'm becoming like a dried-up piece of clay and I can't shape myself into something I'm not. But I never meant you any harm.*

Matt folded the piece of paper back into quarters again as she stood looking at him. It was weird. "Okay, Mom," he said. The thought of reading her diaries, snooping into her private past just felt wrong, even if he *was* curious. "I'll do what you want."

Without speaking she handed him another piece of paper.

I don't want to be a burden, and I don't want to lose my mind irretrievably. When the time comes and things get too bad, you'll know it, even if I don't. Please don't let me live longer.

He stared at the paper in his hands, trying to make sure he comprehended. "You're asking me to help you die?"

She nodded. "When ... it's time."

"I don't know what to say. I don't think I can do that."

"Please, Matty. Please help me."

He reached out and drew her to him, holding her tightly. When he released his grip she took a step back and looked upward through the rattling leaves, away from him. "I'm, I'm sorry," she stammered, shaking her head. She was almost whispering, a catch in her voice. "I've been so ... awful."

He had never heard her apologize before and he stood frozen, not sure how to respond. His instinct was to say that it was all right, to offer her some comfort that she seemed to be reaching for. But it *wasn't* all right. Not the way she had treated him all his life. He wanted to yell to break through to his calcified heart.

He wished he could make the most of her lucidity, her moment of such brave honesty, instead of succumbing to his own stubbornness. But it was only later that he realized what he was struggling with was not anger but instead something so unfamiliar in their relationship.

Forgiveness.

CHAPTER 13

DAVID

That Joe Ariss, David's investment banker, was late again was bad enough. But to have to wait alone in L'Etoile, the French restaurant that had no excuse for its pretensions, David found positively humiliating. Joe had selected the restaurant, asking if they could meet somewhere close to Joe's office so he could slip out quickly at 1:00 when the markets closed. It was already 1:20. What was it with people who were always late? Didn't they realize the message conveyed, with unvarying frequency, was that something else was more important than you?

David pulled out his phone and scrolled through his calendar. He needed to make a trip back to the Okanagan soon, where life ran a little more slowly, where priorities could be screwed back on straight. It was always a relief for David to walk through his vineyard and the orchards inhaling the hot valley air, as dry and crisp as one of his fine chardonnays. In spite of Matt's persistence, David had put off meeting him as long as he could, delaying their meeting until he got back to the Valley, and therefore delaying his return to the Valley even more.

As his thumb glided down the phone he felt a quick stab of pain on the back of his hand where the melanoma had been removed. For a moment he sat paralyzed, then he turned his phone over, putting it down on the table. He stroked the scar where the errant tissue had been, noting how soft the spot had become. Surely it was gone;

he was almost certain just by the feel of it—the pain must mean it was continuing to heal. But when the jab hit him again he quickly removed his hand from the table and placed it underneath the napkin in his lap.

"David, I'm so sorry I'm late," Joe said, rushing to the table. Joe ran his hand backward through his coarse salt-and-pepper hair, trying to tame it back into place from the wind outside. Joe was still in his 30s and wearing a suit that would have cost a waiter here more than a month in tips. These damn investment bankers; they were all kids who had never known any hardship, just a bunch of leaches sucking off the good times. An unavoidable evil in these markets.

"I'm glad to see you value my business," David said, remaining seated.

"I know, I know. You know how things are lately. I'm working on a deal right now that looks like it might go sideways, and I had to stroke the client. I just couldn't get away when I wanted to."

Well, perhaps not the best sales tactic considering Joe was pitching him on putting together an offering. Joe asked the waiter for a glass of California chardonnay without even looking at the wine list, or asking David's opinion. But no matter. Joe wanted his business, and David wanted Joe's money.

"So tell me how you're going to make me wealthier than I already am," David said.

"Well ..." Joe chuckled. "It's really your business plan that makes you successful, David, and when you combine that with our capital, you're bound to do well." He seemed a little twitchy. "The thing is, in these markets it's a little more difficult to get access to that money. Your idea of doing an IPO is going to be tricky in this climate. Investors are sceptical right now."

David had specifically asked for a table in the corner, and for the tables beside them to remain empty. The maitre d' had complied, but David still looked from side to side to see who was listening.

"Really?" David felt his jaw locking. "Are you telling me you're not willing to do it? You know that I need the money for expansion, and I need to pay off my debt."

"I'm not saying we can't do it, just that we might have to look at it in a different way. Maybe a private offering instead, selling a chunk of your business to another interested party."

"What, like a competitor?"

"No, not necessarily." Joe seemed nervous. "There is still private capital out there, but it's just getting a little harder to access. And they're going to make demands, like the kinds of salaries and bonuses you can draw, and most will want to take a majority interest in your company."

"You mean control? There is no way I'm giving up control."

"David, you might have to. From our look at your business, you need to get your debt down, and the credit markets are tight. Your spending has been high, and we both know it would be difficult to continue at this amount of debt load."

What did he know? Young punk. Had he ever built a business from scratch? Maybe he could buy nice suits, but David could buy him out a gazillion times over. Maybe. If he got access to some cash.

After lunch, David walked down Thurlow Street back to his office, his head down, pushing through the pedestrian traffic as he rubbed the scar on the back of his hand. A few drops of rain spluttered on the sidewalk, spreading beside the dark chewing gum blotches that had been ground into the pavement. He realized he had forgotten his umbrella back at the restaurant, but he wasn't about to set foot in that place again. Maybe later. For now it could rain all it wanted.

CHAPTER 14

Matt twisted uncomfortably in Shirley's floral print-armchair, picking at the worn fabric on the arms, trying to find a position where the chair's squeaky springs didn't push into his butt. Sage the bartender had arrived with her rottweiler, Randall, who lay with its head on Liz's worn boot, twitching as it dreamed.

Matt leaned over and raised his beer bottle to Liz.

"Well, here's to you, girl. I see you haven't lost your touch," he said.

Liz laughed and wrested her foot from under Randall's nose, hoisting her boots onto the stack of magazines on the coffee table. "I think it's the cowgirl boots. They do it every time. At least dogs like me. That's about all I can handle right now."

"Girl, if you keep on talking like that I'm going to get you up there singing country songs with me at the bar," Sage said, sitting on the piano bench with her back to the upright Heintzman, a sad-looking instrument that Matt hadn't heard played in years.

"You sing?" Matt asked.

"Yeah, a little. I play at the bar on Tuesday nights. It's a bit hokey, but believe it or not it's actually kind of popular. Tuesday was their dead night, and I used to play around on the keyboard between pouring drinks, and it caught on. You should come check it out sometime."

Sage slid around on the bench to face the piano, pushing her dark hair behind her ears so it bounced down the back of her white shirt.

She studied the keyboard for a moment, then allowed her fingers to stroke the tops of the keys. Matt remembered how he noticed her hands at the bar, how powerful they seemed, almost independent from the rest of her body as she poured drinks, screwed off beer caps or polished glasses and stuffed them into the racks, all the while appearing completely engaged in the conversation. But tonight her hands looked almost delicate, attached to a beautiful woman who seemed a lot more vulnerable this side of a bar.

When she started to play, the old Heintzman creaked to life, as though it was surprised someone had woken it up. The low notes growled off the thinning wood, high notes like a spoon striking a glass full of beer. The gears creaked as Sage pushed the pedals to the floor. But when she started to sing, Matt forgot about the piano's shortcomings and sat entranced by her delicate voice. The song she sang, 'The Way I Am' by Ingrid Michaelson, was one he had played for Amanda in better times.

She finished singing and let her hands rest lightly over top of the keys and then swung her legs around on the bench to face Matt and Liz. "Well, it could use a little tuning, but it's not a bad piece of hardware. You have to exercise pianos just like people so their poor old muscles don't atrophy."

"I'm sure it's been a long time since anyone played it," Matt said. "Shirley used to bang away at it pretty competently." He was out of practice with small talk, and even more with women. He tried not to seem nervous.

"Anyway, if that's what you've got on offer on Tuesday nights, it's worth hauling my ass out of here." He hadn't returned to the Colonial since the day he ended up in a panicked pile on the bathroom floor, and he knew it would be difficult to go back.

"Well then, you should come down," Sage said.

"I don't get out much lately. Taking care of Shirley occupies most of my time."

Liz leaned in, lowering her voice. "How is she these days?"

Matt was pretty sure that Shirley, who they had left sitting in the kitchen, couldn't hear them. "She drifts in and out. She seems to avoid talking, maybe because she realizes that what she says usually doesn't make any sense. It's as though she knows she's making a mistake, like when she points to the salt and asks you to pass that thing, and then gets all upset and frustrated that she can't find the right word or say what she means. Or the other day when she told me the phone wasn't working when I'd just got off it, but then handed me the TV remote instead. The batteries needed changing. Other times I can carry on a pretty good conversation with her. Mostly though, she sits staring out the window."

"What about you Matt?" Liz seemed to be probing his face. "You can't let this run your life, can you? What are you going to do?"

Sage excused herself to go to the bathroom.

Matt's eyes followed her out of the room. "I know, I know. It's like I've been using Shirley as an excuse not to get my own act together. Between you and me, it scares the hell out of me to go anywhere right now, and I sure as shit don't want to go back to the army. And I feel guilty that I've got the farm up for sale. I know Shirley likes it here. The minute I try to take her away from home she gets confused and agitated, and the doctors tell me that if I transplant her somewhere else, it might be the start of a more rapid decline. I've read how that can happen."

This conversation needed a detour. Matt bent forward, a pained look arising on his face as the chair's spring thrust into his thigh. "So tell me something. What's up with Sage?" he whispered, looking toward the bathroom.

Liz smiled. "I don't know how many times she asked me about you since you were at the Colonial. I thought you could use a little bit of interaction with someone other than Shirley or George, or the grocery check-out people. She's a pretty cool chick you know."

"Yeah well, cool or not, don't get any ideas. I mean, she's a babe for sure, but I don't need any more complications in my life right now." He heard the toilet flush and leaned in a little closer. "I thought the way you two were so kissy-kissy …"

"Oh, get over yourself, soldier," Liz said, laughing as she sank back into the couch. "Just 'cause I can stand there with my arm around her doesn't mean she likes girls. And even if she did, do you think I'd be interested right now?"

"Okay, I get your point." Matt played with his wedding ring.

The door latch clicked and they sat back, both taking a swig of their beer. Liz lifted her feet off the *People* magazine and started to flip the pages.

"What?" Sage asked, standing at the living room entrance. "What were you guys talking about?"

"We were talking about your stupid dog, who one of these days I'm going to kidnap." She leaned down to stroke Randall's head.

Sage lowered herself beside Liz on the couch. "So, Matt," she said. "Any thoughts about going back to Afghanistan?" There was a pause as Matt and Liz looked at each other. "I mean, the job's not done over there yet, right?"

Matt wasn't sure where she was going with the conversation, but it felt like she was getting too close and personal, and it made him uncomfortable.

Liz jumped in. "Matt's still on medical leave, Sage. I guess you don't know when you'll be going back, eh, Matt?"

"No, I'm not really sure."

"Oh, I didn't mean to pry," Sage said. 'I just thought you had come home to take care of Shirley."

"Well, that's part of the reason I'm here, for sure."

"Don't get me wrong. It's just that I don't know anyone in the military, so I'm curious about it."

"Yeah, lots of people are, and a lot of them ask dumb questions." The words had sounded harsher than he intended. He tried to soften it by smiling, although he hoped his abruptness might signal the end of the questioning.

Sage smiled back, undeterred. "Well then, what if I ask you some questions that *aren't* stupid? Because I don't understand why we're there and, I don't mean to offend you, but I'd love to hear from someone like you, who is close to it, what the conflict means.

"Don't get me wrong," she continued. "I was as pissed off as anyone when I saw what they were doing. And how they kept women under lock and key, stripped them of their education and rights or blew up those giant Buddhas carved out of cliffs." She paused and looked directly at Matt. "I'm not putting you on. I really am interested."

Maybe she was rattling his cage, he thought, or just trying to find some common point they could talk about—or maybe she was flirting with him. Then again, maybe she really *was* interested in the subject.

"It's pretty simple, really," he waded in. "We're in Afghanistan to restore order, to get rid of terrorists and to help them build and support good government. The Taliban tore that place apart, and we're doing what we can to stitch it back together."

"But the Russians were trying to install their own form of government there not too long ago, with the United States supporting the counterinsurgency. Now the US, along with our help, is trying to get rid of the very people it supported fewer than a couple of decades ago."

"Yeah, the same people who attacked us and would rather see you or me hanging in charred strips from a tree somewhere than hear about peace. It's unbelievable what the Taliban did over there. Most people are still terrified of them and scared shitless that they'll get back in power."

"But I don't understand why we don't let them figure it out for themselves. Why do we have to impose *our* will on them? Isn't it obvious they don't want us there, or any foreigners for that matter?"

These were the kind of conversations he would have with his buddies when drunk, always leading to the same conclusions. Except this wasn't his buddies, and they weren't drunk.

"You seem to know something about the area."

"I've read up," she said. "It interests me."

"Okay, but we're not trying to conquer them," Matt said. He admired her intelligence, even if her opinions missed the mark. "We're just trying to let them live without the atrocities of the Taliban, to let them be free."

"It's a tribal society, which you can't really understand," Sage said.

"What, and you can?" That unintended hostile tone again.

"My people are First Nations Matt. Not that that gives me exclusivity on understanding Afghans who live another world away. But I question what we're doing there, imposing our will and our way of life on these people who have lived differently than us and still managed to survive forever. How different is it to what Europeans did to the native population in North America? We're going to go in there and allow them to absorb our way of life, for what? So they can cry when they watch Oprah and learn how to get drunk?"

Clearly she had given this some thought, drawing parallels between her people and Afghanistan. He was trying to make the leap in his own head. "I think it's a different thing in Afghanistan, Sage. You should see the way they live over there. So many of them have nothing and so little hope of ever improving their lives."

"I'm not sure how different it was here before you guys came along, or that it's so much better now that you're here." She grinned. He could tell she was yanking his chain. "If you looked back at the conditions that we lived in then, I'm sure you would say that they were damn primitive and that some of the customs we had were barbaric. But I think we could have lived very happily without smallpox or alcohol, thank you very much."

He found it difficult not to take her words as an affront. But he was intrigued, even while fighting the rising thought of how attractive she was in so many ways.

"Well, as much as Liz here thinks I'm a Neanderthal, I actually realize we're living in the 21st century. It's just a fact of modern life that the strongest and most wealthy culture is going to spread quickly, and human nature will make sure that the have-nots will then see what the haves possess and then do what they can to get it, even if that means cultural change. It's a force pretty much beyond our control, and if I'm just helping it along as a collateral effect of doing my job, I really don't think history will show I'm wrong."

"Just think, they can all have access 24/7 to the wonderful, unbiased coverage of Fox News."

"Well, at least they'll have their choice of coverage. Al Jazeera isn't exactly a paragon of enlightenment."

"That's the weird thing though. We can't seem to understand that radical Islam would have us all behave in their manner, according to their religion, at least if the different sects could get together and decide what that really meant. They want to dominate and assimilate us because they believe it's right, just the way we in North America or Europe, the free world"—she put quotation marks around 'free' with her fingers—"would have them all doing things the way we do, only in a more secular way. We don't see it as forcing them to assimilate as long as they believe in our democracy, capitalism, free trade and human rights. I really don't see how that makes us so different from them. We stand there defiantly and ask how could we possibly be wrong. Why would anyone question the validity of our ways? And they do the same thing."

"But what they *don't* have is the freedom of choice," he said. "Radical Islam would have everyone live by Sharia law and nothing less than a harsh interpretation of the Koran. Oh, and by the way, the people we're trying to get rid of have a tendency to blow other people up."

She threw her hands in the air, and he had to chuckle. What an incredible package she was.

"So Matt, you said the boys called you yesterday?" Liz had sat silently throughout the exchange, the sidelines apparently a safer place to be.

The three of them looked back and forth and then suddenly started laughing, a pressure-cooker releasing steam.

"Nice interception, Lizzie," Matt said. "It was getting kinda good. But yeah, the boys did call last night."

"You've got a couple of boys, don't you?" Sage asked. She seemed relaxed now on the piano bench and, he noted gratefully, unoffended by the argument.

"Yeah, Callum's 8 and Baxter's 10. They're great kids. I miss them like crazy." *Damn*, there he went, opening up to her again. She probably perceived him as some sort of army grunt with a quick trigger finger. And why should he care what she thought anyway?

"Amanda only allows me to talk to them once a week, which is crazy, and I'm pretty sure she's on the other line while we talk. I don't know what she thinks I'm going to say to them. But I chat with them by computer all the time, which their mother doesn't seem to monitor."

"How are they doing Matty?" Lizzie asked.

"They sound good, but they're boys, you know. Their priorities are soccer and food, and they're not going to realize until later how important it is to have a dad around. Not that they could do much about it right now." He wasn't sure he should say what he was about to. "Baxter let something slip yesterday about a 'Greg' taking them swimming." As he said it, he had a sinking feeling, as though giving words to it made the situation real. "I think Amanda's seeing someone."

Liz reached over and took his hand. He looked at her, expecting her to say something, but instead she just squeezed his hand and smiled at him warmly.

"How could she do that? I mean, so soon? She must think I'm some sort of monster, or maybe she's been planning this all along. I couldn't even *think* of seeing anyone right now."

Sage shifted uncomfortably in her seat. She picked up the *People* magazine and began thumbing through it.

"Well," Matt said, changing the subject again. "How about we get something on the barbecue? I forgot I had those coals heating up for a while."

Shirley was sitting with her back to the wall as they entered the kitchen, staring out the door beyond the porch where the smoke seeped from underneath the barbecue's blackened lid.

"Hi, Shirley," Liz said. She bent down and placed her hands lightly on Shirley's knees. "How are you today?"

Shirley shifted her eyes in Liz's direction, appearing to look beyond her.

"This is a friend of mine, Sage."

"I'm pleased to meet you, Mrs. Graydon," Sage said, extending her hand.

Shirley returned to staring out at the porch.

"Well, Matt, what can I do to help?" Sage asked, turning to the kitchen counter.

"Pretty much everything is prepared. Maybe just set the table." He squeezed steak sauce onto the sirloins. "I haven't barbecued since last year some time, before I went to Kandahar. This should be good."

Matt balanced the platter of steaks on his palm, grabbing the barbeque utensils with his free hand. He gave the screen door a kick. On the porch, prickly branches of a blackberry bush climbed over the wooden railing, the white paint on the handrails chipped in spots, revealing the raw, grey wood underneath. The stairs looked like they hadn't been painted in years; most of the steps were rotting from neglect. The house would be a full-time project to get back in shape to sell.

The breeze that had tempered the warmth earlier in the day had now vanished completely, and the heat hung in the air. Matt lifted the barbeque cover, increasing the temperature a few more degrees, the heat clinging to him like a Kandahar summer. He pierced the steaks with the long metal fork and set them hissing onto the grill. He bumped the flaking railing a couple of times with his hip to test its soundness and then leaned back against it.

The girls were laughing in the kitchen, and looking back through the porch door, he saw Shirley still staring outside, gazing right through and beyond him to some point in time that only she must recognize.

Matt closed his eyes and wiped his brow with his forearm. He was feeling a little dizzy. He thought maybe it was just the hot stillness of the air that was making him so uncomfortable, but as he leaned harder against the railing, the swirling increased and his vision started to narrow, like being siphoned into a dark funnel. Yellow flames had begun to flare underneath the meat, and the smell of the sizzling flesh found its way to his nostrils. His heart beat harder, threatening to break through his shirt. He hung on to the railing with both hands and tried to fight the encroaching nausea.

No. He moaned. *No!* As his breathing quickened, he felt himself being transported away, back to Afghanistan, and suddenly he was there in combat. The LAV was on fire in front of him, and he smelled the searing of flesh as bodies cooked inside the vehicle. *I'VE GOT TO GET THEM OUT OF THE LAV BEFORE THEY BURN TO DEATH! DAWSON! I'VE GOT TO GET DAWSON! GET HIM OUT! GET HIM OUT!*

When Liz and Sage ran outside onto the porch he looked at them as if he didn't recognize them, his eyes wide with terror, then he tore at the lid of the barbeque, suddenly picking up the entire metal mass and heaving it off the porch, screaming as he did. Hot embers bounced and scattered on the ground below, and the half-charred meat stuck limply to the dirt while he stood at the top of the stairs, his face coiled tight, fists clenched by his side.

When he came to, he was sitting at the bottom of the stairs shaking his head in his hands. The air was once again still; the conflict far away. There were no fires, no report of a machine gun, no soldiers yelling orders or screaming in pain. He had no recollection of time; he seemed to have bridged months, time zones and some hellish abyss just by standing on his porch. He saw Liz's and Sage's feet in front of him as he looked through his fingers, the sound of their shoes crunching on the gravel, but he couldn't raise his head. He felt humiliated, as though he was a child who had just lost control in the schoolyard, as if he had wet his pants in front of everyone. How could anyone understand the terror he lived with, how it stalked him nearly every waking moment, like a tiger after its prey? Night upon night he did everything to keep himself awake in his room—listen to the radio, surf the net, play solitaire on his laptop—so he didn't have to face the nightmares that would inevitably come, the dreams of seared flesh and bullet-riddled corpses, of mangled limbs ripped clean from bodies, torn apart by the blast of a grenade or a suicide bomb, the tortured screaming of a buddy downed by enemy fire, the dead eyes on Kareem's disembodied head staring blankly out at a future he would never have. More nights than not he would knock himself out with a bottle of Stoli, drinking until he passed out, but the dreams would still come. And they would carry through straight into his day, like a disembodied soul riding a train over and over with no destination except from night to day. Only a remaining sliver of his rational mind managed to keep everything from exploding like a cluster bomb.

He felt a weight on top of his head, a hand gently stroking his short hair from front to back.

Turning slowly to the side he saw it was Shirley sitting beside him on the bottom step, her hand brushing his head softly, her other hand hooked through his arm. "It's okay, Matty," she said as she gave his elbow a little shake. "Everything's going to be okay."

He turned to her and wrapped his arms around her waist, sobbing into her shoulder.

Was it immoral to tell someone the opposite of a certain future, even if you were simply trying to extend some comfort? Matt had held the hand of dying men before, their organs exposed in a bloody, sinuous cavity of what remained of their bodies, knowing they were slipping away as surely as the day would end, but Matt told them the same thing: they were going to be okay, just to hang on. Even his mother had told him—in an obviously lucid moment—that it would all be okay, even while surely knowing it would not; not for either of them.

But in that moment it still had felt right, and she knew just like he had so many times before that telling a lie was the right thing to do, a mother's—no—a *human* instinct. And when she said those words, in spite of knowing she was lying, his heart squeezed itself back into life. In spite of the fight that rose inside him—the ingrained distrust, the walls and aversion he had so successfully constructed over the years—an unexpected yet undeniable feeling washed over him that felt a lot like love, or perhaps just the need a son has for his mother, who can make everything all right, who can hold the whole world and all of its demons far, far away from her child.

And more than anything, he wanted to believe it was true.

Later they sat in the kitchen, Matt drained from his earlier struggle. Shirley was helping the girls with dinner. She fought to maintain control, her face rigid as she sought not to lose her grasp, as though she knew Matt needed her.

She brought him a cup of hot chocolate and put it down on the table, smiling softly at him. As she turned to go back to the counter she paused, laying her warm hand on the back of his neck, letting it rest there.

When the girls left, Shirley went to her bedroom, saying good night as she did, the only words she had uttered since the barbecue incident. He knew, as did she, that in the morning everything could be different, that she might not even remember any of this. But Matt would. His eyes followed Shirley to her bedroom door, and when it was shut, he sat crying gently.

Minutes later Matt opened his laptop on the kitchen table and Googled 'Military Afghanistan' to see if anything new had been posted. It was a habit he had developed, night after night of changing his searches—Forces, Combat, Kandahar—trying to find new videos, new information, something he recognized so he could hold on to, if only for a moment, what was once so real to him. It was like a modern-day séance, sitting around the kitchen table, electronically conjuring sounds and images that didn't exist in reality anymore, whose time had passed but could still be transmitted through the ether. He would spend hours looking at videos of guys in battle, of tanks and planes, and then of all the pictures he had taken in dusty Afghanistan a lifetime ago.

What if he went back? What if he did what they wanted him to do, got treatment and got better and then returned? What the hell could he do here at home anyway? Or back in Edmonton, even if he and Amanda got back together, or he got custody of the kids? Maybe he really was built for combat, if he could just get the PTSD under control. Yeah, the war had screwed him up, but so could so many other things in life.

He needed something to look forward to. Some goals and objectives. He started a new document on his laptop and began typing.

1. Keep seeing shrink.
2. Sell the farm.
3. Get care for Shirley.
4. Hire a lawyer.
5. Get the kids back.
6. Confront David.
7. Get back into a meaningful job.

He laughed because it looked like the outline for a country hurtin' song. But it was the framework of a plan, and even though he knew it looked a lot simpler on paper than it would practically be, he couldn't help but feel good as he saved his document, calling it simply *Better*, and snapping the lid shut on his laptop.

July 2008
End of 2nd Tour—Kandahar Air Field

I'm finally stable enough to sit up without my head feeling like it's going to float off like a soap bubble. Morphine and ketamine have been my two best friends for the last week, but now they've got me down to Tylenol 3s. So I've recovered my brain, but the rest of my body is now paying the price in pain, and they tell me I can't live on the narcotics forever, Sweet Jesus.

I have to type this leaning back from my keyboard and to the side, balancing on my right cheek so I don't squeeze my balls or thighs too tightly. Or ball, I should say. Seems I 'lost' one in the firefight, although I'm pretty sure the doctors found it, mashed like a potato in cheesecloth, and just scooped it out. They tell me they've managed to remove the shrapnel from my inner thigh too, but the pain is so sharp I swear to god it's still in there.

A major came by and grilled me today, none too gentle about it. Didn't seem to have any sympathy for my medical situation and made it pretty clear I could be up for court martial. What he doesn't know is that I'd do it all again.

We were on patrol back near the border again, checking out a low-slung mud building reported to have been used recently by Taliban. You have to stick your nose through these doorways and creep in like blind rats in a maze, not knowing if you're suddenly going to come face to face with a rifle on the other side. And you're never sure who's watching you from the hills.

We'd gone about a third of the way through the building, encountering nothing but leftover garbage on the dirt floors and feces in the latrines that smelled recent enough. Then I heard this moan, almost a whimper. I was sure it was a boy's voice coming from close to the end of the building. I signalled for a couple of guys to follow me and then stood quietly at the doorway waiting for any other sounds. There was some shuffling noise from inside, so I followed my rifle through the doorway, into the dimly lit space. I sprang around the corner and yelled something, I can't remember what, shining a light toward the noise.

A man, probably in his mid-30s, was bent over a naked boy who couldn't have been much more than 12. I could see the fear in the boy's face, the agony as the man barely stopped what he was doing long enough to sneer at me like I was interrupting his dinner. I didn't pause to think about anything, as though I had stepped outside my body, watching myself. My rifle was already aimed at the man, the safety was off and I pulled the trigger and shot him straight through the head. I heard a scream from the boy, and the man slid over backward. I remember noticing how dirty his long fingernails were and his lifeless, bloodshot eyes as he stared up at the ceiling. And his goddamn erection, which I should have chopped off. The boy was cowering in the corner, and I went over and extended my hand but he didn't take it, so I kneeled down and spoke to him as gently as I could. I reached under him and scooped him up in my arms.

Corporal Bradford retrieved the kid's clothes from the ground and laid them over top of his naked midsection while I carried him out as he whimpered and tried to hide his head in my chest. I felt something dripping on my boot, and when I looked down I saw it was the boy's blood.

We got outside into the light, and all of a sudden we were fired on, machine-gun fire from all around. I leaned over, trying to cover the boy with my body as I ran back toward the convoy. The last thing I remember was deafness from an explosion and the simultaneous propulsion of my body through the air. Then I woke up in the KAF hospital in stoned pain. I'd taken shrapnel in my thigh and crotch, and they'd removed my right testicle.

They tell me the boy died in the explosion. The major also told me the guy I hosed down was unarmed, probably a simple civilian and not Taliban at all, and that this is all quite a mess. And now I'm just sitting here recovering, waiting for the other shoe to drop, wondering if I ever said I'd give my right nut for the army.

CHAPTER 15

George stood in the hallway waiting for Matt to get off the elevator, looking as eager as a puppy. "Hi, Dad," Matt said, giving George a quick hug.

George led them through the living room of the waterfront condo he and Jilly had purchased a few years ago. The apartment was his pride and joy, in George's eyes the reward for all his years of butchering meat. It had a great view of the Okanagan Lake and the hills that sloped up either side of the water as far as anyone could see, and a wide balcony ran the length of the apartment to take advantage of the vistas.

Jill kept a clean house, George was always happy to point out, and he was right: it looked like a cleaning crew had just finished sterilizing every last inch of carpet and furniture. Matt almost expected to see a paper band around the toilet seat whenever he went to the bathroom, and plastic-wrapped glasses. After being in the wide-open spaces of farm country, this felt like being in a dollhouse, actual size. Matt wasn't sure how George, such an effusive and simple country guy, could live like this, but far from minding, George actually seemed giddy about his little palace.

They stepped out onto the balcony, and Matt filled his lungs with fresh lake air, expelling the living room's potpourri of Glade scent, Lemon Pledge and Mr. Clean. From their view on the twelfth floor he noticed the light had already started to change with the onset of fall, the angle of the sun no longer bleaching the streets and buildings below in a harsh summer glare.

They sat in the nylon mesh loungers.

"Beer?" George asked.

"Dad, it's only eleven o'clock." He could have used one to calm his nerves but promised himself to keep sober, at least until after his meeting with David. "Maybe I'll have some wine at the vineyard."

"Nervous?"

Matt nodded slightly, grinning sardonically. "Shit yeah. And angry. I can't say I'm looking forward to staring at the guy's slimy face. But I'm cool. I'm on a mission, so I'm determined to keep calm and businesslike. Hopefully I can appeal to this new human David has apparently become. Maybe he'll offer me to be vice president of his empire. He owes me, after all." He picked a petal from the geranium in the terracotta pot, surprised it wasn't plastic, and pressed it into his palm.

"Hey, George, I gotta ask you something." Matt tore the small red petal in two with his fingernails. "Shirley had a talk with me a while ago about her journals. It looked like she wanted to get some stuff off her chest about what to do when she, um, passes on, and I guess these journals are pretty important to her. She says she doesn't want anyone reading them, that she kept them for herself, but she says I'll get more out of them than anyone else. She had even composed a note about it to make sure she got her thoughts down correctly. Must have taken her some serious time and concentration to do that."

George was looking down at his hands, his fingers intertwined so tightly in his lap that his knuckles where white. "Yeah," he said. "She's kept those all her life, as long as I can remember. She's very private about them, keeps them locked up in a safety deposit box."

"Have you ever seen them?"

"No. I'm sure they're full of all sorts of gossip about somebody or other." George hadn't yet raised his head to look at Matt. "You know how she is though. She's always kept to herself about a lot of things."

"I know. But I think she's trying to tell me something. We haven't communicated in years, and now she's barely capable of it. Maybe this is her way of wanting me to get to know her better." It occurred to Matt as he spoke to his father that Shirley was as unknowable as she had always been. Except now, when she seemed to be pushing on the other side of the door, she had lost the key.

"I'm sure that's true, son," he said, nodding thoughtfully. "Yeah, I'm sure that's what it is."

They both looked out at the whitecaps on the lake through an awkward pause.

Finally George got up from his chair and said, "Is that it then, Matt? That's all you wanted to talk about?"

Matt rubbed the pieces of the geranium petals between his thumb and finger. It was his turn to look at his hands. "Yeah Dad, I guess that's all."

"Well, you'd better be getting to the winery then, right?"

David looked up at the framed review of Estridge's Restaurant on the wall in his winery office, right beside the Board of Trade plaque for Entrepreneur of the Year. He smiled. The restaurant had been open now for more than two months and *The Post* had raved about it. Customers were pouring in for lunch and dinner, and his book was full two weeks in advance, with some reservations already stretching into the winter. *Let the doubters eat cake,* he thought, *or any of my fine food—as long as they pay for it through the nose.*

The Estridge's wine list featured vintages from his Placid Hills Estate, straight from the verdant, undulating fields that stretched below his open window. Row upon row of twisted vines snaked their way over and down the hills, each row marked at its start with a rose bush in alternating pink or red. He could even smell the dirt from outside, the rich slate smell of the soil mixed with leaves decaying in the fall afternoon. He had rebuilt the main house and winery to resemble an old French chateau, a two-storey grey stone beauty complete with arched stone-wall wine cellars and tasting rooms. Tours and tastings were by reservation only; he felt no need to 'Disneyfy' Placid Hills Estate and tolerate the philistine gourmands who tried to present themselves as wine cognoscenti. Most knew the drill: they would say something about the colour ('straw' or 'ruby' were favourite adjectives) of the wine as it was poured into a glass, and then they would swirl it around and finally taste it, pronouncing a thoughtful "hmm" as they finished swallowing (few would spit). Then, if they thought they had anything to say that wouldn't embarrass themselves or reveal their complete ignorance, they would make some comment about how 'rich' or even 'meaty' it was, about its finish and fruity notes. It was ghastly to watch.

He checked his watch. Matt would be arriving soon and along with him some kind of trouble, David was sure. Ever since he had received that first e-mail from Matt, his thoughts ping-ponged between contrived optimism and slit-your-wrists negativity. But David had managed to put him off long enough. David tried to practice the routine he had refined over the years, quite triumphantly he thought, from so many self-help books, of visualizing success and forcing negativity out with positive thoughts, but even when he wasn't thinking about Matt's visit, a gloom hovered over him like big-city smog. He knew it was simply a bad case of nerves, but probably a justifiable one. He had worked so damn hard to get all this, too hard to have his success, and his reputation, challenged by innuendo. Maybe he should have paid more attention to the Buddhist philosophy of letting go, which said giving up striving for things—even including inner peace, which he never really understood—was the way to true happiness. But most of the time he could hardly imagine himself happier, unless of course he had even more of all this great stuff he had acquired.

He questioned why he had gone to the funeral in the first place, but he was curious to see Matt and Shirley after so many years, especially to see what had become of Matt. It was probably hubris, he now knew, to think nothing would come of it.

He walked over to the open French window and sat on the wooden sill, allowing his gaze to drift lazily beyond the vineyard. What a beautiful part of the world this was! Here in the arid hills, life seemed a little more real than back in Vancouver. He considered this his head office, and although he didn't get to it as often as he would like these days, this was the place he felt most grounded, the place where so many years ago his path had started to elevate for the better. It was here that he finally saw something other than a bleak future for himself, where he got his start in the business working for Mr. Cleghorn, learning about the wine trade and how to cook in the winery's kitchen when its restaurant was still open to the public. This was where he first learned about his lottery win, and soon after where he plotted his move into the restaurant business in spite of the scornful reception to the idea he had to put up with from so-called friends.

After he purchased Placid Hills, he approached the neighbouring vineyards and made them offers to buy their wineries at prices they could barely refuse. He mortgaged himself to the hilt, opening his first restaurant and then buying up the vineyards, but in the process he learned about financing, staffing and just plain managing a business. He had left the running of the winery to his former boss, the indomitable Mr. Cleghorn, and then later to Cleghorn's son, Harley, who was now teaching David's son, Adam, the ins and outs of the wine business.

As much as he knew and understood the restaurant business, and for as much money as his Dave's Grills made him, his heart was always with the vineyard. He loved being able to put things in the ground and watch them grow, then produce their bounty each year (although some years admittedly were a lot tougher than others), the fussiness of it all, the way one had to treat the vines like children, coaxing and feeding them, even sometimes withholding from them, tricking them into growing. Then there was the alchemy of the winemaking itself, the intricate dance of the grapes and yeast and complex compounds that create the ambrosia of a buttery chardonnay or the richness of a deep cab.

The irony was that David didn't drink. Sure he would taste the wines—it was part of what he liked best about the process, noting the subtle flavours, the viscosity of the wine in his mouth—but then he would spit the wine out, never swallow. Mr. Cleghorn had been the one to recommend he stop drinking if he was going to go into the restaurant business, and especially the winemaking business, knowing at the time what a lush David was. Drinking heavily would be far too easy. Quitting drinking was part of his turning around, and other than whatever residue ended up on his palate from tastings, he hadn't had a drop to drink in nearly two decades.

He went back to his desk and jotted down some possibilities about his imminent meeting with Matt. He made two columns, one which he headed *Negative* and the other *Not As*. Under the negative column he wrote *Revenge* in black fountain pen. But surely after all these years Matt wouldn't have decided to seek some sort of twisted vengeance? As far as he knew, Matt was a married, fairly well-adjusted man who had never breathed a word of anything. Under *Revenge* he wrote *Blackmail*, which, in the negative column, seemed a more likely scenario. Everyone wanted a piece of him, but few could get it without working for it. Blackmail really wouldn't involve that much work, and Matt probably only recently realized David might be an untapped source of funds. He was sure that if necessary, he would find a way of outwitting Matt, but it all depended on how clever the man was. David remembered him as a smart kid, which caused a thin layer of sweat to form on his brow. Below *Blackmail* he had quickly scratched *Murder?* He had superstitiously added the question mark to the end of the word, as if doing so would dispel the possibility. But wasn't killing people second nature to a military man, and he had heard Matt wasn't all that well adjusted after coming back from Afghanistan.

Just to be sure, David walked over to the hitching post he used as a coat rack and took his keys out of his pocket, walking back to his desk and sliding open the bottom desk drawer. He stared at the black 9mm Browning lying in the drawer. He slowly lifted the gun from the desk and turned it over in his hand, releasing the clip to check the magazine. Loaded.

He looked back at the paper, to the *Not As* column where he'd jotted down a number of less daunting possibilities. A job? A loan? Sponsoring Matt or some charity he was involved in? All of them their own form of benign blackmail, he supposed, since Matt knew David could hardly say no, but these were easily dealt with. Finally, he had written *Shirley*.

He had heard Matt was now living with his mother, at least temporarily. He also knew Shirley was losing her fight with dementia. When he heard she could no longer work and that money had become a problem, he had tried to contact her but received no response, so instead he started sending her $1,000 a month to give her a hand. He never heard a word from her, but the cheques did not go uncashed. Maybe $1,000 wasn't enough money, and with Matt now appearing to be her guardian, that might be why he wanted the meeting, to increase her allowance. Again, a problem easily solved.

David was jolted out of his daydream when Adam walked through the door. David wasn't quite sure when his son had crossed the threshold to manhood, but since he started working part time at the winery, he seemed to have acquired a maturity that made David breathe a sigh of relief. His body was clearly a man's, although he still possessed a boyish face, topped by wheat-coloured hair and eyes the blue of a welder's flame. He looked a lot like his dad when he was young is what everyone said, and they should both consider that a compliment. Fortunately, Adam seemed to have bypassed the bad stage where David got stuck when he was that age, when his comportment would have made a horny alpha orangutan seem gentlemanly. A stage where—and how he regretted this—he had been stuck for far too long.

David placed the piece of paper with his notes in the shredder beside him.

"Matt's here, Dad," Adam said. "Do you want me to bring him in?"

"Sure."

"And his mother is in the car outside. Apparently she doesn't want to come in."

"Well it's the whole damn family then!" he said, laughing—not that there was anything funny about it. "Adam, just get him and bring him up, okay?" David suddenly found it harder to hide his irritation. "When we're finished here, maybe you can give them a tour afterward if they want."

David realized he could be overly protective of the boy, almost compulsively so. How could he not be? He knew the kind of threats kids faced in the world and couldn't handle the thought of something happening to Adam; he didn't want him to run into the likes of, well ... the likes of the way David used to be. He felt his face flush red with the embarrassment of this admission, which he quickly dismissed, and watching Adam leave the room to get Matt, his heart filled as he thought, *How could anyone possibly do anything awful to a beautiful kid like him?*

Adam held the door open while Matt entered the room. David stood from behind his desk and nodded toward his son. "Thanks, Adam," he said. "I'll let you know when we're done." He leaned forward, supported by his splayed fingers, on the edge of his desk.

David tracked Matt's move to the window where he looked out at the parking lot, no doubt checking on his mother. Before Gwen's service, it must have been more than fifteen years since David had last seen him, when Matt was still a kid, really.

Matt stood with one side facing into the room and the other facing the window, glancing back and forth between the parking lot and the office. Of course Matt was a man now; what else could David have expected? But there seemed no trace of the naïve kid left in him. He was all brawn, and rugged toughness was etched on his face. He was a military man, and as he stood there in his leather jacket with his arms by his side and legs spread like a gunslinger, David thought not so jokingly that he should have had him frisked at the door.

Finally Matt walked over to the front of David's desk and extended his hand, giving David a small sense of relief. "Thanks for seeing me, Uncle David," he said while David waved to one of the leather chairs facing his desk.

"It feels funny to be called that again," David said. "Uncle, that is." He cleared his throat, looking Matt up and down. "I see you're no longer on the crutch. Life seems to be treating you well."

"Treating me well enough, I suppose. I guess I could say the same thing for you," Matt said, gesturing wide.

David wasn't sure if Matt meant for the smile on his face to look ironic, but it did. "Well I'm sure your mother feels lucky to have you here right now. By the way, why don't you bring her up instead of leaving her in the car?"

"She didn't want to come. You know how stubborn she can be."

"Ah, yes, I think I remember that. How's she doing?"

"It's good of you to ask," Matt replied.

Again it was hard to tell if Matt was being polite, matter-of-fact or sarcastic, which would have been the same thing as rude. In any case, David couldn't shake the impression that Matt was looking at him like George must look at a pig about to be butchered.

"Why are you giving my mother money?"

David was taken aback by the abrupt question. "I've known Shirley a long time. I feel sorry for her. I know she doesn't have much, and it must be hard for her, especially now."

"Is it about guilt?"

"Guilt? For what?"

"David, stop fucking around. You know what happened back then. I want you to admit it. I need to hear you say it."

"Say what, Matt?" At least Matt had come straight to the point. "That I took care of you when Shirley was in the hospital? That I've helped your mother out for years? You have to understand I'm not the same person anymore Matt. All that stuff that happened was a very long time ago."

Matt took a deep breath, letting his words out slowly. "I killed a man in Afghanistan because of you."

"I thought that's what you were supposed to do there. Kill people, I mean."

Matt's eyes narrowed. "Sometimes I wish it had been you. Jesus, David, why can't you just say it? Why can't you admit what happened?"

David slowly untwisted a paper clip and started to clean his nails. "What are you doing for work now?"

"Fuck, you're impossible!" Matt said. "You have a son out there. Should we worry about him too?"

David ignored the implication, even though he felt his indignation rising. He needed to deflect the conversation. "George told me you've got some personal challenges on your hands." The paper clip hit the metal waste basket with a *ping*. "If you need a job, I know I could find something for you here. You probably don't have much business experience, but neither did I when I started out, and I'm sure the army has at least given you some valuable leadership skills." Keep your friends close and your enemies closer.

Matt sat blinking, shaking his head. "I'm not your lap dog, David."

"Maybe I haven't been very clear. I'm giving you the opportunity to get into something great here, and to help out your mother at the same time. But do what makes sense. You can always sell the farm and put her in a home."

"The farm is too important to her."

"Matt, from what I hear, she's failing. It's only a matter of time. Why not get started now while you're here and I can arrange everything?"

Matt sat silently.

"You know, something just occurred to me that I think is worth considering," David said, a self-satisfied smile rising on his face. "I really would like you to think about joining us here at the company. If you sell the farm, I'm going to think about giving you the equivalent in stock here at Estridge Holdings. You can still use the money to put Shirley into a home, but this is so you don't feel like you're losing anything. Consider it a little incentive to sell the farm and come work here. We both gain something, and Shirley is taken care of."

"Damn!" Matt cried, slamming his fist on the desk.

It startled David, who started stretching toward his bottom drawer.

"What the fuck, David? Do you think this is atonement for what happened between you and me? That this is some sort of redemption and I can be paid to forget about it? Do you think I've forgotten what happened?" The vein in the side of his red face looked ready to pop.

The truth is, somewhere inside, David had hoped, irrationally, he realized, that maybe Matt *would* forget what happened. He had hoped Matt had blocked it out, somehow closing off the synapses that linked that memory with reality.

"And what if it is atonement Matt?" David asked. "We're both different men today, you and me. There are certain things in our past that should remain there. In the meantime, I think I've made you a very generous offer." Maybe he was crazy throwing out such an impulsive proposal, but Matt was losing what little family he had in Shirley, not to mention his wife and kids back in Alberta.

Matt was on his feet. "Stuff your offer." He leaned over the front of David's desk, looking down on him.

David could almost feel the heat from Matt's face.

"I can't believe I'm asking you for something so simple—an acknowledgment, an apology—and you have the balls, after all that's happened, to sit there so smugly. What the hell's the matter with you? There is no way I'm going to be your little poodle. In fact, the less I have to do with you the better."

If Matt was trying to appear intimidating or threatening, he would learn in time that it was not the right tactic to use with David Estridge. David remained seated behind his desk, controlling his breathing, his gaze not moving from Matt's. "If you change your mind, then maybe we can talk."

Matt pushed the armchair out of the way and spun around. "I should turn you in is what I should do. I should tell everyone about the marvellous David Estridge, entrepreneur, philanthropist, child molester. Should I ask Adam how *he's* doing?"

"You can leave, Matt," he spat. "Now."

When the door shut, David leaned back in his seat and allowed his shoulders to sag. He couldn't believe he had gotten nowhere with Matt. He wasn't sure if Matt was serious about the threat, but he was convinced Matt still didn't know the entire story. Because if he did, there would be no way Matt would let it go. He had hoped that by making him a generous offer, they would become a little closer and in time Matt would realize David wasn't such a bad guy after all.

David had so carefully manipulated every element of his life after his reprobate days, meticulously plotting each goal and smashing through any barriers that stood in his way. It had gone so well! Not only materially but spiritually, he thought. A good Catholic, a charitable man—what else could even God ask for? Yet all his wealth, his reputation, his stature in the community now looked like the winning side of a Faustian bargain that was reaching its best-before date.

∽

"Are you sure I can't give you a tour?" Adam was following Matt down the hall. "I'm sure my father would love to have you sample some of the wines."

"Thanks, Adam," Matt said, continuing toward the door. "Maybe another time." He needed to get some fresh air.

"Hey, Adam?" Adam had followed Matt outside. "Do you like working here?"

"Yeah, sure," Adam said. "It's okay. Sometimes I'd rather not be working with my dad, but it's like a family business."

"Is everything okay with you and your dad?"

Adam fixed on Matt with his fire-blue eyes. "Sure," he said, his expression suddenly changed to something less friendly. "Yeah, everything's fine."

"It's just that I've known your dad for a long time. Since I was a kid. He used to babysit me sometimes."

Adam walked him to the car. "Well, maybe I'll see you sometime," he said, apparently dismissing the subject.

Matt hung on. "Hey, why don't you say hello to my Mom?"

Shirley was in the backseat, fidgeting with the clasp on her purse.

Matt leaned on the door and looked through the window. "You all right, Mom?"

"Why did you leave me here locked up?" she growled. "Locked up in this, this taxi?"

"It's not a taxi, Shirley. It's my car. And you're not locked up."

"I can't open the door. I'm locked up."

"Here," Matt said, pulling up on the lock. "That's all you have to do."

She scowled at him. "Why did you lock me up here?"

Matt gave a small, knowing smile at Adam and opened the door, extending his hand to Shirley to help her out of the car. He glanced over his shoulder at David's office window to see if they were being watched. They weren't.

Shirley crossed her arms over her chest.

"There's someone here who wants to say hello to you. Why don't you just come out for a minute and stretch your legs? It will do you some good."

She flipped him off with her shoulder, clutched her purse and exited the car without taking his hand, standing up and smoothing her dress. She snapped open the clasp on her purse and started rummaging through it.

"Mom, this is Adam, David's son."

"I can't find my … my." She was clawing through her purse like a dog after a bone. "Oh, I just need my …"

Matt placed his hand gently on her arm, stopping her search. She looked up at him. "This is Adam," Matt said, nudging the young man toward her.

Matt saw Shirley's gears trying to engage as she shuffled back into her jumble of yellowed mental files. He watched her process Adam's face, her look changing slowly from a questioning stare to what seemed like recognition as something in her memory clicked, like an arm retrieving a scratchy record in an old Wurlitzer. Suddenly her face tightened and her eyes teared up, and she took small steps backward, sliding with her back against the car's front fender.

"No," she said, the word barely audible as she shook her head. "No." Again, but this time louder, and the fear on her face grew.

"What is it?" Matt asked.

Adam stood silently, not sure what to do.

"What's wrong, Mom?"

"Stay away from me," she said, looking at Adam. "Get away from me, David!"

"It's Adam, Mom, not David. This is David's son, Adam."

She latched onto Matt's arm and dragged him backward with her, away from Adam. Her voice was nearly a panic. "Get away from me, David! Leave me alone!"

Adam looked quickly back and forth between Matt and Shirley. "I guess I'd better get back," Adam said, his voice shaking. He turned and practically ran back to the building.

Matt tried to calm his mother. "It's okay, Mom. It's all right. We're going to take you home, okay? Back to the farm." It broke his heart to see her like this. He wished he could reach back in her mind, to be there with her for an instant so he could interpret the confusion clawing at her, maybe find a way to give her comfort. Sure, Adam looked a lot like his father, but Matt couldn't understand the intense reaction.

Matt opened the car door and guided Shirley gently back into the seat, feeling more protective of her than he realized he was capable of. Then as he walked around to the other side of the car, he glanced up to the second floor of the building, to David's office window. David stood there with his arms folded across his crisp white shirt, expressionless as he watched the small group below.

CHAPTER 16

The crisp fall air had arrived along with the earlier nights, and it blew gently through the open kitchen window where Matt and Sage played cribbage.

Matt answered the ringing phone like a chipper inn receptionist. "Graydon House."

There was no response on the other end. He was about to hang up, thinking it was a telemarketer, but then he heard a quiet hello.

"Amanda?" he asked. She had never called him at the farm before. Any dialogue they'd had taken place mostly by perfunctory e-mail. He was tethered by the phone's cord to the kitchen wall and ducked around the fridge for more privacy. "Amanda," he said in almost a whisper. "Is that you?"

Sage got up discreetly. He heard her go into the living room and turn on the TV, and he couldn't help feel a little guilty. Sage and Liz had formed a kind of relief team lately that took a lot of pressure off him, allowing him to force himself to get away from the farm. Therapy made him realize he was hiding out there, and now the more he got out, the easier it was becoming. Lately when he went into the supermarket he was less anxious; he didn't sit sweating in his car beforehand contemplating escape routes or coming up with excuses not to go in at all. Even gas stations had become a little easier.

But it was already 9:00 p.m. in Edmonton. The boys were probably in bed, so she wouldn't be calling to let them speak to him.

"What's up, Amanda?" He was treading softly, his tone friendly.

"I just wanted to talk, I guess," she said.

He thought he detected a bit of a quiver in her voice. Had she been crying? "What's up, baby? Is everything okay?"

Baby? He hadn't called her that in so long. But it was an emotional semaphore, he knew, a sign the door was open, shorthand that you develop after being married a while. He also knew the flipside of the telepathy was that anything negative could be conveyed just as quickly, setting tempers spattering like water on a greased grill.

"No, I'm fine, Matt."

He didn't hear any of the tough-chick attitude in her voice, which had been the only attitude he had experienced since he got back. And he was such a sucker for her vulnerability.

"I just wanted to talk to you about the boys." She paused and then sighed, so lightly he barely caught it. "I think they miss you."

The words shot through him like a bullet. "I miss them too, Amanda," he said when he recovered himself, trying not to let her hear his own voice shaking. "I really want to see them." He was choosing his words so carefully, knowing he couldn't blow this. "I hope you don't think because I'm in Summerland that I don't miss them. I'm doing everything I can to get things in order so I can get back to Edmonton. I even put the farm on the market."

"Really? What about Shirley? She loves that place."

"It's the only way. Honestly, most of the time I don't think she realizes where she is anyway. She'll adjust."

"Oh." There was meaning in that little word, but he wasn't sure what.

"Why, you don't think it's a good idea?"

"No, I'm not saying that. I was kind of hoping the boys could see it again, I guess." Was she suggesting they come down? He put the brakes on his rising optimism in case she was about to let him down.

"I thought maybe it would be good for them to see you, and to spend a little time on the farm as well."

He stuck his toe in. "Do you want to send them out?" He waded in deeper. "Or maybe come out with them?" He held his breath through a moment of silence.

"Yeah, Matty, I think we'd all like that, and it would be good for the boys. I could probably pull them out of class for a couple of days, and we could make it a long weekend."

He extended the cord on the phone as far away from the wall as it would go, trying to peek around the corner and down the hall to where Sage was sitting in the living room. "When were you thinking?"

"How about next weekend? We could come out a week Thursday and leave on Sunday. I can leave Wednesday night and drive through the night."

He couldn't understand the sudden thaw, but he felt like a teenager, almost the way he had felt when they first started seeing each other. He couldn't help it, even though he lectured himself to slow down and be realistic. Amanda had been impetuous before, and she could always change her mind.

"Matty?" There was hesitation in her voice.

"Yes?" His defences were up.

"I'm not sure how to tell you this, but I might as well get it right out on the table. There was someone else."

Matt felt his heart skip a beat. She only paused for a moment, but it was enough time for him to parse her sentence, to analyze the situation and his own reaction to it, just like they say when you're in a car crash and everything is happening in slow motion. She had said there 'was' someone else, which implied there isn't anymore. It must have been this Greg guy the boys had mentioned.

"Jesus, Amanda." He did his best to rein in his exasperation.

"I'm sorry."

He didn't know how to respond.

She didn't let him. "You were so distant, and so scary. I was scared for the boys too, and I was lonely. It was stupid."

His jaw tightened. "Anyone I know?" He couldn't help the icy response.

"No. A reporter. He was interviewing wives of soldiers who were in Afghanistan for an article he was doing back in the spring, and it just kind of happened."

"His name's Greg?" The guy would be easy enough to Google. Not that he wanted to do anything about it other than check out the competition.

"Yeah. I guess the kids let it slip, eh?"

He thought of Sage sitting in the living room, and how close he had been to asking her to stay over. He wanted so much to be close to someone, to be held, to know someone cared about him.

"I don't know what to say, Amanda."

"It was a mistake Matt. I know you're pissed off, but I was angry and stupid. Please forgive me."

After a moment he said, "Are you sure it's over?"

She was sure. He listened to her breathing for a while, knowing she was waiting for whatever came next.

He let out a long sigh through his nostrils. "I know I made it hard, but I'm not about to take the blame for you running off with someone else. It's not like you. It's not like us. Normally you're a bigger fighter than that."

"If you could have seen yourself though."

"Please, Amanda. Let's not go there. I'm sure I wasn't easy to live with. *None* of the guys are after they get back from tour. But I've had a lot of time to think out here. I'm getting treatment for the PTSD."

He looked out the window into the night, at the grey outline of the fruit trees just beyond the Grand Am. The wind seemed to be chasing itself through the fall leaves. The porch light cast flickering shadows through the trees onto the gravel drive. It would be hard; just imagining another man touching his wife made it hard to picture himself getting near her. But then he thought how close he had been to attempting to sleep with Sage.

"I miss you, babe." He choked up. "The boys are too important. I promise I'll try my best if you will too."

The boys were coming, and the days couldn't possibly pass fast enough before they got there. Their mother too. For a moment he let the thought envelop him like a favourite scratchy sweater, allowing himself the odd pleasure of knowing it felt right.

CHAPTER 16

Even though he knew he had the full legal authority to handle Shirley's affairs, Matt felt like a sneak, as though he were a kid about to be caught with his hand in her purse. Just because he was now her legal guardian didn't mean he felt any more comfortable digging into her affairs. There was so much he had to get used to, so much to discover of this woman he barely knew, like stripping layers of paint off an old house. There was no other way but to dive in, even though he knew she would have bridled, like it was an affront to her dignity. There was so little left for her to feel dignified about, and he had to be more intimate these days with her than he ever would have imagined, bathing and changing her, or rescuing her from the toilet when she became confused.

This was a little different. Going to the bank, taking control of her accounts and pillaging her safety deposit box—at least that's what it seemed like—felt too close and almost dirty, like having to clean her soiled underwear. To have to deal with the bank in Penticton, a busy, noisy branch in a high-ceilinged building with nowhere that he felt safe, nowhere to run for cover and to sit across from a bank clerk who eyed him suspiciously even while she complied with his requests; it all made him sweat. The fact that Tracy—the name on the clerk's badge—looked a lot like his grade 4 teacher didn't help. She was probably in her 20s but dressed more like she was in her 50s, with her dark-framed rectangular glasses and the yellow cardigan draped over her shoulders. Her fat breasts and gelatinous belly squirmed to escape the paisley polyester dress she undoubtedly had made herself ten years ago when she was considerably slimmer. As she was filling out her forms and tapping away at the computer, she looked up only once, without saying a word, glancing over her desk at his hands, which had been nervously clicking the plastic clasp on his knapsack open and shut. She was pure schoolmarm, looking down her nose over her glasses and then back up at him. He smiled sheepishly at her then let go of his knapsack, folding his hands into his lap just like he would have in elementary school.

"Would you like to access the safety deposit box now?" She sighed.

For a second he pondered the question. That's what he had come for, to get the diaries, nothing more, even though Ms. Tracy was undoubtedly convinced he was scavenging for jewels or forgotten stock certificates. He suddenly knew what Pandora felt like. If he went in there and opened the box, who knew what hell he would release? He had never been a superstitious person, although the PTSD had turned him into a bit of an obsessive-compulsive—stepping over bumps in the grass like they were mine fields, making sure a dozen times the doors were locked at night—which in a way was its own form of superstition. But Shirley had asked him to look at the diaries only when she was dead, and now he almost feared a curse if he examined them any sooner.

He laughed quietly at how ridiculous he was being.

In the vault the bank clerk took Matt's key and looked around the steel-lined room for the correct box. There must have been hundreds of them, three different sizes as far as he could see. "Ah, there it is," she said, bending down to insert her key and then his. He was sure he could hear the seams of her dress straining.

The box was one of the large ones, about half the height of a file box, and he was surprised how long it was as she pulled it out of the wall. With some effort she heaved it on top of the counter.

"You're welcome to take it to a private room if you like," she said.

Matt flicked open the latch on the box and pulled back the lid. Shirley's wedding ring lay at the bottom—she hadn't worn it since she and George split—alongside a gold Longines watch, the only other things he could see besides four stacks of notebooks. The sticker on one of the books said 2003–2005, and it sat atop eight or ten identical Grand & Toy blue-covered bound notebooks. The rest of the piles contained groupings of notebooks of various colours and sizes. He looked at the bottom of the leftmost pile to a wire-bound school notebook, its thin green cardboard cover stained with water rings and crumpled. He pulled it out. On its cover, a girlish handwriting spelled her name and "1970," the oldest of the lot. She would have been fourteen.

He stood back from the box and took another look at it, as though he were looking at a coffin and uncertain if the body was really dead. Then he held his breath and reached in, scooping up the piles of notebooks and stuffing them into his knapsack. He took one more look at the ring and watch before closing the cover, struck by how sad he was thinking back to a time when Shirley's life would have been happier, less complicated. These were remnants of a life, perhaps of happier times, certainly with no idea of what would become of her later. She couldn't have expected this end; the last thing she would have wanted was to lose her mind.

He closed the lid on the box and turned to the clerk, who had her back to him, aimlessly examining the boxes on the far wall. "I'm done, thank you."

The clerk lifted the box from the metal table, prepared to struggle with its weight but raising her eyebrows as she easily picked it up, sliding it into its dark crypt. She handed him his key, which he dropped into his pocket with a simple thank you then walked out of the vault and through the bank, oblivious now to the intrusion of sounds and shapes of people around him. He couldn't help feel a rush of nerves and excitement thinking about reading the diaries.

As he stepped onto Penticton's main street he took a breath of the crisp fall air and felt oddly relieved, the sense of something new washing over him. He looked up, his eye drawn to the cumulous clouds floating against the deep blue of the autumn sky. Even as this small corner of the world slowly tilted a little farther away from the sun, he realized it had not stopped turning, nor were frogs and locusts descending from the sky. He felt that tingle again, like a child certain of the promise of something new and big that was about to come his way. Whatever the heavens had in store, for once he felt unlike he had in a long time, convinced that no matter what crazy universe he was about to enter, he would emerge on the other side, intact and whole.

Shirley's Diary
December 23, 1974

I am so unclean! I wish I could take a knife and just gouge out my vagina. Oh, God, forgive me! Would having an abortion be a greater sin? If I told Mom and Dad who the real father is, then maybe they'd see some reason and let me go away and come back suddenly unpregnant. But if I told them or anyone else, then David would carry out on his threat and kill me, I know he would. It might be better to be dead instead of carrying his child. Oh, God!!! Even saying it makes me feel like I've been poisoned, infected by his filthy, demon seed. Having sex with him was bad enough, but pregnant by him? What kind of child will I have? It might have two heads or a tail, or at least his psychopathic genes.

Lord, what have I done to deserve this? I know maybe I haven't always been the girl You wanted me to be, but I've been so much better than a lot of my friends. Are You angry at me, so much to allow this to happen? Yeah I've been drunk a bunch of times, and I have fornicated once or twice (okay, four times—You would know), but in my heart I've been faithful to You. And it's been months since I've been with anyone. If only there could be some doubt in my mind that this child wasn't David's. Can you not make this go away?

He was drunk, having a party with my brother and his friends upstairs while Mom and Dad were away. I was on the phone in my bedroom talking to Jilly, and he was standing in the door with this stupid leering grin on his face, leaning up against the doorframe in his Wranglers and dirty white T-shirt. I told Jilly to hold on for a second while I asked him what he wanted but he didn't say anything, just kept on standing there looking stupid.

Finally when I hung up I told him to get the hell out of my room, and instead, he stepped in and shut the door, and started rubbing his crotch. I could see his erection through his pants. I said "David, that's gross," and I threw a book at him and told him again to get out, but he kept on coming toward my bed. Then all of a sudden he grabbed me and threw me down and started ripping at my clothes. I was screaming at him and punching him but no one could hear us. He told me to shut up and held the pillow over my head until I thought I was dead, and when I was too weak to fight back he did it to me.

I stayed in my room for what must have been a whole day after that, throwing up and sobbing. I was terrified to leave the room even though I wanted to run as far away from there as I could. I locked my door and pulled the dresser in front of it, and then I lay under my blankets and shook for hours. More than anything I wanted to get out and wash myself, to disinfect myself with Mr. Clean or spray a can of Raid up inside me to kill his seed. But I stayed in my room because I had no idea if he was still around, and if he did it once maybe he would want to do it again.

The phone rang so many times but I didn't answer it; I couldn't talk to anyone. I had to pee so badly I went in the Coke can, but it overflowed and I started crying when it spilled on the floor. Every second I listened to see if there was someone in the house, and after hearing no one for hours, I finally told myself I had to get out. I grabbed my keys and wedged them between my fingers so I could use them for a weapon, and then I finally went through the house locking all the doors and windows, hoping David wasn't still around. Then I ran a bath and scrubbed myself so hard I thought my skin would rub off. I must have added another five gallons to the water just by crying.

Every time I've seen David since then he gives me this stupid little grin and points his finger at me as if to tell me I should watch my step. How the hell do I keep far away from him when he's bunking with my brother? I've tried so hard to forget about it, that he ever touched me, but how can I when I'm carrying his child?

And now I'm marrying George! Mom and Dad are merrily carrying on as though the wedding had nothing to do with my pregnancy, as if I wasn't even pregnant at all. Of course people know I'm 'in the family way', but everyone is being condescendingly sweet, as if they don't know. And all of a sudden, when this baby pops out, everyone in town will forget their basic mathematics and biology and be all gleefully gooey over my spawn.

George has been amazing to put up with this. I suppose I could have asked for a worse husband than him. We've only gone out for six months, and I've never even been all that serious about him, although I know he's crazy about me. He would have to be to marry someone who he knows is pregnant with a child who's not his own. I told him it happened one drunken night in the back of a car with a guy from out of town, when George and I were going through a bit of a rough time. It doesn't seem to matter to him. Sure he was upset about it at first, but the whole idea that we've been able to get married as a result of this seems to have completely erased his memory of the 'car' incident, and he's happier than a robin in a rain shower. He even said something about having David in the wedding party, but I convinced him we have to keep it small, that Jilly should be my bridesmaid and that's it.

If I lose the baby, I don't suppose I can call off the wedding, can I?

CHAPTER 17

Matt hurled the book at his father, barely missing him. "Why didn't you tell me?" He marched back and forth across the thick carpet in George and Jilly's living room, embedding boot prints in the fresh vacuum tracks. The vein on his temple pulsed while George and Jilly looked on him silently.

"You could have told me. You *should* have told me. All these years I've been thinking you're my father and you're not? Instead it turns out to be that bastard child molester?"

"Matty, please," George said meekly, not daring to move. "I didn't even know. I'm as angry at him as you are."

As *if* he could be that angry, Matt thought. This wasn't about *him*. "There is no way you could be as angry as I am, my man. And you knew. You knew you weren't my father, even if you didn't know it was David. This changes everything." He felt filthy, like he had just wriggled through a sulphurous hole, spawn of Lucifer. Oh God, what about Adam? What about his half-brother?

"But I *am* your father Matt. Not biologically, but in law and in every other way. Your mother didn't want you to know. She wanted to give you as normal a life as she could. Both of us did. I was in love with her." He glanced over at Jilly. "But I knew she couldn't be pregnant with my child. We weren't even having sex. She told me it happened with some guy from out of town."

"But you married her anyway?"

"Of course. Like I said, I was in love with her. I didn't mind people thinking it was me. I knew she wasn't a loose woman Matt. We all make mistakes. It wasn't like her to mess around. I figured she just got out of control once, and I knew her well enough that I was pretty darn certain it wouldn't happen again. She was an eighteen year-old Christian kid Matty, and this was more than 30 years ago in small-town Okanagan. Getting an abortion was right out of the question, thank God." George smiled wanly at Matt then continued. "Marrying your mother was the right thing to do."

George sighed and looked down at his lap. He was crying. "I loved you like my own son from the minute you were born. We didn't talk about it because *nobody* talked about it. It was just swept under the carpet." He looked up at Matt and wiped the tears from his cheeks.

"I often wondered why your mom let him hang around."

"He threatened her, George, so he could do whatever he wanted. That's why." Matt sat in the wingback opposite George. He knew he shouldn't take this out on him. George had always treated him well, and Matt had never had any reason to suspect George wasn't his father. That he would marry Shirley under the circumstances just proved what a good man he was.

"It's obviously something your mother wanted you to find out eventually, otherwise she wouldn't have asked you to read her diaries once she had passed on. Think of how difficult it must have been for her. She just wished it had never happened."

"And here I was a constant reminder of it." He looked out the window, beyond the balcony and through the driving rain, past years and decades of sludge. He rolled the movie backward, wondering how things could have played out differently if she had acknowledged the truth, if Matt had known. Shirley had lived her life feeling it was a lie, and Matt had lived his own life alienated from her and confused. He had a right to be angry, although it seemed far too late.

"David should be in jail. Or better yet, dead. He's a fucking menace to society. I don't care what he's done in all the years since. He raped her, then twelve years later molests *me*, his own *son*? Who's to say what he's done in the meantime? What about Adam, for god's sake? What might have gone on there? All of this goody-goody stuff he does is just a psychopath's disguise as far as I'm concerned." He shook his head. "I can't believe I called him Uncle David all this time. Fuck."

"I didn't know Matty. I just found out last week what he did to you, and now you're telling me this. I knew David was a screwed-up kid, but I thought he'd redeemed himself. I'm so sorry." George looked down.

Jilly got up and stood beside his chair, taking his hand. "Maybe this explains a lot about your mother, Matt," Jilly said. "I remember how crazy she was when she was a kid. She was so carefree, so funny. After she got married, everybody figured she was unhappy with George, or just resentful about her pregnancy. And I guess maybe she was." She was suddenly flustered. "I mean, not about you, Matt. Just about the way it happened. I guess I would be too in the same situation. She started to retreat more and more. We used to be good friends, all the way back to school, but pretty soon she started seeing less and less of everyone. She was holding this lie inside. It must have been killing her. But I don't think she loved you any less."

She had been looking at him, studying him for his reaction, but now she turned away.

"Jilly, you know as well as anyone that's not true. She didn't love me. Most of the time I'm sure she even hated me. You know how she's treated me."

Silence hung in the room. If he had known earlier, the truth would still have left a wound for sure, but a different one that maybe could heal over time. They could have worked on it as a family. Now he was starting stale, not fresh.

Thoughts bounced through his head. It was as though he had to go back and stitch his life together again, like ripping apart a fine needlepoint tableau and reusing the thread on a different background. Who knew what picture it would create? But it would never be the same.

Even while he struggled against the knowledge that had just pulled him so far from the safety of familiarity, he knew giving up would mean defeat. Only in the last few weeks had he begun to feel as though he was regaining strength. Yet he was sure his hatred toward David was entirely justified, perfectly placed. And the proper way to address it was to make sure David went to jail. Or maybe dead was a far better idea.

I know everything now.

The first words of Matt's e-mail pounded at David's head like a migraine. *I know everything now,* it said, hitting him again. He had wondered if there would be repercussions to their meeting, especially after watching how Shirley reacted to Adam in the parking lot, apparently convinced he was actually David. It was true that Adam's resemblance to his father at Adam's age was uncanny, but David had never expected it would trigger such hysteria in Shirley. The thought of it made him shudder.

David had been hoping for the best, that after thinking about his generous offer Matt would come back and accept, but as much as David tried to shut down the thought, something told him that after the parking lot incident, his future had taken a different turn. The thought needled him. Now after reading Matt's e-mail he cringed, waiting for the impact after the detonation.

> *I know everything now. I know what you did to Shirley, and as vile a thought as it is, you are my father. The fact that you could have raped her and then molested your own son, actually getting away with it for all these years, is beyond*

> *comprehension, beyond fairness or justice. I am mortified that I chose never to act on my own account out of fear. But now there has to be retribution for this, David, although nothing could redeem the horror you have inflicted on my mother and me.*

Attached to his e-mail were the scanned pages of Shirley's diaries.

At first he thought it was a physical threat, but Matt couldn't be that stupid; he wouldn't have given David any notice and certainly wouldn't document it by e-mail.

He scrolled through his e-mail contacts for his lawyer's phone number but stopped before connecting. How would he ever explain this to him? David Estridge was an upstanding citizen in the community, a superstar fund-raiser and philanthropist. What will people say? Would they even believe Matt? Maybe he should call his public relations firm instead and tell them about the story that this whacko concocted for blackmail; start a campaign now to discredit Matt. Were they going to believe a prominent benefactor like himself, or some fucked-up two-bit obsessive-compulsive Afghan vet with PTSD? Still, the publicity would be damaging right from the get go, putting David on everyone's radar. People would eye him suspiciously wherever he was, in supermarkets or at his restaurants; they'd probably hide their children from him. He couldn't believe the horrible timing, so close to putting his company on the market. There was no way he could allow this to happen now.

Who else had Matt told? George? The police? What if the police came? Could they take him away based simply on Matt's accusations? What would Adam say? Before anything he had to find out who knew, and perhaps then he would know what kind of damage control would be necessary.

He went to his desk and pulled out his chequebook. He wrote *Matt Graydon*, and then the amount, $250,000. Not many people could look the other way from that kind of money, and Matt had to be hurting for cash. He would ask Matt to meet him right away and present him the cheque. He could soft sell it a little, not like he was buying Matt's silence but that as David's son, it was something he should have given Matt long ago, an amount David easily would have spent on him growing up or going to university. There would be more, yes; certainly he could convince Matt that there would be more. He would wave his hand out the window and over his vineyards, showing Matt that all this before him could be his, at least partially. It was his birthright after all, and David had every intention of taking care of him. He would tell him that he had always provided for Matt and his mother in his will, and he would have done it all sooner only he had wanted to keep quiet about this for Shirley's sake. But now that the cat was out of the bag he could accelerate it all, make sure Matt never hurt for anything. And he would do whatever was necessary to ensure that Shirley was taken care of in an appropriate manner.

He hit the Compose button on his screen and sent Matt a response, asking to meet with him at his office that evening. Then he slid the cheque into the bottom drawer beside his gun and contemplated how to make this all go away.

CHAPTER 18

When he heard the tires crunching on the gravel through the kitchen window, Matt closed the lid on his laptop, not wanting Amanda to see that he had been checking the highway websites for delays or accidents. He fought rushing to the door, slowing his pace as he walked onto the outside porch.

Amanda looked flustered as she drove up, but then his eyes went to Baxter and Callum, who came bounding out of the car practically bowling him over. In a matter of months they were already different versions of the same kids, as though each time he saw them their changes were revealed in a time lapse that had missed so much between frames. As he kneeled down and tightened his arms around them, he realized he couldn't live like this, watching time put more distance between him and the boys, feeling his heart drain like an infected wound when they left and then practically explode each time he saw them again.

Amanda regarded him almost shyly, supporting herself against the car hood with one hand, looking weary from the long drive. For once she seemed more dressed for comfort than style with her jeans fitting more loosely than normal. Her hair was shorter and lightly spiked, which made her look younger than her usual coiffed and blown set. He tried to read her as she approached, and he knew she was doing the same thing, like animals circling to check out each other's scent. He made the first tentative move, opening his arms a little by his sides, and after a slight hesitation she stepped forward, hugging but keeping some distance, mindful, it seemed, not to touch crotches. He rubbed her back and whispered hello. He was glad she made it.

"Can we go play on the farm, Dad?" Callum asked.

The boys were standing in the glow of the porch light, on the edge of the dark orchard, which they leaned into like sprinters getting ready for a race. He stood between them, a hand around their shoulders.

"First thing in the morning, boys, I'll take you around the farm."

"Where's your mom?" Amanda asked when they got inside.

"She's in the living room watching TV. She likes to watch nature shows. You may as well come in and say hello, but don't expect much." The thought pierced him that Shirley probably would no longer know her grandchildren.

He told Amanda about David. Everything. He told her about what had happened to Shirley and what had happened to him. He told her about shooting the pedophile in Afghanistan. They cried about Kareem's beheading. Afterward he would kick himself for not telling her any of it sooner, at least the stuff he knew.

And they talked about her affair. It was hard not to be angry, but he had to admit something unexpected had happened. It was like a fissure had opened up in the earth, but instead of swallowing them whole it had spit them back out, hurt but grateful to be back and together.

"And what do you think you'll do about David?" she asked.

The question stopped him, lodging in his chest.

What he really wanted to do was to kill David; he deserved it. Matt had killed men that he hated less, and the reason to take their lives was less clear than this.

He had been thinking back to Afghanistan, of those men he was trained to think of as the enemy, one conglomeration of amorphous evil. The rationale was high on emotions and patriotism, low on compassion or individualism.

You didn't want to peek too far beyond the veil, into the private lives of the enemy, for fear of getting tangled in emotions and morals. How many of those people had families waiting for them when they got home, defended their beliefs as fiercely as *he* was expected to defend his own and then returned to their wives and kids who were never sure their father or husband would make it back? How many of those men had sons like he had, kids they loved beyond anything in the world, who they would die to protect? Matt shielded his conscience in moral duty, no doubt the same way those men did, and it allowed him to blow them away without prejudice, his motivation the same as theirs, the flipside of the same coin.

But there was evil that was launched upon the unsuspecting and defenceless. Matt had been the subject of such evil as had his mother, having been defiled by it. Matt had been born of it. With David he knew. If he had ever looked for rationalization in his job—his *duty*, as the military called it, to kill the enemy—it was far less clear than the ease with which he could justify killing David.

But if he needed justification *not* to kill David, he didn't have to look further than Baxter and Callum. They would not suffer for this. He wanted to be there for them without the jarring gaps, to take them to soccer games, to show them a world he never took the chance to see, to protect them and be an example to them. If he were to take matters into his own hands, then what would it say to his children? An eye for an eye makes the whole world blind.

"I think I'm going to let him cook in his own juices for a while," he answered Amanda. "He e-mailed me saying he wants me to come and see him. I haven't responded yet."

"You're not going to do anything stupid, are you?"

He felt embarrassed that she would have jumped so quickly to the assumption. "I have to do something. What if he's the same person but just in a different guise? We don't know. But I think I'll let the police handle it. I want to see him suffer. I want to see him dragged through the courts and ruined by this first and then put away."

"Are you sure you're ready for this? It's going to be hard on you too you know."

He laughed and pointed at his injured leg. "Have you forgotten how tough I am?" Then he leaned over and messed her gelled hair.

By Saturday morning, with only one day left in her visit, they still hadn't discussed her and the kids leaving. The thought of not seeing the boys for a while turned his stomach. The boys had set up quarters in the basement in his old room, around the corner from the cold cellar where the bushels of apples from the orchard were stored. Bosley, the golden retriever, loved it there they said, and Matt could only laugh when Baxter quietly suggested that if they had a horse, they could keep it there for when they returned.

More surprising was how he felt about Amanda leaving. He knew these few days were a false bubble but was surprised at how well they had done, how much stronger he felt with her around. The thought of her going back didn't feel right.

"You know there are some people who are interested in the farm?" he asked at breakfast, poking at the hardening remnants of egg yolk on his plate. He tried to sound casual.

Amanda chewed on her lower lip as she looked at him and then followed his gaze out the window, saying nothing.

"The realtor figures we'll probably sell it pretty quickly, and I've got a place lined up that will take Shirley. I'd like to have her close to where I'm living, but I think she'd rather be near her church friends, at least when she recognizes them. They really seem to care about her."

"But what about *her*? She knows where she is here. You've always told me how much she loves this farm. I'll bet the minute you take her out of here she goes right downhill. It happened to my friend Sandra's mother. She just got more and more confused and then shut down, mentally and then physically."

"I know, I know," he said. "But there's nothing else I can do. I'm certainly not going to take David's blood money."

Amanda stood up and walked over to the door, leaning up against its decaying frame as she peered out at the orchard. The apple trees had shed almost all their rotting fruit to the ground; the morning air was chilled with the feeling of winter approaching.

She spoke in the direction of the trees. "What if we come and live here?"

It took him by surprise. Whenever the thought had occurred to him before he pushed it back down, not wanting to have his optimism shattered.

She turned around to face him. She was grinning, obviously expecting his surprise. "I'm serious, Matty. I don't think I ever got how wonderful this place is. I know you've always tried to push the farm out of your mind, but you still love it. The boys do too. They've already made me promise we have to come back here any chance we get. They miss you Matt." She paused and stared at the floor tiles. "I miss you too."

Her words seeped into his brain in a fog, making him wonder whether he was hearing her correctly. But without saying a word he wrapped his arms around her shoulders, squeezing her hard. As he looked into her soft gaze he felt relieved, as though he had found home. And suddenly he let go, his body heaving in spasms, feeling his tears melt into her sweater. He wouldn't have dared imagine this joy.

CHAPTER 19

Walking through his vineyards always had a calming effect on David. Making wine from the earth up, like caring for anything from birth, requires full attention, and it tended to take his mind off everything else. Many of these vines he had planted himself so many years ago: tilling and ploughing the soil, planting the gnarled grey vine cuttings into the rich mounded terroir, watching the vines twist their way up the trellises shooting their new growth of leprechaun green leaves along the way. Then finally the grapes, first in tiny garnet-coloured pods like a palm's worth of precious caviar, growing into the plump, luscious fruit that wouldn't reveal its true personality perhaps for years to come. And not unlike a child, you had to hold certain things back, in the vines' case stressing them by strategically withholding water, forcing their roots to grow stronger and deeper and produce more fruit than foliage.

He turned around and began trudging his way back up the hill toward the stone house, puffing a little as he went. He wasn't as young as he once was, even though he was still in fine shape, but these hills took more breath out of him than they used to. More than once over the past week he had thought that maybe he would semi-retire here sooner than he had planned, sell his restaurants now and get away from the stress of all that business. He loved the challenge of running his restaurant empire, but when he was at the winery he realized he loved this land more than anything.

Instead of returning to Vancouver, he had decided to stay these last few days, waiting for an opportunity to see Matt, waiting for a response to the e-mails David had sent. Damn him! Two e-mails now and still no reply, yet he knew full well that Matt must have received them. The man was obviously toying with him. He had even driven by Shirley's farm to see if Matt's car was still there or if maybe he'd gone out of town. The car was there.

He tried not to let the situation get the better of him, attempting to convince himself that Matt simply needed time to process everything, that maybe Matt would speak to no one in the meantime. There was little David could do without seeing Matt or talking to him, except maybe run. And he wasn't the fleeing type. Even his lawyer had advised him to stay put and wait it out; better that he should try to convince Matt first to keep his mouth shut and let this go, something the money would surely help. But first Matt had to surface.

David's insides felt wrung like an old dishrag, squeezing every drop of patience out of him. It was so damn frustrating! How would he make people understand he wasn't a monster? The thought of what had happened—of what he now so cringingly admitted he had done—all those years ago made him vibrate even now. He wasn't the same person now. He had turned his life around, done everything he could to remake himself into a compassionate, upstanding citizen, a practicing, repentant Catholic and pillar of community. Wouldn't people see that? They *had* to see that.

Inside the house he sat down behind his desk and ran his fingers along the grain of the honey-coloured oak. He opened his laptop and glanced at the date: November 11. His life was so busy that the growing season and harvest had flown by, yet he still wished he could speed up the clock. Not that he wanted to avoid any of this; he simply wanted to arrive at the point now where he could deal with everything, confront the problem and solve it, bring things to a logical conclusion. He clicked on his inbox again. It was the same stuff he had already seen: a report of the overnight numbers from his restaurants, an Okanagan Growers newsletter. And as he watched, a note from Matt popped onto the screen.

"They're on their way" was all it said.

He fumbled with his phone and frantically looked for Matt's phone number, almost dropping the device through his sweating hands. What the hell did that mean? Was Matt sending someone there? The police? Whomever it was, David had to try to dissuade him from whatever madness he was contemplating. David would do anything, give anything at all to make it up to Matt if only he was given the chance. Surely it wasn't too late.

He stood up from the desk, steadying himself against it. His entire body felt swampy; even his eyes had become wet with nerves. Through a daze he heard a car pull into the parking lot. He stumbled over to the window like a drunk man, angling his head to peek around the thick stone sash of the window. Two RCMP officers sat in their cruiser below the window while they checked the computer before getting out and heading toward the building.

David knew how to handle this. He took a deep breath, exhaled slowly and then stepped around the window and walked calmly to his office door, intentionally slowing his pace. His leather shoes clicked on the oak plank floor as he stepped over the Persian carpet at the entrance to his office, exiting into the hallway. He heard the officers talking to Adam in the reception area below but continued walking in the opposite direction, toward the winemaking room.

He stepped through the glass door of the winery onto the catwalk that overlooked the huge stainless steel fermenting tanks and oak barrels beneath him, scanning the room. One of his men swept the floor in the far corner while another examined the temperature gauges on one of the large tanks.

"Get out!" he suddenly screamed at them. "Get out now!"

They looked at him, surprised, and then scurried through the exit to the yard.

David took a deep breath and stood calmly for a moment, admiring the expanse of the room, its thick wooden beams supporting the eighteen foot ceilings. What a lovely winery he had built! The row of stainless tanks, each eight feet high by six feet wide sat glistening within the stone walls, their tops the shape of space cones. With the door shut behind him and the staff having fled like trained dogs, all he could hear was the low hum of the room's climate control system.

He had entered on the second-floor catwalk that clung to the wall in a U shape, its floor suspended near the top of the tanks so their contents could be inspected. He liked to occasionally remove the manhole-sized opening in the cone-shaped lid and punch the grapes down manually, just for fun, or take a sample of what was fermenting in the tank below. It was one of his favourite things about winemaking, all this chemistry, the natural process of fermentation building the initial character of the ultimate product, and he was always fascinated how carbon dioxide would settle above the thick cap of grape skins on top of the juice as a weird but dangerous by-product. How many times had he told his employees to be careful not to reach too far into the tanks or they would be overcome by the deadly fumes?

He stopped in front of tank #2 and leaned out over the catwalk, crawling onto the tank's cone and spreading his torso against the cool stainless steel. He smiled and hugged his baby as he felt his body relax, his sweat-soaked shirt cooling against the chilly metal. After a moment he reached to the side and unhooked the lid, discarding it behind him on the catwalk, then he poked his head slowly into the tank to take a final look at the thick ambrosia below. He knew that once the carbon dioxide entered his blood and brain he wouldn't even know he had hit the liquid; he would pass out before he realized he was drowning. So he reached his body a little farther into the hole, supporting himself with his hands on the rim of the opening, taking one deep breath and exhaling, and then another even deeper than the first, until his hands relaxed around the cold steel, and he finally slipped head first into the liquid below.

CHAPTER 20

Matt sat in the dark kitchen, the light from his laptop's screen illuminating his face like a fluorescent mask. The eleven o'clock news was over with no reports of any casualties in Afghanistan. He had given Shirley her medication at nine and helped her into her bed.

He typed "Canadian Forces Afghanistan" into the YouTube search box and did a quick scan of the results. Nothing new, although he knew he would play one or two of the videos anyway. He had seen all of them except one, the one that a video journalist had documented of their battle at Shah Wali Kot. He had heard about it from the other guys; they said that it was largely due to the video that Matt had been awarded the Medal of Military Valour, pulling Corporal Dawson out of the burning LAV. He hadn't been able to bring himself to watch it. Nor had he responded to the military's request for him to attend a ceremony to give him the award. To accept it would have cheapened the efforts of the rest of the guys, especially of Dawson and Hutch, to deface the humanity of it all. Any of them would have done what he did.

It used to be when he played the videos that he wanted to be back there with them, but the feeling was no longer as strong. Now he played them to lessen the tyranny of distance, the 10,000 kilometres that meant people only remembered a war when they lost another soldier.

The chat window on the side of the screen popped open. Rayner.

"Hey, man, you still up?" it said. Rayner had been back in Afghanistan for a few weeks already; signed up for another tour when the call went out for experienced guys and they'd made him a sergeant. It must have been morning in Kandahar.

Matt typed back. "Yeah, just playing some lullabies before I go to sleep. What's going on over there?"

"The usual. They pop up. We shoot 'em. Just like Nintendo. What's up with you?"

"Killing time before Christmas when Amanda and the kids arrive. They're moving here."

"Get the fuck outa here! Good going, man! You said things were good but I wasn't expecting thatJ."

"We're keeping the farm. The boys love it. Shirley's going to live here with us."

"Congrats, Graydon. I'm glad you're working it out. How are the demons?"

"Hey, you know. This shit never leaves you. But I'm beating the crap out of them best I can."

"Listen, gotta go, buddy. Hang in there."

"Keep your head down, Rayner. Say hi to the boys."

He sat with his fingers resting on the keyboard, the chat session having sucked his thoughts half a world away to Afghanistan. He closed his eyes and for a moment sat bundled in his sleeping bag in the desert facing Kareem once more, the young interpreter's green eyes twinkling with life.

He held out his palms and Kareem let his hands rest on Matt's. "Everything's going to be all right, Kareem." Comfort to a dying man.

"George! *George!*"

Matt jumped up from the kitchen table, catching the chair to prevent it from crashing backward. He ran and opened Shirley's bedroom door.

Shirley was sitting up in bed, a nearly transparent silhouette in the moonlight, squeezing her pillow to her chest. She shook her head as he approached her, her milky eyes watching a scene that was somewhere beyond the walls, anywhere in time. He sat on the side of her bed.

"It's me, Mom. It's Matty."

"Help me," she mumbled between small gasps. She was looking beyond his shoulder to a place that only she could identify. "Help me," she said again, this time looking straight at him. "Please help me."

"Shhh," he whispered to her. "Shhh," he said again and again as he watched the branches outside her window shivering in the wind. Matt put his arms around her then gently lowered her head to the bed. He unravelled her cold fingers one by one from around the pillow, slowly taking it from her. He took her hands in his and softly rubbed her little chicken-bone fingers. What a life she had had, this woman who was once so strong, who had endured so much alone.

"Everything is okay, Mom. I'm right here." He stroked her damp hair as he spoke to her. "We're not going anywhere. We're not leaving the farm." He took her pillow and squeezed it to his chest, still feeling the warmth from her body as it radiated against his, and then he kissed her clammy forehead.

"It's going to be okay, Mom. Everything is going to be all right."

ACKNOWLEDGMENTS

Thank you to the Humber School for Writers and David Adams Richards for mentoring me through a first draft, to Anne Giardini, who wasn't afraid to tell me how much work I still needed to do, and to Douglas Coupland for his encouragement.

A special thanks to everyone in the Canadian Forces who helped me research this book, especially to corporals Gordon Whitton, Fraser Logan and Jason Tabbernor and to Sargent Darryll Newsham for sharing their stories. Also to Dr. Greg Passey for giving me a deeper understanding of PTSD in the military. I am grateful as well to the people at the Alzheimer Society of Canada for their assistance.

To my sister, Tracy, who will always be the family's best writer, thank you for always supporting me. And as always, a huge thank you to Luc Bernard, who not only helped me with many of the military aspects of the story, but whose encouragement, strength and artist's soul are a constant beacon.

ABOUT THE AUTHOR

Mark Prior was born in Toronto, Canada. He is a media executive and author living in Los Angeles, California.

CPSIA information can be obtained at www.ICGtesting.com
Printed in the USA
LVOW12*1513021114

411678LV00010B/300/P